CELL7

ALSO BY KERRY DREWERY

A Brighter Fear
A Dream of Lights

CELL 7

KERRY DREWERY

HOT
KEY
BOOKS

First published in Great Britain in 2016 by
HOT KEY BOOKS
80–81 Wimpole St, London W1G 9RE
www.hotkeybooks.com

A CIP catalogue record for this book is available from the British Library.

ISBN: 978-1-4714-0559-4
also available as an ebook

This book is typeset in 10.5 Berling LT Std using Atomik ePublisher

Printed and bound by Clays Ltd, St Ives Plc

Hot Key Books is an imprint of Bonnier Publishing Fiction,
a Bonnier Publishing company
www.bonnierpublishingfiction.co.uk
www.bonnierpublishing.co.uk

To Rebecca Mascull and Emma Pass,
who know the journey

There is a higher court than courts of
justice and that is the court of conscience.
It supercedes all other courts.

Gandhi

Prologue

There are two sounds in my head.

The bang of the gun through silence.

And my own voice shouting, 'Go!'

They both echo loud.

There's tightness in my chest. Hotness. Like nerves walking in the dark at night, or a knock at the door when I'm home alone. That tip in my stomach.

I'm dizzy but I'm breathing. I'm conscious. Alive.

What have I done?

Those words repeat over again.

Same, same, same.

The darkness is crushing.

My breath screeches through it; my heart thuds.

I hear a siren in the distance; see headlights, dim.

You could run, I think.

'No point,' I reply out loud. '*This* is the chance to do something. Change things. Have to.'

Siren's louder now, brighter headlights too.

The headlights turn, drowning me in white. I lift the hand holding the gun and shield my eyes. Blue lights flash on my skin.

On, off, on, off, on . . .

And flash on the body at my feet. Show me red pouring from him.

What have I done?

Still that echo in my head.

'What you had to,' I tell it. 'It was the only choice. Only chance.'

Headlights dip. Dark uniforms pour from cars, talking, ordering. I'm not listening.

I drop the gun, rest my hands on my head.

'I did it!' I shout. 'I shot him! I killed Jackson Paige.' I can't tell their reply.

Their eyes on me are full of disgust, handcuffs on my wrists cold as their hearts.

They live in the bubble of the Avenues and the City, let the gloss reflect and not wonder what's outside.

I'll die in seven days because I have to, but after that, their bubbles will burst and everyone will know the truth.

CELL 1

News

'The breaking news this morning is the shocking murder of celebrity Jackson Paige. Paige, who won the nation's hearts with his appearances on reality TV and his tireless charity work, was shot just metres from where I'm standing here on Crocus Street, in the area of the city known as the High Rises. In a bizarre twist, the culprit, who stayed on the scene following the shooting, has already confessed her guilt and been named by police as sixteen-year-old Martha Honeydew.

'Honeydew has since been arrested and, in accordance with the Seven Days of Justice law was this morning placed in Cell 1 of death row. This will be a landmark case – Honeydew, at sixteen years of age, is both the first teenage girl to face the death penalty *and* the first to be tried by our country's unique Votes for All system, the most democratic justice system in the world, where you, the viewer, decide on the fate of the accused.

'We'll certainly be following what is most likely to be her final seven days very closely indeed. You can keep up to date via all our usual social media portals, as well as our dedicated twenty-four-hour TV channel, *An Eye for An Eye*. Our show *Death is Justice* – on air every evening from 6.30 p.m. – will be analysing the details of this truly horrendous crime and the life of the accused, asking what could have led her to become such a cold-hearted killer.

'Her willingness to admit her crime may have already reserved her a place in that electric chair when public voting is calibrated and results are given in seven days but, viewers, do not miss your chance to vote on this historic case.

'This is Joshua Decker signing off and handing you back to Kristina in the studio.'

Counselling

Martha sits at a table in the centre of a room in half light. Her long hair has been shaved to her scalp and her clothes have been replaced by white overalls.

She glances to the wall, watching the second-hand of the oversized clock tick loudly on to 9.05 then, puffing out her cheeks and sighing heavily, she turns and stares out of the barred window to where a sparrow is perched in a tree, next to leaves curling and turning orange and red. The sparrow opens its beak and closes it again; Martha knows what it should sound like, but she can't hear its song.

The chains around her wrists and ankles clank as she shuffles in her seat and looks to the middle-aged woman with thin blond hair and watery blue eyes sitting opposite her.

'Did the guard explain to you who I am?' the woman says, her voice warm and smooth against the chill of the room.

Martha shakes her head.

'My name's Eve Stanton. I'm your designated counsellor.'

'I don't need a counsellor.'

'You might appreciate someone to talk to as it gets closer to . . .' She pauses, rubbing at her chewed fingernails as she searches for the right word.

'. . . to my execution?' Martha glares at Eve as she finishes the sentence. 'I know I'm going to die,' she says. 'I'm guilty. I killed him.'

Eve's gaze flickers and she looks away. 'So you say,' she mutters.

'Why would I lie?'

'Exactly. Why would anyone lie about something like that?'

'Yeah.'

They both fall back into silence.

The clock ticks.

The sparrow flies from the tree.

'Why do I have a counsellor?' Martha asks. 'Because I'm a teenager?'

'No,' Eve replies. 'All prisoners do.'

'Why?'

Eve crosses her fingers. 'Some people disagree with the death penalty, especially for teenagers. This is a . . . a *concession* for them. Something that the government can point to and say, "Yes, but look at this kind thing we allow".' She smiles with her lips pressed together. 'A glimpse of the humanity some feel we have lost.'

'Humanity? Is that what we've lost?' Martha says, running her fingers over the stubble on her head. 'What do you think?'

Eve watches the tension in the girl's face and the worry behind her eyes, nothing matching the words she says and the attitude she gives off. 'It doesn't matter what I think,' she replies. 'It's the law.'

'What? An eye for an eye?' Martha asks.

'Don't you agree with it?'

'Don't you?' Martha fires back.

Eve gives a wry smile. 'I asked you first.'

'So what? Whatever I think isn't important, is it? You tell me. Do *you* agree with voting on whether people live or die? No courts. No witnesses. No evidence . . . juries . . . nothing.'

'Doesn't a system of the whole public having the right to vote *mean* that everyone is a juror? That they all affect the outcome?'

Martha rolls her eyes. 'Do you always answer questions with questions?'

Eve doesn't reply.

'You're just like all the rest from the City,' Martha says, looking away. 'And those who live in the Avenues around it. No, you're worse, cos you think you're doing something worthwhile, and you're not. Anyway, laws can change, can't they?'

'I don't live in the City or the Avenues. Not quite. I'm more on the outskirts.'

'Yeah, well, same thing. You don't come from the Rises, do you?'

'True.'

'Like I said – you're just like the rest of them.'

She sticks her legs out as far as the chains will allow and folds her arms across her chest.

'How often do I see you?' she asks.

'Every day,' Eve replies. 'Apart from day seven.'

'Day seven? My last day?'

'Potentially your last day.'

'What about visitors?'

'No,' she replies.

'What? None?'

Eve shakes her head.

Outside the conversation the sparrow lands back in the tree, a worm in its beak. Martha watches it, then leans forward. 'What about a message?' she whispers. 'Can you pass a message on for me?'

'I can't do that,' Eve replies. 'I'm sorry.'

'But nobody would know.' She looks around the room. 'There aren't any cameras in here. Nobody would see.'

'I can't . . .'

Outside, the wind blows at the branches of the tree, pushing them against the glass as the sparrow bobs up and down.

'Who would it be for?' Eve asks.

'Why do you care? You just said you wouldn't do it.'

'Your mother is . . .'

'You read my file?' The chains on Martha's wrists clank against each other as she taps at the folder on the table. 'Then you know my mother's dead.'

Eve leans back slowly and pulls in a deep breath. 'I know your mother's dead," she replies gently, 'and I'm sorry about that. I was going to say that as your mother isn't with us any more and your father ran off before you were born, who would the message be for? Who would you be writing the message to?'

'I have friends.'

'Do you?' she says, and she takes the folder from the table and opens it. 'Because it says here, and I quote – "Martha was never a social girl at school. She struggled to make friends, casting herself on the outside and not making any effort to join in with her peers."'

'That's teachers for you. They never liked me.'

Eve raises a finger. '". . . although she was a very intelligent young lady, and if she had applied herself, had the ability to go far."'

10

'*If she had applied herself?*' Martha gives a snort of derision. 'Is that another way of saying, *if she could've been arsed?*'

'No, I think it's another way of saying, *if she'd had opportunity.*'

They stare at each other.

The clock ticks.

The branches of the tree scratch against the window.

'I had to drop out of school,' Martha whispers. 'To pay the rent. Y'know?'

Eve nods.

'If I couldn't . . . if they started questioning . . . I didn't want to be . . .' The air jutters in her chest as she sucks in breath.

'The authorities missed the fact that you're an orphan because you were paying the rent?'

'Suppose they must've. Otherwise they would've taken the flat away and made me live in one of those *care institution* places with all those kids. I couldn't . . .' She rubs her hands over her eyes and turns to the side.

Eve pushes the box of tissues towards her. 'I understand,' she says.

Martha looks back with tears in her eyes. She sniffs loudly and swipes the box of tissues off the table.

'Bollocks,' she says. 'You can try but you never will.'

Minutes pass in silence.

The box remains on the floor.

'I had a friend,' Martha whispers. 'A good one.'

'What was her name?'

Martha glances to Eve. '*His* name,' she said. 'It was a he, a male. Boy.' She sniffs again.

'What was *his* name?' Eve asks.

Martha turns to face Eve again. 'Is this confidential?' she whispers. 'Like in a doctor's?'

Eve nods. 'Of course.'

'If I tell you something, you won't go off to the newspapers or go on that *Death is Justice* programme and tell them?'

'No,' Eve whispers.

'Or write it down?'

'No,' she replies. 'I promise.'

Martha leans across the table a little more and swallows hard. 'He . . . I met him . . . after my mother was killed . . . he . . .'

The metal door behind them flies open and slams into the wall.

Martha spins around as a prison guard strides in, his stomach wobbling over the top of his uniform trousers and the buttons of his blue shirt straining. He swings a baton in his right hand.

Eve stares at the guard. 'I said I'd call when we're done.'

He shrugs. 'Thought I heard you.'

'No . . .' she begins.

Martha's eyes flash around the room. 'Are there cameras in here?' she says, the guard moving closer to her. 'Is this recorded? Does this go out to the TV?' Her voice is louder and louder. 'I thought this was confidential.' The chair grinds against the floor as she stands up, and the chains clatter as she lifts her hands in desperation.

'You said –' she says, leaning over Eve.

But the guard grabs the chains, yanks her backwards and she falls to the floor, lying near his feet with him towering over her, baton above his head and a sneer on his face.

'Stop!' Eve shouts.

'Go on!' Martha shouts back. 'Hit me! Hit a defenceless girl if you think you're man enough!'

The guard leers down at her.

'Stop it!' Eve shouts.

'She's a killer, this one,' he says. 'An animal. Should be treated like one.'

Martha kicks out at the guard but he pulls her sideways and her head and shoulder bang into the door frame.

'Martha,' Eve says. 'Everything in here *is* confidential, I promise you that.'

The guard snorts. 'Yeah, unless I can hear it, then . . .'

Martha pulls back against the guard; for a moment her strength catches him off-balance and he lurches forward, but he heaves against the chains again and raises the baton higher above her.

'Stop it!' Eve rushes forward, taking her phone from her pocket and pointing at him. 'You want this in the papers?' she asks. 'On the television? Want voters to see what it's really like in here?'

He stares at her. 'You wouldn't do that.'

'Try me,' she hisses.

'Bloody softies like you,' he says to Eve, dropping the baton and jabbing at her face with his finger, 'are how this country got into such a mess before. Getting murderers off on some technicality, letting paedophiles go cos there weren't enough evidence.

'Best thing we ever did was get rid of the courts – that weren't no justice. This –' he points out of the door to the cells and the corridor – 'this is justice. Death is justice and *you* haven't got no place in this system with your stupid softie ideas.'

He shakes his head, sweat beading on his forehead.

'I know how I'll be bloody voting and more than once too.' He drags Martha to standing. 'I don't care how much it'd cost, I'd spend my whole month's wages making sure you fry, girl. If it were up to me, you'd be in that chair tomorrow.'

He wraps the chains around his fist and pulls her to his face. 'How could you do it?' he hisses. 'How could you kill Jackson Paige? The man never hurt no one. Look at all them people he helped. All his charity work. He could've left this country with all that money he had, but he din't. He stayed and helped the likes of you. He was an icon!'

'He was a fucking liar!' Martha hisses.

The head butt forces her backwards, and as he lets go of the chains she slams into the wall and slumps to the side.

Too shocked, Eve doesn't move.

'Did you get that?' he says to her. 'On your phone? Did you get a good shot? Cos I don't give a bloody hoot. Go sell it to the papers. They'll put it on the front page and I'll be hailed a hero.' His cheeks puff out as he grins. 'They'll pay me to do it again.'

Martha watches as his raucous laugh wobbles his whole body. Her face tightens, her eyes narrow and as she stands and stares up at him, she spits in his face.

Before he can react, Eve grabs Martha, pulls her out of the room and into the corridor.

'Calm down!' she shouts behind her. 'I'll see to this. I'll sort her out.'

14

In the corridor are six metal doors, closed but for a small panel, some with anonymous eyes staring out. The seventh, the final one, is at the very end, locked up and silent.

'What you do, girl?' a deep male voice comes from one of the cells.

'Spat in his ignorant face,' Martha replies.

The voice booms a hearty laugh. 'You made my day,' he says. 'You from the Rises?'

'Come on,' Eve says, 'you're not supposed to be talking to anyone. The guard will be out in a minute.'

'Yeah,' Eve replies to the voice.

'Uh-huh. What got you in here? What did a girl do that was so bad?'

'I shot Jackson Paige,' she replies.

'No shit?'

'No shit.'

'Girl, you just made my *year*! Power to the Rises!' he says, and from the gap in the cell, a clenched fist appears, a tattoo of a rose down the side of his hand.

'Come on,' Eve says, but before she can lead her forward, Martha rushes towards the door and rests a hand on the man's fist.

She presses her face up to the gap. 'What did you do?' she whispers.

Dark eyes peer back at her. 'Only thing I ever did wrong, girl, was to be born in the wrong place.'

'Martha, move! Come on, quickly.'

'Good luck,' she whispers to the man and walks away.

Eve pulls open the heavy cell door. 'You shouldn't have . . .' she starts. 'That guard, he's . . .'

15

'What difference does it make?' Martha replies as she steps inside.

'He'll make your life a misery,' Eve says.

'What's left of it, you mean?' Martha shrugs. 'What happens in here doesn't matter. It's what happens out there that does.'

Martha

He doesn't follow me into the cell. I wonder if Eve stops him. Can I trust her?

The cell's small and cold. The walls are bright white without a single mark. There's a window high up on the outside wall, with white bars across – I don't think it opens – and on the wall opposite is a white metal door. It's closed and locked now, the flap in it too. It's like I'm in a box. If there was a fire in the corridor, I'd roast like a chicken.

In fact, everything in here is white – the bed against the wall is white with white sheets and a white pillow, and there's a white toilet in the corner and a white sink.

But that's it.

No shelves, desk, table, lamp, wardrobe (why would I need a wardrobe?), books, pens . . . nothing. Why would I need anything?

The only thing superfluous in here is a clock, high up on the wall above the door, ticking away every second left of my life. And that's white too, with neon hands.

It's totally devoid of anything. Any kind of stimulus. It's like my eyes have been turned to mute or I've been struck down with some weird colour blindness, not where I can't tell the difference, but where there is no colour.

These prison overall things they've put me in are bright

white too and even my brown hair has gone. Shaved off and in somebody's bin.

I feel like I've lost half of myself. My hair was me, my clothes too.

What did I expect? It's prison, for Christ's sake. It's death row. It's not going to be nice, is it?

It's so bright in here it's hurting my eyes and giving me a headache. I can't tell where the light's coming from – there's no bulb dangling in the middle of the cell or strip across the ceiling. I think maybe it's coming from right at the top where the wall joins the ceiling but . . .

Are the walls glowing?

Is that some kind of light-emitting paint?

Is this some torture they've dreamt up?

I'd like to close my eyes, lie on the bed and drift away from here, but even when I close my eyes it's still bright. Shouldn't think I'll sleep much in here and I don't think they want me to.

Torture? Yeah, think I was right.

Maybe they figured out that the best way to cope with this is to sleep the time away. They don't want you to cope; they want you to suffer.

I couldn't really sleep away my final week though, could I? My last seven days of breathing and living. Less than that now. How many hours is it? Minutes? Seconds? I don't want to know. But what else is there to do but sleep and remember?

I lie down, close my eyes and pull the sheets over my head, trying to make it dark, but I'm sure it just gets brighter. Why torture me when I'm going to die anyway?

18

I bury my head in the mattress, screw up my eyes and concentrate on the dark inside them, trying to remember you.

We met in the dark. You were hiding in the shadows just like I was, watching the street, the old cars tearing across the broken tarmac, the stench of exhaust fumes. You weren't there every evening like me, sometimes you didn't stay very long, but I had to go there, see? Couldn't sleep 'til I'd said goodnight to her.

God, I don't want to remember. I miss her, miss you. Hate that I do. Don't want to be soft.

When I picked up that gun she was in my mind, but I didn't do it just for her. I told you to go that night for everyone else who can be saved, for justice and for right.

You wanted to bring down the system; at first all I wanted was to bring down the man.

Not kill him, actually, although that's how it happened, but show him for what he was.

By the end of my seven days here, even those who love him at the moment will have dragged his memory off that pedestal they put him on and my part will be done. I'll rest in peace and so, finally, will the others.

We've got our roles, me and you, defined by where we were brought up – you can be the fighter while I can be the martyr. After all, that's all a girl from the Rises like me can do. I'm not clever enough, confident enough, I haven't got enough money, had no future even before I ended up in here. We thought we could be together but that was bullshit.

Love me enough to let me go.

TV STUDIO

6.30 p.m. The programme –
Death is Justice – is beginning.

On a dark blue screen, flecks of white buzz and crackle like electricity. An oversized eye with an ice-blue iris appears in the middle. It blinks and the words 'An Eye For An Eye For' spin in a circle around the black pupil.

MALE VOICEOVER: An Eye For An Eye Productions brings
you . . .

The words stop spinning. The sounds of electricity fizzes again and the style of the words goes from smooth to jagged. The eye reddens and closes.

MALE VOICEOVER: . . . tonight's show *Death is Justice*
with our host . . .

The blue fades and lights come up on a glitzy studio. The large floor reflects the many studio lights from its silver-blue surface. To the right is an oversized screen filled with the eye logo – the words slowly spinning and the eye blinking – while left of centre is a shiny curved desk with high, glossy stools placed around the back and sides, facing out to the studio audience, who are hidden in shadow.

MALE VOICEOVER: . . . Kristina Albright!

Lights come up on Kristina standing on the left of the stage. She's tall and slim, her blond hair frames her perfect face and her white teeth smile into camera. Her red dress is tight and matches her lipstick and shoes.

KRISTINA: Hello, and welcome to *Death is Justice*!

Applause sounds around the studio. Kristina smiles and nods at the audience.

KRISTINA: My name's Kristina Albright and tonight we have some very exciting news for you.

Kristina's high heels click as she strolls across the floor to the screen on the right. The eye is replaced by a photograph of a handsome, smiling man with a pretty wife and teenage son.

KRISTINA: Breaking news last night brought us the shocking story of the violent murder of multi-millionaire celebrity Jackson Paige.

21

The photograph changes to one of the man with his arms in the air in triumph while a crowd of people applauds.

KRISTINA: Jackson won a place in the hearts of millions after a string of appearances on reality TV shows over the last decade. Originally from the deprived area known as the High Rises, named after the row of tower blocks built to solve the housing crisis . . .

The screen fills with a panoramic of the High Rise area – a dozen concrete towers stretching into a dull sky; a skinny stray dog, empty takeaway wrappers in dirty gutters and a young boy smoking a cigarette, a can of beer in his other hand.

KRISTINA: He invested his winnings wisely, worked hard and took himself out of poverty and became an inspiration to all . . .

The grey of the High Rises disappears, replaced by a large white house with big metal gates and a lush green lawn stretching across its boundary. Pink, orange and yellow flowers pour from baskets and fill borders. A red sports car in the driveway shines in the sun. The smiling man – Jackson – poses next to it.

KRISTINA: . . . with his public appearances, his unrelenting charity work, and of course, not forgetting . . .

Images of Jackson flash onto the screen: him smiling at a camera at a red carpet event, a still of him giving a speech dressed in a tuxedo, another as he passes an oversized cheque to a row of nurses.

KRISTINA: . . . the selfless act of adopting a young boy after a tragic accident left him orphaned.

A black and white photo comes into focus. Jackson, his forehead creased, his eyes watery, his mouth downwards, holds a crying six-year-old boy to his chest. Behind them the tower blocks of the Rises are blurry and dull, but on the cracked pavement, just visible, is the only colour – a trickle of red.

Kristina presses her palms together and holds them in front of her mouth as if in prayer. The studio is silent. She lifts her head, bats her eyelids and looks back into camera.

KRISTINA (quietly): But more about Jackson Paige later. Let's turn our attention to the crime and the perpetrator. What kind of person could commit such a terrible act? Let's go to our roving reporter, Joshua Decker. Josh?

She turns to the screen. A blue banner stretches across the top, a small eye logo blinking in the left corner, the words 'Joshua Decker – roving reporter' sparkling across the middle, while running perpetually along the bottom is 'Cell 1 – teen killer – Martha Honeydew'.

In the middle, his black coat collar up against the wind, leather gloves holding a microphone and his eyes twinkling and smiling despite the November cold, is Joshua.

JOSHUA: Yes, Kristina, hello. I hope you can hear me against this howling wind. It sure is cold here in the Rises. I'm looking forward to getting back home to a hot bath and a glass of wine, I can tell you.

He winks. Female voices mumble around the audience.

JOSHUA: I'm standing about a hundred metres from where the crime was committed. This, for our audience who've never been here, is close to the main rail station that leads to the City and the surrounding Avenues, aptly named the underpass.

His gloved hand points above him. The camera pans away from him, showing the underside of a large by-pass, dark and dank with broken railings and half-crushed bollards that were to stop motorists taking short-cuts. Beyond and out of its shadow is a smaller road followed by a row of shops with smashed or boarded-up windows, and just visible in the distance are the rows of tower blocks with pinpricks of lights in windows.

JOSHUA: This side of it, away from the station, is an area frequented by drug dealers and the homeless.

KRISTINA: Tell us what's happening there, Joshua. What are people saying about our killer?

The camera focuses again on Joshua.

JOSHUA: Well, Kristina, thing is, they're not. Nobody's talking. For the residents of the High Rises it's as if it never happened. Unlike the rest of the population, that is, as I'm sure you can see around me.

The camera follows Joshua as he walks, panning out as he stops to see flowers, cuddly toys, photographs, handwritten messages and burning candles left on the ground. A woman on her knees places more flowers, two men hug each other as they sob.

JOSHUA: This is the site where he was gunned down. These people can barely contain their grief. There's been a steady stream of them all morning. Teenagers who've had their parents drive them here on their way to school, a couple of doctors taking a detour before surgery, some nurses paying their respect after a night-shift. Most too upset to speak, or even if they can, unable to put their feelings of grief and shock into words.

But . . . try to ask the opinions of shopkeepers around here, young mothers taking children to school, teenage boys on street corners, people queuing for their benefits . . . nobody wants to talk.

KRISTINA: Very strange.

JOSHUA: That it is. Ranks are closed, it seems. But, I hasten to add, this roving reporter has managed to get an exclusive for you . . .

He gives a lop-sided smile and tilts his head sideways.

KRISTINA (smiling to the audience): I'm not going to ask how he managed to get an exclusive, but I'm guessing it's something to do with that charm of his!

The audience laugh.

JOSHUA (with a wink): Yes, Kristina, we have some video footage of the moments following the crime. I think it speaks for itself.

His image flies into a frame on the left of the screen, on the right another frame is filled with a shaky video image.

JOSHUA: This is footage from the police head-cam. It was thought initially that the alarm was raised via CCTV, but it appears the cameras in the vicinity were broken.

The footage shows half-lit streets flying towards the camera, rain and windscreen obscuring all but the obvious. In the distance the darkened shadows of the tower blocks loom as if they are gravestones in the evening sky, and around them roads flow like blackened rivers. Flashing blue from police lights reflect off wet streets and metal shutters on buildings, and sirens wail in anger.

The changing of the scenery slows. Headlights turn a corner and flood white into an area beneath the underpass. The car stops. Drowned in light is Martha, long dark hair wet from the rain and eyes wide like a rabbit's, her hands are in the air; in one is a gun.

The image wobbles as it moves out of the car. In front of it a pair of arms are extended, hands clasped around a gun pointing at Martha.

POLICE OFFICER (off-screen): Drop the gun and put your hands on your head!

She bends and drops the gun on the ground. Shaking, the camera moves closer to her. She puts her hands on her head. The camera focuses on her face now filling the screen.

MARTHA: I did it! I shot him! I killed Jackson Paige.

On the screen in the studio, the frame on the right pauses on Martha's face, while on the left, Joshua sighs and shakes his head slowly.

KRISTINA (quietly): Thank you, Joshua. We look forward to catching up with you again tomorrow.

She drops her head a moment, then lifts it back to camera.

KRISTINA: Martha Honeydew may look as sweet as her name suggests, but in reality, is she a cold-hearted killer who has stolen from us one of the most famous and well-loved characters of our time? She says she is.

MARTHA (off-screen, recording): I did it! I shot him! I killed Jackson Paige.

KRISTINA: Her words, viewers. The gun in her hands.

The word 'KILLER' is stamped in red across her paused image. Still facing into the camera, Kristina strolls towards the curved desk, the lights above it dimmed.

KRISTINA: An open and shut case then. She is the first female teenager on death row and it seems she's very likely to be the first executed. After all, why would you, the voter, doubt her word?

The still of Martha disappears, the screen filled instead with the eye.

Kristina eases onto the stool at the end of the desk, her long legs positioned neatly to her side. The lights brighten,

28

revealing a small man on the stool to her left. His shoulders are hunched and his head is low, his hair sticks out in tufts.

KRISTINA: But before we move on to another occupant of death row, we'll turn our attention for a moment to what our celebrity-killer, Martha Honeydew, will be doing right now and how she'll be feeling.

She smiles at the man.

KRISTINA: Gus, welcome.

His face lifts. He flicks a smile at her and his eyes dodge around the audience. Twitchy, he runs a finger along the inside of his shirt collar and tugs at his jacket sleeves.

KRISTINA: Five years ago you *were* one of those people. Incarcerated for a crime the public voted you not guilty of. You are ultimately experienced to tell us how she'll be feeling tonight. What will be going through her mind?'

GUS (quietly): Ummm . . . Well, yeah, as you said, I was accused of murdering . . .

His low voice quivers with nerves.

KRISTINA: I'm sorry, Gus, can you speak up?

His body jutters as he takes a deep breath.

GUS (slightly louder): Yeah . . . yeah . . . erm . . . five years
    ago I was accused of murdering someone but . . . but
    thanks to you viewers . . .

He turns to camera, smiles widely but awkwardly; the
audience applaud.

GUS: I was let off.

KRISTINA: And how was it, Gus? How was that first night?
    How will it be for our prisoner facing the final
    days of her life?

GUS: Well, first, just so viewers know, right, she was arrested
    yesterday but been charged and put in the system
    and that, so wouldn't have arrived on death row 'til
    this morning, so like, as you said, today's her first day.
    Day one – Cell 1. 'Til sunrise, that is. At sunrise, you
    change cell.

KRISTINA: And what is Cell 1 like?

He runs his finger along the inside of his collar again, now
soaked with sweat. He looks down, frowns.

KRISTINA: Gus, we know this must be hard for you and we're
    asking a lot, but as I'm sure you understand, it's

vital for us, the voters, to have a full comprehension of the situation in order to make sure we vote correctly. I've suggested many times that video feed into the cells would provide voters with a far more complete understanding of the accused.

She turns to the audience.

KRISTINA (nodding): Don't you agree?

The audience cheer and clap.

KRISTINA: Gus? Cell 1. Tell us.

GUS: Er . . . yeah . . . it was . . .

He looks up and around at leering faces, sits upright, touches a hand to his right ear and takes a breath.

GUS: . . . basic. There was a bed and . . . erm . . . a sink and . . . a toilet . . .

KRISTINA: A toilet in the same room as you *sleep* in?

He touches a hand to his ear again and forces a laugh.

GUS: Er . . . no . . . no, there's a bathroom. That's what I meant. Not a sink neither, it's a hand basin – and a toilet, in the bathoom. And a shower.

He swallows hard and takes a breath.

GUS: In the cell . . . there's . . . books, loads of books, and a
      TV. . . . erm . . . and pictures on the walls . . .

He wrings his hands together.

KRISTINA: Not how you'd expect a criminal to be treated, Gus.

GUS (quietly): S'pose not . . .

KRISTINA: It sounds to me as if our Martha won't feel like
      she's being punished at all. Next you'll be telling
      me that the doors are left open!

Gus touches his ear, glances to camera, and back to Kristina.

GUS: They are.

Kristina leans backwards, her mouth falling open, her palms
opening out.

GUS: And . . . they . . . the prisoners . . . they can talk to
      each other.

Kristina tuts audibly.

KRISTINA (to camera): Let's think about that, shall we,
      voters? This girl has said she did it. She's admitted

she gunned down a man in cold blood and watched the very life seep from him, she's freely admitted that and has shown no remorse and she is sitting around watching television, chatting . . . and eating . . . Gus, what would she be eating?'

GUS (muttering): Fish and chips today, and sticky toffee pudding. Vanilla custard.

KRISTINA: Well, justice, viewers, is in your hands as always. Let's take a look at those all-important numbers and voting information. Across the bottom of your screen now, you can see the numbers to vote for Martha. Dial 0909 87 97 77 and to vote *guilty* add 7 to the end or to vote *not guilty* add a 0. You can also vote by texting DIE or LIVE to 7997. To vote online visit our website www.aneyeforaneyeproductions.com, click on the 'Martha Honeydew Teen Killer' tab at the top and log your vote. Calls are charged at premium rate, please seek bill payer's permission, texts cost £5 plus your network provider's standard fee, voting online is also £5 after an initial registration fee of £20. For full Ts and Cs visit our website.

A blue band with the numbers and details written in silver glides across the bottom of the screen.

KRISTINA: Gus, as always it's been fascinating speaking to you, and we have so much more we could discuss: motive, broken childhood, missing father, dead mother, but we have seven days to debate.

GUS (muttering): And the counsellor.

KRISTINA: Counsellor? Explain.

GUS (slow, as if copying): Her counsellor is Eve Stanton. The only counsellor who's never been on this show. Never does interviews or nothing. Never comments on stuff.

KRISTINA: Excellent point, Gus.

The camera focuses only on her.

KRISTINA: And an exciting one, viewers, one we'll be leading you through over the next seven days; much to discuss and many stones not to be left unturned. Join us again after this message from our sponsor – Cyber Secure – when we'll be looking at the last few hours of the accused currently in Cell 7 – what will judgement bring to him? Life? Or death? And in seven days what will it be for our newest resident – teen killer, Martha Honeydew?

The lights in the studio dim. Gus rips the earpiece out and storms off set.

Eve

'What you watching, Mum?'

Eve takes off her glasses and rubs her eyes. A brief smile flickers as she watches her son, Max, bound into the kitchen-diner, put his laptop onto the table, open the fridge and peer inside.

Instinctively she shuffles together the papers spread out on the table in front of her, turning some over or placing others into files to hide all the images and names from view.

'Nothing really,' she mutters. 'It's just on.'

Max glances to the TV in the corner of the room. '*Death is Justice?*' He pulls off his headphones, heavy guitar bleeding out. 'You *never* watch that!'

He grabs a bottle of juice and slumps down at the table opposite her, peeling open the lid and watching her gathering together the files.

'Are you her counsellor? That girl? The one who killed Jackson Paige?'

'Who *says* she killed . . . ?'

'Whoa, you are, aren't you?'

'And you don't know if she . . .' She closes her eyes, props her elbows on the table and rests her head in her hands.

For a moment he watches, then he picks up the remote and turns off the TV.

'Don't watch it,' he mumbles, and he stands back up, pours her a coffee from the machine and places it in front of her. 'It's junk. And they manipulate you.'

'Max . . .'

'Everyone knows it, just no one says it. It's horseshit, it's not justice.'

She flinches.

He takes a swig of his drink. 'Have you eaten?' he asks.

'Not yet,' she mutters. 'Earlier . . . breakfast . . . sandwich at lunch.'

He shakes his head. 'Come on.' Taking her by the elbow, he leads her across the room to the sofa.

'I don't need you to look after me,' she says.

'Who else is going to? Sit down.'

She slumps into the cushions and he lifts her legs onto the seat.

'Stay there. I'll make you some food.'

When he returns with a bowl of pasta, she's fast asleep.

He throws a blanket over her, dims the light, and retreats to the kitchen area. Back at the table, he lifts the food to his own mouth and stares at the files and papers in front of him.

Chewing the first mouthful, he glances back to her; her face is against the comfort of the sofa and her breathing is heavy. He puts down the fork, and turns over the first page.

Martha

Something wakes me. Didn't realise I'd slept. My eyes hurt in the bright as I open them. I hear voices. Someone chanting or praying, someone else crying.

Is there someone in every cell? Seven cells and seven people all waiting to die?

Doubt it. I heard it's never full. Threat of death will do that, they said, make people behave. Talk of building a death row in Birmingham, Manchester, other cities, stayed as talk – no more needed.

Ship the accused from wherever to this one here in London. No loved ones near them? No family? What the hell does that matter? They don't see visitors anyway. A prisoner loses all rights when they're accused.

You said they rule with an iron smile – the folks it suits only see the smile, while we feel the iron. I didn't really care – I just wanted to see that scumbag Paige brought down. Or that's how it started. But life isn't that simple, is it?

How many people then? Who's awake and crying? Does anyone manage to sleep more than five minutes? Wonder if I'll see them when we change cells at dawn.

No hint of that yet though; it's dark out the window.

I want to see outside.

I drag the bed over; it scratches along the floor but nobody comes at the noise. I stand on it and stretch upwards, but the window is angled so all I can see is sky. Now I'm facing away from the light, I can see it's not black like it seems, it's a deep, velvet blue, pinpricked with stars. I cup my hands around my eyes to block more of the light. The moon's full, staring down at me like it stared down at me and you together last night. Before this crap happened.

Maybe we should've run away together. Forgotten Paige and the pain he caused, made our own lives and futures . . .

Who am I trying to kid? The pain would've carried on eating me 'til there was nothing left and we would've both been forced to watch corruption make the rich richer and the poor poorer and justice disintegrate further.

'The sky was all we could ever share, Isaac,' I breathe.

I move a hand through the bars as far as I can, letting the moonlight fall onto my skin. 'Are you looking out now as well?'

Clouds pass over and the moonlight fades. 'I hope this is worth it.'

CELL 2

Counselling

Martha sits opposite Eve in the counselling room, her face almost as white as the room she spent the night in. Her prison overalls have turned grubby around her wrists and ankles from the chains, and grey lines have formed down the front where they're joined together.

She clinks as she moves in her seat and jangles as she rests her hands on the table in front of her, her fingers fiddling with the edge of Eve's folder, notebook and pen.

'How did you sleep?' Eve asks.

Martha shrugs.

'A bit too bright? They do have some funny ways here.'

'Hilarious,' Martha replies.

Eve leans in slightly. 'Designed to shake you,' she whispers.

'Great. Does that mean there's something else today?'

Eve ignores her. 'It's less than six days now,' she says.

'You know just how to cheer someone up,' Martha replies.

She looks away and out of the barred window, the wind brushing the branches of the tree against the glass.

'They shouldn't have planted a tree so close to the building,' she says.

Eve glances over her shoulder. 'Why?'

'Isn't it obvious? The roots will attack the building's foundations. Cause subsidence or something. Make the

41

building fall down. Bet they wouldn't know 'til it was too late.'

Eve nearly smiles. 'You know a lot.'

'Why would they plant it there?' Her face screws up as she thinks.

While the clock ticks on, Eve watches Martha as she opens her mouth to speak, but closes it again, and she watches as she shuffles in her chair, folds her arms across her chest, stretches her hands across her shaved head then drums her fingers on the desk.

'I planted it,' Eve says.

'*You* did?' Martha turns to her with her eyebrows raised. 'Huh. Why?'

'I thought it would be nice for the prisoners to see it,' she replies. 'A sparrow has a nest in it.' She turns to look at it again. 'He's not there right now, but he'll be back.'

'I saw him yesterday. Can you open the window? Let some fresh air in?'

'No,' Eve replies. 'It's locked.'

''Course it is,' Martha mumbles. She looks back to Eve. 'You look tired,' she says.

'We're not here to talk about me. Tell me how you are.'

'I don't see the point of this,' Martha replies. 'It's not going to change anything. I'm still going to die in six days.'

'If they vote you guilty.'

'I told them I did it, why wouldn't they vote me guilty?'

'Maybe they won't believe you. Maybe they'll think that it's too easy, or wonder why you would admit to it, even if you did do it.'

42

Martha folds her arms again. 'People don't question, it's too much effort. Why bother?'

'What do you mean?'

'They don't want to know the truth, they just believe what's fed to them. "Let someone else do the thinking, we'll just follow the crowd," they say. "We don't care if you make it up as long as it sounds like a scandal." Sheep.'

'Martha . . .'

'Nosy sheep that like to ooh and ahh, and read gossip headlines that are all just a load of made-up shit to sell newspapers and make money.'

Eve frowns, leans forward and rests her arms on the table. 'Martha, you told the police that you're guilty. They have you on record as saying, "I did it, I shot him, I killed Jackson Paige."'

Martha nods.

'Are you trying to tell me that you didn't do it? Do you want to change your plea? I can tell them that for you.'

Martha stares at the counsellor.

'Do you want to change your plea?'

Martha blinks and her eyes glisten with worry.

'Tell me,' Eve hisses at her. 'You didn't do it, did you? It wasn't your gun. Somebody else was with you, weren't they?'

Martha doesn't move.

'If you're innocent, you have to speak out. You can't take the blame for someone else's crime.'

'I'm not,' she says and roughly brushes a tear from her face. 'Why are you going on about it? Just shut up.'

'Who did it? If you tell me I can help.'

Martha swallows and breathes heavy. She stares at Eve. 'I told you,' she whispers. 'I did it. It was my gun. I bought it from a guy who lives in the Rises.'

'But there was someone else with you, wasn't there?'

'I told you I did it!' she shouts. 'What more do you want? Nothing else matters! Not whether someone else was with me, or if it was my gun or not. *I* did it! *I* shot Jackson Paige!'

'Why?'

'Because . . . because . . . This isn't one of your old courts! I don't have to answer that. I just killed him because I wanted to. OK?'

'If it was a court, if we still had courts, they might ask you why you shot him in the exact spot your mother was killed.'

Martha's face turns to stone. 'Coincidence,' she mutters.

Her eyes blink and blink and her breathing is heavy in her chest. She stares at Eve, her eyes full of venom, her mouth open to say something but no words come. She stands up and strides to the window. As the branches sway in the wind, she lifts a hand and touches the glass between the bars.

Behind her, Eve stays seated.

In their own worlds, they're silent.

The clock ticks. Outside in the corridor heavy boots move towards them, then away. In one of the other cells, somebody shouts, something unintelligible, guttural, painful.

'It was a hit-and-run, wasn't it?' Eve asks through the stillness. 'It left you orphaned and alone.

Martha doesn't reply.

'Your neighbour's son was arrested for it, wasn't he? He was here, on death row. He was executed.'

The chains clink as Martha folds her arms across her chest. 'Shut up with the questions.'

'I imagine it's hard to think that you're in the same cell that your mother's killer was. The same bed . . .'

'I thought counselling was supposed to make you feel better?' Martha says.

'Why don't you sit down?'

Martha ignores her.

'You must've been relieved they caught him so quickly, your mother's killer? What was his name? Oliver . . .'

'Ollie,' she says. 'Everyone called him Ollie.'

'You must've been pleased.'

'Did you read it in the tabloids, what they said about him?'

'I don't read the tabloids . . .'

Martha turns around from the window, brushes a hand over her head and sits back at the table. 'The people who vote on *Death is Justice* do. They read it and believe it. He used to look after me when my mum worked, Ollie did, but they didn't write that. They didn't put that he taught me to play chess, fixed the motor on the washing machine when it broke or that we celebrated with him and his mum when he got a job, that I baked him a cake when he bought his first car.'

'The car he hit your mother with?'

They stare at each other. 'Yeah, of course I was relieved when they arrested him.' She doesn't take her eyes from Eve. '*Thrilled* when they executed him. Who wouldn't have been?'

'You don't think he did it?'

Martha tuts. 'Why are you even interested?'

'Because it's obviously important to you.'

45

'You must've met him. He was in here.'

'I'm not everyone's counsellor,' Eve replies. 'There are a couple of us.'

'Were you his?'

Eve puts her hands together and lifts them to her face. 'I don't remember,' she whispers.

Martha stares at her. 'Time's up,' she says, and she stands and moves to the door.

'Martha . . .'

'Press the button, call the guard.'

'It's not easy, watching people through this, knowing they'll more than likely die.'

'But we deserve it, don't we?'

Eve doesn't say a word.

Martha strides back to the table, puts her palms on the surface and stares at Eve. 'Don't we?'

'If . . .' Eve mutters, folding her arms across her chest and leaning back in her seat. 'If . . .' her voice is low, '. . . you did . . .' She shrugs her shoulders. 'The law states that should the accused be found guilty of the crime of taking another life, then their life shall be taken from them.'

'Culpae poenae par esto,' Martha says. '"Let the punishment fit the crime." I know what the law says. I asked what you think.'

'What I think doesn't matter; what I do does. I do this job because I believe everyone should have support in what could be their final days. Nobody should approach death alone. And I do it because,' she swallows hard and brushes a loose strand of hair from her face, 'because, believe it or not, I do care.'

46

Martha sits down, watching Eve while seconds tick by on the clock above them. In the window movement catches her eye and as she glances over Eve's shoulder, sees the sparrow is back in the tree.

'Prove that you care,' she whispers. 'Do something for me.'

Martha reaches across the table, pulling the notepad and pen towards her.

With her left arm draped in front of her, hiding the pad from Eve, she starts to write.

'I want you to take this to someone.' She doesn't look up. 'But I don't want you to read it, OK? You said you care – if you do, then do this for me.'

'I'm not supposed to . . .'

'I'm guessing you weren't supposed to plant a tree outside the window either.' She finishes writing, tears the sheet from the pad, folds it over and writes on the outside.

'Where am I taking it?' Eve asks.

Martha glances up to her, a smile touching the edges of her mouth. 'The address is on it.' She pushes the note across the table and under the folder. 'Promise you won't read it.'

'I promise.'

'Now I'd like to go.'

Sliding a hand under the table, Eve presses the button to call the guard.

As the key creaks around in the lock, Martha looks back to Eve and frowns. 'You said your name was Stanton.'

'Yes,' she says.

'Are you related to Jim Stanton?'

The guard steps into the room. 'Done, are we?' he says.

Ignoring him, Eve nods slowly at Martha, lifts her hands onto the table and turns her wedding ring around on her finger.

Martha shuffles to the doorway, the chains rattling against each other, but she pauses and looks back at Eve.

'If it means anything,' she whispers, 'he seemed a nice man.'

Eve

Eve drives past the cluster of flowers and tributes to Jackson that are starting to be left and pulls up at the side of the road.

She stops the engine and chews at her fingernail as she looks around at the landscape outside the car. The pavements are dirty, some broken; empty crisp packets, chip wrappers and burger boxes collect in corners or gutters, and past them dry, scrubby grass leads to a park with two rusty swings, a broken climbing frame and a wooden bench with only two slats left for the seat.

A gang of kids sit around it, hoods up and huddled close against the winter cold. Over the grass is a shop with boarded-up windows and a half-illuminated sign flickering in the dark as the last few bulbs struggle to keep going. Outside of it a couple of young men and women chat with hands stuffed in pockets and collars turned up against the wind.

Casting everything and everybody in darker shadows are the High Rises. Tall, dull, grey concrete flats blurring against a cloudy and grey sky. Concrete trees in a concrete jungle.

Eve steps out of the car, pulls her coat tight; wraps a scarf around her neck and pulls a woolly hat onto her head. In her pocket, Martha's note crinkles.

As she crosses the road and heads across the grass towards the High Rises, she feels the eyes of the kids on her.

'Hey, woman!' one of them shouts. 'You lost? You come off the motorway too soon!'

She dips her face into her scarf.

'There's nothing here for you and your folk. Not unless you want to end up like Jackson Paige!' His laugh cackles through the icy air.

Eve keeps facing forward, eyes on the High Rises, watching them get closer, but she hears footsteps running towards her, louder and louder, until they slow and she senses someone next to her.

'You press?' he asks. 'Tourist? I can show you where he was shot. There's still blood on the path. You can take a photo of it.'

She ignores him.

'I can tell you loads about it. For a price. I know everything what goes on round here, see? I could get you a scoop for your newspaper.'

She glances sideways to him as she walks. 'I'm not press,' she says.

'TV then. Reckon I could get one of them women to give you an interview for the right price. As long as you don't mention my name, that is.'

Eve stops. 'What women?' she asks. 'Are you talking about Jackson Paige? Are you suggesting he was having an affair?'

He scoffs. 'You folks put yourselves in your ivory towers and haven't got no clue as to what goes on outside of them. Everyone round here knows he was having affairs! And they know the truth about what happened the other night.'

'You're Gus. I saw you on *Death Is Justice*.'

He looks down, shaking his head and shuffling his feet. 'Nah, you're wrong, that weren't me.'

Eve takes a tentative step forwards and stares at him, and as she lifts her face from her scarf he recoils slightly.

'Yes it was.' Her voice is quiet and she watches his dirty fingernails scratch at his face. 'Why did you lie?' she asks. 'Why did you say all that about the cells? That's not how they are.'

'Yeah, well, I know that, don't I?'

'Were you lying about being on death row too?'

He pauses for a second. 'You tell me.'

'No. You tell me what you know about Paige.'

'I know information's important. Know not to give nothing away what folks like you'll pay for.'

Eve walks on. 'I won't pay,' she mutters.

He chases after her. 'But you want to know, don't you?'

'I don't think you know anything,' she shouts over her shoulder.

'Well, I do. I hang around here, see? Watch stuff, people going about their business and that. I'm not thick, can put it all together, y'know?'

'I still don't believe you.'

'Well, I know he'd been having affairs with women round here.'

'You already told me that.'

'Know I could get one of them to talk to you, for a price. Y'see, that's why he was here all the time. That and selling drugs.'

He stops walking, shoves his hands deep in his pockets and kicks at the dirt by his feet. The cold bites at him and his eyes water as he watches her.

'I don't blame you for not remembering me!' he shouts through the wind. 'I mean, we only talked for what, seven hours all together?'

She pauses.

'There's no need to feel guilty or nothing. I get that there's more important things in your life than folks like me dying. Or not dying, as it happened.'

She strides back to him, shouting across the parkland. 'Are you a pathological liar? Is this some ridiculous game you're playing with me? What is it you want? Money? Is that it?'

'Money, money, money, everything's money with you folk.'

'You're the one trying to charge me for information.'

'Man's got to eat.'

She spins away from him. 'You make no sense.'

'Five years ago. Summertime. July 20th to the 27th. Hottest summer in God knows how many years. No air-con in that room of yours. They, the police, said I throttled a man for nicking my drugs. They had the body and everything. Woke up and it was there in my flat. Scared the crap out of me. Next thing they're barging my door down.'

She stares at him.

'Told them I never did no drugs, but they found some in my flat, didn't they? Told them it was planted there. The body too. Asked them for a blood test to prove it but they refused.'

The wind batters them both, rubbish blowing past their feet and off across the scrubby grass, the sound of the air through the chains of the swing in the distance like ghosts whistling around them.

Gus kicks at the ground. 'Had to do something. Couldn't just give up, could I? Didn't want folks to remember me as some murdering druggie. Weren't right. So I did the only thing I could. I stopped . . .'

'You stopped eating,' Eve interrupts, her voice quiet as memories flood back.

'Yeah,' he says.

'Then you refused water too.' For a moment she does nothing but watch his expression.

'You look so different now,' she says. 'I didn't recognise you.'

Gus shrugs.

'I'm sorry,' she continues, 'I should've done more for you back then, but . . .'

'You tried,' he says. 'Snuck me chocolate in, didn't you? Tried to tempt me but it didn't work. Don't matter now though.'

'It does but . . .' She rubs a hand across her forehead. 'At least you got off.'

He laughs. 'Yeah, right.'

'What? I don't understand.'

'Come on! It was rigged! The whole thing. It was a set-up cos they wanted someone. You remember that doctor who came to my cell? He weren't no doctor. Gave me an option, he did. I can get you out, he says, sort the stats, he tells me, but you have to do things for us. What kind of things? I ask and he just laughs, but don't say nothing. Got you, he's thinking.

'Y'know what it did, all that? Proved to everyone here that they own us. They can do whatever they want. Accuse, set up, lie about. Y'know where I am now?'

He takes her hand and gently peels open her fingers. 'Right there,' he says, touching her palm. 'Right where they want me and I can't do nothing about it. Can't change it, can't get out, can't do nothing. They want to know something, I've got to find it out. They want me watching someone? I've got to watch them. It's like I'm their stooge or something. And as soon as I do something they don't like . . .' He squeezes her hand into a fist. 'I'll be a goner . . .'

'How do I know I can trust you then?' she asks. 'How do I know you won't tell them I've been here? Whoever *they* are?'

He shrugs. 'If I was going to blab about you being here, why would I be telling you all this? I'm just a decent guy in a crap situation. I tell them *some* shit, I don't tell them other.'

'Isn't that a dangerous game?'

'Well, some folks don't deserve telling on.'

'Like Martha?'

Gently he moves her hands back down to her side.

'Different that, isn't it?'

For a moment they stand in silence. Above them clouds grow darker and lower; a storm is in the air, the damp of threatening rain, the thrill of static waiting for lightning. Eve pulls her coat tight around her and shuffles her chin into the collar.

'Tell me where you're going then and I'll see you there safe.'

'Are you going to try to charge me for that?' she asks, a hint of a smile in her voice.

'Nah,' he replies, 'I'll do it for free just cos I'm nice like that.'

She glances at him from the corner of her eye.

'Daffodil House,' she says. 'Floor eighteen. Flat eleven.'

He frowns at her. 'That isn't Martha's place, that's next door, Mrs B's. Why are you going there?'

Eve ignores him.

'OK, OK, don't tell me.'

'You knew Martha, didn't you?'

'I'm saying nothing about that. Not even if you *do* pay me.'

'I'm trying to help her,' Eve mutters.

'Yeah,' he replies. 'Reckon you are. C'mon then.' He starts walking. 'It's the one in the middle. Don't look much like no daffodil, does it?'

'Thank you,' she says.

'For what?'

'For telling me things for free.' She flicks him a brief smile.

Martha

I didn't think I'd feel this lonely.

I thought I'd be allowed visitors or something. Or there'd be something to do. Reading, maybe, or be allowed out of the cell, talk to the other accused. Not just this. In a cell for twenty-three hours a day. Nothing but thoughts and worries. Old memories, few good.

I've never felt so alone.

When Mum went to work at night and I'd lie in bed listening to bumps and creaks around me, I'd know she'd be back in the morning. After she was killed, the TV kept me company and Mrs B was always next door and popping in to make sure I was OK.

I miss you, Mrs B. Miss having dinner with you and Ollie after Mum had gone, both of us as sad as each other but not saying anything. What could we say? You were like an auntie to me and I'm sorry. You've suffered so much and were so good to me, and to Mum too. I hope you understand.

When Ollie was arrested and you cried in my arms, saying over and over that he didn't do it, I believed you because I already knew – so did the whole population of all the Rises put together – but it didn't matter, did it?

'How could he have hit her when his car was stolen?' we screamed at the television and that *Death is Justice* programme.

Everybody we knew voted for his innocence, even people we didn't know, who'd come up to us on the street and tell us that they'd voted and so had their mother, brother, father, sister, aunt, uncle, next-door neighbour, even the bloody dog if it could!

Because we all knew who did do it – that slimy toe-rag of a man, with all his money and celebrity friends, and police influence and all that crap.

Jackson Paige.

We were no match for his money, were we?

He could leave his phone on redial, voting hundreds and thousands and millions of times. We were ripping apart sofas to find enough change for one more vote.

'We can eat properly next week,' I remember telling you. 'Pay the bills, the rent . . . everything, next week.'

I went with you to his execution; the press had a field day.

'Victim's Daughter Escorts Killer's Mother' – was a headline – 'Forgiveness As Justice Is Served?' was another.

Justice?

What justice?

You didn't even get to hold your son one last time.

When the press shoved microphones into our faces afterwards, I opened my mouth to tell them what I thought, but before we could speak, we were dragged away by Jackson's men, bungled into a car and thrown back out again at the bottom of Daffodil House.

Then you're old news, aren't you?

Nobody's interested. Someone else is facing the chair. Who cares if they're innocent or guilty? It's entertainment, isn't it?

Bitter?

Yeah, you know what? I am bitter.

But I'm also determined now.

I can be lonely for a week.

And I can be dead.

People will see, hear what I have to say and maybe, maybe, they'll understand. Maybe they'll finally get it and be shocked and all that, and I'll have done my bit. Then it'll be up to you, Isaac, to use that shockwave and change things for good.

Eve

The lift doors of Daffodil House judder open and Eve steps out and into the corridor of floor eighteen, the lights above her flickering onto the bare walls and dirty floor.

'It doesn't smell much like a daffodil either,' she mumbles to herself.

The yellow police tape and no entry signs outside lead her like a beacon towards number twelve. Next to it, plain and innocuous, is number eleven. With a deep breath, she knocks, waiting as police sirens and car alarms sound in the distance.

After a few minutes she hears the shunt of bolts and the turn of keys, and as the door creaks open, a crinkled pair of eyes behind horn-rimmed glasses peer out from the gap spanned by the safety chain.

The eyes widen. 'Eve Stanton,' the woman croaks. 'What brings you to my door?'

'I have a message for you.'

The eyes continue to stare.

'Well?' Mrs B says. 'What is it?'

Eve takes the folded-up paper from her pocket, pauses a second as she looks at it, then holds it to the gap.

Mrs B pulls it from her and before Eve can say a word the door slams in her face.

59

She shakes her head and closes her eyes, both aching from the lights flickering across the darkness.

'Great,' she says to herself, 'what do I do now?' But before she can decide, the chain on the other side of the door jangles and the handle creaks down.

'Come in if you want,' Mrs B says.

Eve steps inside and closes the door behind her.

'I have nothing to say to you but I make you cup of tea, if you want.' Mrs B disappears through a doorway to the side. 'You're first visitor I've had in long time,' she shouts through. 'Maybe I have biscuits . . .'

'A cup of tea would be lovely, thank you.'

The entrance leads into the living area, which is calm, clean and welcoming; a sofa covered in wool, knitting needles and magazines, a television on a stand next to a potted plant that stands on top of a small three-legged table. Eve steps further inside, pausing at some photographs on the wall.

In one is a young man with unruly hair and a wide smile, leaning on the bonnet of a red car; in another is the same person, although much younger, wearing school trousers that look baggy from the knees down, a blazer slightly too wide at the shoulders, and a jumper with arms that cover his hands. He's holding a postcard, his fingers touching the domes of Saint Basil's Cathedral in Red Square, Moscow.

'First day of secondary school,' Mrs B says from behind Eve. 'My smart boy. We could never afford to go back and see family, so we sent them picture showing he think of them.'

'Is that Ollie?' Eve asks.

Mrs B nods as she places a tray on the table, with two odd

cups with saucers that don't match either, a teapot with a cracked lid, a faded sugar bowl and a gravy boat used to hold the milk. Amongst it all is an unopened packet of biscuits.

'Then you must be Mrs Barkova.'

'You call me Mrs B. Everyone does.' She pours the tea into the cups. 'You see photo at end with white frame? That is happiest memory of my life.'

Eve takes a step across, leaning in to see the faces.

'Who is it?' she asks.

'Christmas Day nine years ago. On the right is me, next is Beth, Martha's mum, then little Martha, about seven I say. Next to her, with no Christmas hat, is my Ollie.'

'Of course,' Eve says. 'He has the curly hair.'

'That he does.' She replaces the teapot on the tray. 'Did,' she whispers. 'Sit, enjoy your tea; you look tired.'

Eve sits down next to her on the sofa. 'You're the second person who's said that to me today.' She takes a sip of tea. 'Martha was the first.'

With her hands in her lap, Mrs B watches Eve.

'And how is our Martha?'

Eve blows the steam across the surface of the tea. 'Stubborn,' she says.

Mrs B smiles.

'Worried, I think. Sad. But she wouldn't tell me so.' She takes another sip and places the cup back on the tray.

'She didn't do it,' Eve continues, 'although she insists she did.'

Mrs B doesn't move or say a word.

'Was the message for you?' Eve asks. 'Can you write back to her and tell her to change her plea?'

'Message was not for me. I pass it on to right person.'

'Why didn't she ask me to do that?'

Mrs B laughs. 'Didn't want you to know who it was for! But you will work it out I think. Probably you will meet before this is over. Other question? No, I can't tell her to change her plea.'

'Why?'

'Why? Why what? Why everything? Mrs Stanton, when person with loud voice steps forward it is easy for majority to follow, and follow they will wherever it is, as long as everyone else does also. It takes braver person, braver than them following leader, to break from pack. Brave person to voice different opinion.

'Sometimes most unlikely person is best for job. Most unlikely wins battle, most unlikely steps forward.'

'Are you saying Martha . . . ?'

'I'm saying nothing but listen and look and hope. Hope good can come from bad. Hope God can win. Hope balance is . . . what is word now . . . clothed?'

Eve frowns at her.

Mrs B's face wrinkles in thought. 'Still English harder than Russian. What is it? Balance is *dressed*?'

'Oh,' Eve replies. 'You mean redressed. Balance is . . .'

'Yes, yes, that. I've watched Martha grow to lovely girl and turn into strong young woman, though everything taken from her. She fell into pit I thought she'd never get out of. Then, Mrs Stanton, I watched glimmer of hope walk into her life and her face light because things *could* be better. There was happiness in her eyes and smile on her face I'd not seen in long time.' She looks away.

'Broke my heart when it went.'

'What happened?'

'Not for me to say. There are a hundred Marthas in the Rises, thousands out there, million more all over. What she's doing is for her own reasons but for all of them Marthas too, and all Ollies.'

'But all she's doing is sacrificing her life for something she hasn't done. She's going to die.'

'No it is not! You do not look around you and you do not listen!' Her finger jabs into the air. 'We hope and we pray and keep voting with every penny we own. Justice will –'

'Mrs B, clearly you know more than me about Martha's motives, but I can guarantee you that unless she changes her plea she will die in five days' time.'

Mrs B watches her over the top of her glasses. 'You are not fortune teller. You do not know everything. There is time and chance for her to be voted innocent.'

'I'm telling you there is no escape from this. In fact, even if she does alter her plea now, it would take a lot of work to change people's minds about her.'

'Mrs Stanton, it's time you leave.'

'Why are you giving up on her?'

'I'm not.'

'You've watched her grow up and now you're going to watch her die?'

'No, Mrs Stanton.'

'Is that how you want people to remember her? As a murderer? Because that's what will happen.'

'I want you to leave now.' She stands up, grabs the biscuits from the tray and strides to the door, Eve following behind.

'I'm disappointed . . .'

Mrs B pauses with her hand on the latch. 'I am disappointed also. In life. System. Justice. Disappointed my friend was killed, my son executed and now the only person in my life may also die. But her decision is her own. And . . . and I must respect that. I'm sure, Mrs Stanton, that of all people in this world you understand that.'

'But –'

'There is no but. There is nothing for me to say or do.'

Weary, Eve rubs her forehead. 'There is something you could do for her though. You could be her representative. She needs someone.'

'What, go on that show?'

'Yes, and speak for her. Tell them what she means to you. Tell them about . . . about *Christmas* and . . . her being special to you.'

Mrs B falters.

'That wouldn't be breaking any promise, or going against her, or anything like that. People need to see her as a person – you can do that. I think it may be her only hope.'

Mrs B turns the key in the lock.

'Maybe I do it. Maybe. Need to think.' She pulls the door open.

'Take biscuits,' she says, thrusting them into Eve's arms. 'They're for Martha.'

6.30 p.m. *Death is Justice*

Dark blue screen, flecks of white buzz and crackle. The eye logo, the words 'An Eye For An Eye For' spinning.

MALE VOICEOVER: An Eye For An Eye Productions brings
        you . . .

The words stop spinning. The fizz of electricity, the words turn jagged, the eye reddens and closes.

KRISTINA: Good evening, ladies and gentlemen, and welcome
        to this evening's *Death is Justice*!

The studio lights shine on her white teeth. Her dress is tight and blue, high-heeled shoes to match. Jaunty intro music with a heartbeat undertone plays as the camera lifts and pans over the applauding audience, scans the studio and focuses in on Kristina shuffling papers at the desk from her usual seat at the side.

With a final drumbeat the music stops and the lights over the audience dim. Kristina smiles.

KRISTINA: On tonight's programme . . .

The camera pulls back, the large screen visible on the right.

KRISTINA: We'll be examining crime stats.

The words zip onto the screen.

KRISTINA: Looking at how crime rates in so many areas have fallen since the introduction ten years ago of Votes for All . . .

The words are replaced by a photo of a man in a dark suit with a light blue shirt, cufflinks catching the light, and an expensive watch on his wrist.

KRISTINA: Discussing why this City banker, currently in Cell 6, is accused of killing a drug dealer and why so many believe he's been framed. Will we have an execution for you tomorrow, viewers? That, of course, is up to you. Although more importantly . . .

A photo of Jackson Paige now fills the screen, in soft focus and with a gracious smile.

KRISTINA: . . . is the ongoing and tragic story of Jackson Paige. The senseless and brutal murder of one of the country's heroes. We'll be taking a journey through his influential and quite astonishing life, looking at how he used his rise to stardom to benefit others, supporting his chosen charities and those less fortunate than himself. It'll be a sad one, viewers; don't forget your tissues. But first, we have an exclusive interview for you. Joining us by live video-link is . . .

The crumpled face of an older man takes Jackson's place on the screen, his moustache obscures his top lip and his thick glasses blur his eyes. More hair covers his head than his age would suggest, yet is speckled with grey.

KRISTINA: . . . former Lord Chief Justice to the Supreme Court, the Honourable Mr Justice Cicero. Justice Cicero rose to notoriety long before the advent of the Votes for All public voting system for many of the cases he presided over, notably the Castle killings. Famously, after being acquitted by Cicero following claims of insufficient evidence, the perpetrator, Antoine Castle went on to commit a number of truly horrendous murders of innocent people.

She turns to Cicero on the screen.

KRISTINA: Justice did final prevail though, didn't it, My Lord? He was, in fact, put to death?

CICERO (slowly nodding): After seven years on death row, the old death row of course, yes, he was executed.

KRISTINA: And this was one of the cases that led to the changes in our justice system?

CICERO (sighing): That's correct. Among other arguments the government thought it too expensive to have someone on death row for that length of time.

KRISTINA: *Inhumane*, I think was the word used, My Lord. After all, he was guilty, of that there was no doubt.

CICERO: There was a system in place to be followed . . .

KRISTINA: . . . that needed updating.

CICERO: Should I remind you of the case of the State versus Dasher? Dasher was accused of murdering three of his own family, and was on death row for ten years, constantly proclaiming his innocence. Finally he was acquitted when technology caught up to prove it was impossible for him to have committed the crime. If the system hadn't been followed, that innocent man would be dead.

KRISTINA: But we have that technology now.

CICERO: Yet our current form of *justice* neglects to use it!

KRISTINA: Exactly.

CICERO: Not exactly. Now we don't ask for evidence, we don't even ask for motive. It is not a *justice* system, it's a butchering ground, completely open to corruption, fraudulent activity, bribes . . .

KRISTINA (smiling): We're getting off the point, Judge Cicero. Oh, I'm sorry, I believe I've got your title wrong . . .

She puts her hand to her ear, nods and turns back.

KRISTINA: As you don't practise law since the change in the court system, you're no longer a judge, you don't sit on the bench – actually you don't have any power at all. You are in fact, just plain *Mr* Cicero now, aren't you?

CICERO: You know damn well, Kristina, that we no longer have any kind of court system. First we were given telephone votes for murder and manslaughter charges and now we have this quite ridiculous *Buzz for Justice* show for lesser charges! So, no – I am no longer a judge because there are no courts for me to be a judge of!

KRISTINA (smiling): So good to hear you got the name right! Yes, the highly successful *Buzz for Justice* show, which you can catch every weekday from twelve o'clock until one and again from five through to six.

CICERO (interrupting): Who in their right mind ever heard of a legal system, a *justice* system, where a buzzer is pressed if you're thought to be guilty?

KRISTINA (laughing): That's to simplify it, Mr Cicero, I think! After all, there is a panel of people who all get to buzz – a majority *is* needed.

CICERO: Five people, Kristina, who've all bought tickets for the privilege.

KRISTINA: And what a privilege it will be for the programme designers to hear they have an ex Supreme Court judge as an avid viewer!

CICERO: I'm hardly an –

KRISTINA: Anyway, we're getting off the point again, Mr Cicero; I believe we're starting to bore our audience.

She looks across the studio audience then to camera. Her smile falls, her face is serious.

KRISTINA (voice low): We're here to talk about Jackson Paige and Martha Honeydew. The senseless killing, the unfairness society feels at having such an icon taken from them.

She turns to Cicero.

KRISTINA: Tell me, as someone against our current system, against the public having a right to vote on what they believe –

CICERO: You're twisting my words.

KRISTINA: Do you think she did it?

Cicero closes his eyes. The audience are silent. Kristina waits.

CICERO: No.

A gasp sounds from the audience, the shuffle of bodies, a murmur of opinions shared.

KRISTINA: But she admitted it.

Cicero leans towards the camera.

CICERO: Ask yourself – ask *yourselves* – why she would do that. Think, question . . . don't rely on a ridiculous buzzer or picking up the telephone!

KRISTINA (incredulous): Because she's *guilty*?

CICERO: Ask yourselves why she would kill him? Why was he there? What was he doing near the High Rises? What was her motivation? Question things!

KRISTINA (to camera): Audience, viewers, fellow voters, let's not forget that she had the gun in her hand when the police arrived. We saw the head-cam feed of that yesterday.

CICERO: Just because she was holding the gun, doesn't mean she pulled the trigger. Has anyone checked the gun for prints?

KRISTINA: Why would they waste time and money doing that? Cicero, it sounds to me like your thoughts on justice are stuck in the past. *We've* moved on. Today justice is sleek and quick, efficient and rewarding . . .

CICERO: No. There is too much apathy. It *can't* work. Mistakes are being made! Innocent people are being killed and guilty ones are getting off!

KRISTINA: Mistakes? We spoke about your mistakes earlier, *Mr* Cicero, and certainly the Castle killings wasn't the only case. I could name the Moss murders – released early on a technicality – the Shepherd shootings – case dismissed because of leaked evidence . . .

CICERO: And I could name hundreds of thousands in the long history of our court-based justice system that have got it right, *and* dozens and dozens since the introduction of this *ludicrous* Votes for All system that have got it wrong. For every person who is wrongly put to death is another who is wrongly free.

KRISTINA: History tried abolishing the death penalty, Cicero, you should know that. Or have you not done your homework? In 1965 the death penalty was suspended, but *re-introduced* in 1970 following public pressure and a number of high profile cases. Shall I go into those cases for you in case your memory fails you? Three policemen shot dead, the Moors . . .

CICERO: I know the cases!

KRISTINA: Ten years ago, we as a society *chose* to take powers from the court; we decided that the best, the *fairest*, the most equal way to deal justice was to give a voice to every person in this land, every opinion counting, every person from every background becoming a juror. Everyone equal.

CICERO: But they're not equal!

KRISTINA: Let's remind ourselves, viewers, of the horrendous crimes . . .

CICERO (shouting): They're NOT equal!

He slams his fist on the desk in front of him.

CICERO: And they DON'T have a vote each! They have as
many as they can AFFORD! That's the difference!
It is not the most democratic system in the world,
it's probably the most *undemocratic* . . .

The screen flickers; lines and static over his image.

CICERO: People think the government is giving them
power but it's an illusion! A misconception!
The government controls the press and the press
manipulate the people! The government doesn't
care if proper justice is served – these people only
care about power. That's their aim . . .

His voices distorts and breaks up.

CICERO: On paper, crime stats are low . . . makes them look
good . . . public feel empowered . . . vote for them
in elections . . . It's not the whole story.

The sound is lost.

KRISTINA (frowning): We seem to be experiencing some
technical problems. Cicero? Can you hear me?
Cicero?

His image returns, his finger jabbing at the camera, his mouth opening and closing but to no sound. The picture flickers again.

KRISTINA: While we try to re-establish a connection, let's recap what Mr Cicero, *Former* Lord Chief Justice for the Supreme Court, who has lost his career since the introduction of public voting, had to say.

She strides across the floor towards the studio audience.

KRISTINA: *People are not equal* – he stated – the Votes for All system is *ludicrous*, that it is *undemocratic*, and he claimed that you, the public, are *apathetic* and *manipulated*. This *former* judge, who presided over the Castle killings amongst other travesties of justice, went on to state that he thought Martha Honeydew to be innocent. Well . . .

She glances behind, Cicero's face blurs onto screen again, his mouth still moving, still no sound.

KRISTINA: . . . it appears we haven't managed to reconnect with Mr Cicero, but let's take a look at a quote about our justice system by former lawyer to the stars, and our current PM.

The crackling image of Cicero finally disappears, replaced on one side by lines of text over a light blue background, and on the other side by a photo of a slender man in his thirties – perfect hair, a smile and white teeth – the Prime Minister. Kristina steps back as his pre-recorded voice, authoritative yet warm and calm, sounds across the studio.

PM : *Our unique justice system is proof of ultimate democracy in our country. Inclusion is a right, exercising opinion is a right, being a valued member of society is a right. Our system promotes all this, giving all of us a voice to affect the safety of our nation. Together, we are world-leading. Together, we are the voice of justice.*

The audience applaud and whoop. Kristina smiles wide and dabs at her eyes with a tissue as she is brought centre-camera.

KRISTINA: I am certain, ladies and gentlemen, that our PM, although on his well-earned holiday, will be *glued* to the screen in his villa, watching this thrilling case develop – our first ever teen on death row.

She dips her head, as the audience applaud again.

KRISTINA: Thank you to our guest this evening and apologies for being unable to continue our fascinating discussion of his interesting, if somewhat out-dated, views on justice. Do remember to log your vote for Martha Honeydew. Do you believe her guilty of the terrifying murder of celebrity charity worker, Jackson Paige, or think her innocent, as our controversial guest did today? Do we want another killer let loose on our streets? Let's take a look at those all-important numbers and the voting information. Dial 0909 87 97 77 and to vote *guilty* add 7 to the end or to vote *not guilty* add a 0. You can also vote by texting DIE or LIVE to 7997. To vote online visit our website www.aneyeforaneyeproductions.com, click on the 'Martha Honeydew Teen Killer' tab at the top and log your vote. Calls are charged at premium rate, please seek bill payer's permission, texts cost £5 plus your network provider's standard fee, voting online is also £5 after an initial registration fee of £20. For full Ts and Cs visit our website. Her fate is in your hands. Don't go anywhere though, viewers, because after the break we'll be joined by the former employer of our Cell 6 occupant, who will explain to us why he believes the devoted father of three has been framed.

The eye logo spins on the screen as the lights dim.

Eve

Eve turns off the television.

The living room is dark and the house is quiet. Behind her, rain patters against the blackened window and in front of her the table is strewn with files and papers; flickering orange from the open fire casts forever moving shadows, while a small table lamp lights the smallest circles underneath it. A cold cup of coffee is abandoned in the middle and a half-eaten sandwich balances on a text book.

'You cocked that up, Cicero,' she mutters to herself.

As she leans back in her seat a photograph on the hearth catches her eye – Jim, Max and herself.

She rubs her hands over her face and glances back to the photo. 'It's like you all over again,' she breathes.

The fire pops and crackles as if talking to her.

'Why is she saying she did it? She's the same age as Max and they're going to kill her and I don't think I can stop it.' She shakes her head and tears fall down her cheeks. 'I couldn't before.

'I did this for you because you had nobody. I *fought* for counsellors. *Fought* so they, you'd, have someone to talk to but ...' Her voice breaks and her chest stutters. 'It hurts every time and this time is ... worse ... you know it's worse ... because ... because ... and I can't ... do it ... any ... more. She has to be the last one.'

She tips her head forward and her whole body trembles as she sobs and sobs. 'I miss you,' she says. 'I miss you, I miss you, I miss you and it's my fault. Without you it's . . . if it wasn't for Max . . .'

The doorbell rings.

Ignoring it, she puts her face in her hands.

The doorbell rings again. For a moment she listens to the rain outside, then lifts herself out of the sofa and pads through the house to the front door, blotting her face and nose on the sleeve of her jumper.

'Hang on!' she shouts as she reaches the hallway, her voice croaky and broken.

She unlocks the door and pulls it open. 'Max, did you forget your –' She stops. 'You're not Max.'

In the darkness outside, she can't make out the person's face; his hood is pulled up and his head hidden, his clothes are dark and wet. There's nothing to distinguish him as anything but anonymous.

'No.' She pushes the door, but he rams his foot in the gap, stepping closer to the light of the hallway, taller than her and intimidating.

'Eve Stanton?' a deep voice says.

'Get out,' she replies. 'I'll call the police.'

'Don't,' he says. 'I don't want any trouble. I know your son is out. I know you're alone, but don't scream. I'm not going to hurt you.'

'What do you want? Money?'

'No,' he laughs. 'A favour, and a promise.'

'I can't . . .'

'You went to see Mrs B today with a note from Martha.'

'How do you . . . ?'

'Did you read it?'

'Have you been following me?'

'Did you read it?' he asks louder.

'No,' she replies. 'No.'

He watches her. 'I've looked into you. I know what happened to your husband. I know your son goes to Foxton School. I know he's in his last year.'

'Are you threatening my family?'

'No. I want to know I can trust you.'

'Well, you can't, so go away.' She shoves the door again but his hands block it. His face is closer to the light now; she can see dark hair under his hood and the outline of a thin face.

'I can't,' he replies. 'I need a favour and a promise.'

'What?' she asks.

He takes his hand off the door, reaches into a pocket and pulls out a white envelope. 'The letter you gave to Mrs B was for me. This is my reply. Please, give it to Martha.'

'You can't correspond with prisoners; they can't have contact with anyone outside.'

'Except you,' he replies. 'But you have to promise not to read it.'

'I'm not supposed to do this. If they find out they'll strike me off.'

'But they won't find out.'

'What if I say no?'

'I don't think you will, because I think you're different. I think you actually care.'

80

She stares into the darkness inside his hood, trying to see more of his face, but he leans back into shadows.

She takes the letter. 'Who are you?' she asks.

He steps away from the door. 'You haven't worked that out? Shame on you.'

With another few steps, he's gone.

Martha

I read once that if people are left alone too long they start seeing faces in things, like their brains are looking for company, but I can't see any.

Cell 2 looks pretty similar to Cell 1, but muted. The walls are more a dirty white, the bed sheets too. Like everything's used and old, and it smells damp too. I think the window's smaller. The cell definitely is. Maybe the next will be smaller, then smaller still, until the last cell's just a box. A coffin.

It's dark in here today as the sun goes down outside. There aren't any lights, not any candles or burning torches or anything like that, it's not like medieval times apart from the cobbles on the floor in the corridor and I can't see them from here anyway because the door's shut. The door's always shut.

There's moonlight coming through the glass and the bars at the window. I like it. If I squint my eyes together so I can just see the dark and the moonlight I can nearly forget about the walls holding me in.

It's raining out there too. I can hear it on the glass, and there's a leak at the side of the window too. The rainwater's coming in, dripping. Drip, drip, drip. Maybe it'll rain and rain and rain and it'll drip and drip and drip and this cell will fill up and I'll drown.

Drip, drip, drip.

I'm lying on the bed
Drip, drip, drip.
watching the drops
Drip, drip, drip.
catch the moonlight and
Drip, drip, drip.
I wait for each one to
Drip, drip, drip.
tap a rhythm.
Drip, drip, drip.
Guilt, guilt, guilt.
Drip, drip, drip.
Dead, dead, dead.
Drip, drip . . .
Oh fucking hell. Drip, drip fucking drip! Stop with your fucking dripping.
Drip, drip, drip.
Bang, bang, bang.
Gun, gun, gun.
Dead, dead, dead.
Gone, gone, gone.
Drip, drip, drip.
Arghhh! Stop!
Stop, stop, stop.
Shit, this is relentless.
Shit, shit, shit.
Stop, please.
No, no, no.
Please.

Mum, Mum, Mum.

No.

Ol, lie, Ol . . .

I'm not listening.

I, saac, I –

Enough! I'm not being tortured by some bloody dripping water. I'll stop you.

I leap from the bed and go to the window. Where it's coming from the wall and dripping onto the floor is about my shoulder height and I put my fingers into it and it runs down them and up my arm instead.

'Stopped you,' I whisper to it.

The water's cool and my heartbeat slows; it's like I'm touching outside again.

'Tamed you,' I breathe.

I rub my hand in it and smear it on my face. Then I stand underneath, lean my head against the wall and let the rain run down my shoulders and on my skin and I'm not there in that cell any more.

I'm outside.

I'm on Crocus Street again as I am every evening since she was killed. I'm in the shadow of the underpass – the shortcut from the station to the Rises where the homeless seek shelter in concrete corners with the rubbish that's blown in, but where the rain can't reach.

The homeless know I'm here, we see each other from a distance every night, but I stay clear of them. They don't bother me, I don't bother them.

The one with the dog on a piece of string, he saw her die. Told the police. Said it wasn't like a hit and run because the guy wasn't in his car at first. Said he got into his car, started the engine and then ploughed straight into her on purpose. He told them, and me, that after, the car stopped long enough for a stocky, well-dressed man to get out, see what he'd done, get back in again and drive away.

'Weren't no Ollie B,' he said to me. 'Weren't his car neither.'

But I already knew that.

In my memory, I'm at the underpass. I'm standing in the only place where rain leaks through from a gap above. I don't have a coat and it's dripping onto my head and running down my face. I pull my hood up and step sideways into the shadows. Across the road is a row of old shops, some with broken windows, others boarded-up, graffiti on them or fliers for something or other stuck to them. None are open.

I take another step sideways and I see something – no . . . some*one* in the doorway of the old sweet shop. A dark shadow steps out into the rain, a hood pulled up covering his face, and his hands in his pockets.

He's tall. His shoulders are wide and he's staring at me.

He's walking forwards, striding purposefully, confidently across the street, towards me and I can't move.

'I've seen you before,' I say as he approaches. 'Hiding in that doorway. I know who you are and I'll report you. And those men over there? Those homeless guys? They're looking out for me. You can't do anything. They'll tell the police . . .'

My heart's pounding as he steps closer and closer. His head is nodding.

'Of course,' he says, 'because nobody could be killed here without the police and the media knowing exactly who the culprit is.' His voice is low. Warm, friendly yet controlled and unwavering.

I stare up to his face half hidden in shadow.

'What do you want?' I ask.

He pauses, lifts his hands up and takes down his hood, and there, in the orange tint of dim, far-away street lights, is a face I've seen a thousand times in newspapers, magazines, and on television. Jackson Paige's son.

'To apologise,' he says.

CELL 3

Martha

They moved me into here, Cell 3, before the sun had even come up. Some guard I've never seen before marched in at 5.30 this morning and dragged me away from the wall where I'd fallen asleep soaked to the skin.

I shouted at him, 'What you doing? What you doing to me?'

'Shut up, scum!' he shouted back.

Then I woke here. My head hurts, my fingers are swollen, and I feel wet still and cold to the core, but a crack of dull sunlight filters through the even smaller window and melts away the shadows, and I watch the dust particles playing in it and I wish I was as carefree as them, and as small as them so I could float out of here, up to you and feel you with me one last time.

I lean my face into the warmth of it and close my eyes.

'Take my coat,' he said.

I was cold and wet, standing in the rain with him looking down at me, but I shook my head.

'I don't want anything to do with you.' I walked away from him, across Crocus Street and past the boarded-up shops. 'I've seen you watching me!' I shouted back. 'You can leave me alone.'

He strode along next to me.

'How are you coping?' he asked. 'How are you doing for money? Why are they letting you live in that flat without your mother? Are they going to take it away from you?'

I stopped and stared at him. Rain was pouring down my face and soaking through my clothes. He'd taken his jacket off and was shivering in a T-shirt sticking to him and wet jeans. His hair, which must've been perfect before, was plastered to his head.

'What do you care?'

'If I didn't I wouldn't be here.'

I carried on walking, cutting through the park. 'Thought you'd come to gloat,' I shouted over my shoulder. 'Look down at us all from up there on your podium with all your money and opportunity and influence and all that shit. Like *poverty tourism*, or something.'

He trotted after me, his coat still in his hand. 'I know Oliver Barkova didn't kill your mother.'

'Ollie B?' I shouted through the wind and rain. 'Yeah, so do I. So does everyone.'

'And I wanted to apologise to you.'

My shoes squelched across the grass. 'Wasn't you, was it? It was some stocky bloke. What do you want to apologise for?'

The rain had soaked through my clothes and my feet were in puddles. In the background the Rises stood like sentinels overlooking our people.

He rushed up next to me and threw his coat over my shoulders. I wanted to shrug it off, or for it to fall, but it didn't. I didn't want it to feel warm, or smell of him.

'I don't know . . . I just thought.'

'Think it was one of *your* people, did you? Heard some rumour that the car seen was so new and shiny that it couldn't possibly have belonged to someone here?'

'Why? Who saw it happen?'

I snorted at him. 'Well, you've apologised, so now you can go,' I said.

'Aren't you angry?'

The rain came down heavier, the sky became darker and lower like it was hemming us in and holding us to the ground. In the distance thunder groaned. I picked up my pace.

'Yeah,' I said. 'No. I don't know. What does it matter anyway?'

'I want to do something for you.'

I laughed but kept on walking. 'So that you don't feel guilty for having your millions when we have nothing?'

'No . . . because I want to make things better for you.'

'I don't need your charity,' I snapped back.

I reached the entrance to Daffodil House as thunder roared above and lightning split the skies. I stopped and rested my hand on the door.

'I know what you can do to make things better for me.' I pushed the door open and his coat fell to the ground.

'Anything,' he said.

'You can fuck off,' I replied.

I slammed the door behind me.

'Meet me tomorrow by the underpass!' he shouted through the door.

Eve

Cicero places a cup of coffee in front of Eve and sits down opposite her.

'White, no sugar,' he says.

'You remembered,' she replies, watching as he tips two sachets of sugar through the froth of his cappuccino. 'You know, you shouldn't really . . .'

'I'm beyond caring,' he says.

She shrugs and turns a spoon in her drink.

'Do you know you're being followed?' he asks.

She lifts the spoon out and watches the liquid drip from it. 'You mean the man by the window with the blue scarf?' she says. 'He works for the *National News*. He's been following me since this began.'

'He'll have photographs of us together now.'

'I should think so,' she replies. 'Yet I can't imagine it could do any more harm.' She takes a slow sip of coffee and places the mug back on the table. 'You cocked up yesterday.'

'They twisted my words.'

'You didn't *expect* them to? Why the hell did you go on? You must've known . . .'

'It had to be said, Eve! I shouldn't have got angry, but I had to do something.' His voice is low and urgent. 'Day three now! And do you know what the stats are?'

'I don't follow the stats . . .' Her eyes drop to the table.

'No, of course you don't, but . . . I know they were wrong with Jim, I remember how it was looking for him, we all thought he'd get off. I remember.'

'He was at ninety-five percent not guilty on day six, Cicero.'

'I know, and everyone thought he was coming home to you.'

'Ninety-five percent!' she hisses at him. 'You can't trust stats!'

'Martha's ninety-nine percent guilty.' He leans towards her, his eyes peering over his glasses.

She looks back up and glares at him. 'And since you went on that programme it's probably a hundred.'

'Eve –' his voice lowers – 'they're going to kill her. I had to do something. I had to try.'

She turns away from him and looks out over the sea of customers. One lifts a newspaper, with the headline 'Murderer Martha In Gang Rampage', another: 'Honeydew Steals Prisoner's Stash'.

'It's all lies,' Eve says.

Another customer, closer to them, drops his newspaper onto the table; a photo of Martha at the crime scene takes up the whole of the front page. Most of the picture is dark, but the police car headlights bathe her in white in the middle, showing her arms in the air and the gun at her feet. They shine on the wet pavements as if they're silver, obscuring the grime and hiding the dirt, and turning it into a scene from a play or a still from a film.

Behind her is the underpass where the homeless live, the orange of a fire glows dimly on faces around it.

Eve frowns as she stares at it. There's something she can't quite see. The shadows look strange. Uneven.

Movement near the window of the cafe catches her eye. 'He's going, the guy from the National News. He must've got what he wanted,' Cicero says.

She watches him leave.

'I had a visitor late last night.' She reaches into her bag, pulls out a white envelope and rests in on the table. 'He gave me this for Martha. Apparently a reply to the note I took to Mrs Barkova, Oliver Barkova's mother – you remember him?'

'Yes, of course.' Cicero frowns and leans forward. 'You took a note? From Martha?'

'Yes, and I know I shouldn't have, but . . .'

He tips his head to one side in thought. 'Strange,' he says, picking it up. 'Who was it?'

'I don't know. A man. A young man. Taller than me. Dark hair. I couldn't see his face. Nicely spoken; a familiar voice I couldn't place.'

'You spoke to him?'

She nods. 'He didn't say much. He said he was surprised I hadn't worked out who he is.'

Cicero frowns. 'How would we know that? How does he know Martha?'

'I've no idea. I don't know how he knows Mrs B either.'

Cicero runs his fingers over the indentations of the name on the envelope. 'Are you going to open it?' he asks.

'No,' she replies.

He holds it up to the light. 'It must be someone she knows. A school friend, perhaps.' He turns it over, toying with the sealed edge. 'It could say something that proves her innocence.'

'I can't open it. That's not right.'

'Shame,' he says, placing it back on the table. 'When your solution could be right in front of you.'

'What difference would it make anyway? Even if it was a signed confession from the murderer, they've got the killer they *want*.'

'You're losing your faith in society too, Eve . . .'

'It's already lost. I fought for this job because it was the only way to make a difference. Because I couldn't fight the changes to the legal system, but I could help those caught in it. But, do you know what? I don't know if it does help them. And caring hurts. It's so painful. I can't do it any more and I can't fight the system. This isn't justice, it's their interpretation of it. All we can do is pray to our bones that it never happens to us.'

'But it did happen to you.'

'Not *me* . . .'

'Your husband . . .' He moves to rest a hand on hers but she pulls it away and covers her mouth. There are tears in her eyes. 'Jim was a good person,' he whispers.

She nods.

'Killing that man was self-defence and you damn well know it. You were *there*.'

'There's no number to vote for *mitigating circumstances* though, is there? It's guilty or not guilty. We've had this conversation a thousand times, Cicero . . . It's a grey area . . .'

'But there is no grey allowed! It's black or it's white!' Cicero's voice is raised and cold with fury.

95

Faces start to turn towards them. She takes her coffee cup and slumps back in her chair.

'An eye for an eye,' Cicero says with a grimace. 'The law has gone quite mad.' He picks up his coffee and takes a slurp; froth sticks to his moustache. 'If he hadn't acted, he'd probably have been beaten to death. Or both of you would've been. He saved your life.'

'Or I cost him his.'

'You can't think like that, Eve. Do you think that's what he'd want?'

She passes him a serviette.

'Maybe there's something about this Martha girl.' He dabs away the froth. 'Something more than we're seeing.'

'What do you mean?'

'I'm not sure, but it seems she has something up her sleeve.'

'Nothing that could change anything.'

He shrugs and picks up a teaspoon, toying with the remaining froth. 'Someone needs to fight,' he says.

'Not me,' she replies. 'I can't . . .'

'Then who?'

She thinks back to what Mrs B said: *it takes a braver person . . . the most unlikely . . .* She pushes the coffee cup back on the table and slides the letter into her bag. 'I have to go,' she says. 'I'm seeing her in an hour.'

As she stands, so does he and together they move between the tables and to the exit.

On the pavement outside, they stop.

Cicero leans forward and kisses Eve on the cheek.

'Go on the programme,' he says. 'What harm can it do now?'

They both turn and leave in opposite directions, but she barely takes a dozen steps before she stops again. In front of her is a newspaper vendor.

'See the evidence for yourselves!' he shouts. 'Exclusive photos of celebrity killing.'

She lifts a newspaper from the stall, the same one she saw in the cafe – the photo of Martha at the underpass, the gun, Jackson Paige, the homeless. She tilts it towards the light, holds it closer to her face, staring at it.

In the shadows of the underpass is the shape of something, only clear if you look and easily dismissed if you don't care.

Eve drops her money into the vendor's hand and walks away.

Counselling

The guard leads Martha through to the counselling room. Today her hands are tied behind her back.

'What's going on?' Eve asks.

Martha lifts her head and stares at Eve with a black eye and a swollen face.

'What happened?' she asks.

'Walked into the door, she did,' the guard replies. 'Had to move cells early and she was all sleepy and that, and walked into the door.'

'Then why are her arms chained behind her back? She's not dangerous.'

'She's a killer,' he says.

'Just take the chains off her and get out of here!'

He stares at her for a second.

'And make sure they're always off now. We don't need them.'

'Whatever you say.' His tone is mocking, and he takes his time choosing the right key and pulling off the chains.

'Thank you,' Eve says as he finishes.

'Hope you feel safe,' he mutters.

The door slams behind him as he leaves.

Eve moves round to the other side of the table and she and Martha sit down.

'How did it happen?' she asks. 'And why is your hair wet?' She looks her up and down. 'Your overalls too. Why are they wet?'

Martha doesn't answer.

Eve watches her. 'It was raining last night, wasn't it? Of course.' She takes her jacket from the back of the chair and wraps it around Martha's shoulders. 'I'll make sure they get you some dry overalls,' she says. 'Most people use the mattress . . . if the . . . the dripping . . . I should've told you, but they change things round . . . sometimes they don't do anything . . . sometimes they have new things.'

'Doesn't matter.'

'I've tried to argue with them, but they deny it or quote the contract you signed when you came in.'

'I said it doesn't matter,' Martha replies, and she shuffles back in her seat, props her feet on the edge of the chair and hugs her knees to her chest. 'The sparrow's back,' she continues, nodding to the window and the tree.

Eve spins around to see it.

'All's well in the world if the sparrow's in his tree, hey?' Martha says.

'I wish that were true,' Eve replies. 'Then world peace would be easy and I'd know the truth of what happened between you and Jackson Paige.'

Martha smiles. 'Shall I spell it out for you? I shot him.'

Eve places the letter on the table and Martha's smile disappears. She stares at it, stretches her fingers out to it and glances them down the edges and across her name. 'Did you read it?' she whispers.

'No.'

99

Martha picks it up and lifts it to her face, closing her eyes and breathing heavy. 'How did you get it?' she whispers.

'It was hand-delivered to me.'

Martha's eyes shoot up to Eve's. 'Who . . . ?'

'Who do you think?'

Martha stares at her, her face not moving, her expression not changing. 'I don't know,' she says.

'I think you do.' Eve leans down to her bag, takes the newspaper from it, and rests it on the table.

Martha looks at the photo of herself on the front page. 'Who took that?' she asks.

'It's a still from the police head-cam.'

'Told you I did it.'

'This image is appearing everywhere. The video's been on *Death is Justice*, it's been on the news. They were discussing it on the radio too. "Proves her guilt without question," they said.'

'See?'

'But I don't think it does. You're not pulling the trigger. You're not pointing the gun at him.'

'I shot him, though. I dropped it when the police arrived. They told me to. I didn't want them to shoot me.'

'Why? So you could spend seven days here and die by a different method?'

'No . . .'

Eve taps on the photo. 'Look there,' she says. 'Look. See? Around the fire are the homeless men. They probably know what happened, but oddly, they've all gone now. Yesterday when I went to see Mrs B I parked there, and I drove past again after I saw this photo. Seems since the day of the shooting they've all found somewhere to live and all have enough money for some new warm clothes and hot soup.' She shrugs. 'But look there.' She taps her finger on the shadowy edge of the photo. 'See that figure?'

Martha stares at Eve.

'In fact, you don't need to look because I think you know. That's not a homeless man. His clothes are too good.'

'You can't see that properly,' Martha interrupts. 'It's blurry. That's probably just some kind of splodge from the printing.'

Eve looks up at her. 'No, you're right, I can't. Which is why when I've finished here, I'm thinking of going to see someone who could enhance this for me.'

'You're wasting your time.'

'Because I think this person here,' she jabs at the photo again, 'is the same person who came to my house last night and gave me that envelope. Maybe he can tell me why you're willing to die for something you didn't do.'

Martha doesn't move or say a word.

'Or maybe it's something to do with what Mrs B said about standing up against the majority . . .'

'Screw the majority, I'm not interested.'

'I think you are.'

'Think what you like, it doesn't bother me.'

'I don't understand why you would shoot him.'

Martha leans forward across the desk. 'I don't need you to understand, but you will, everyone will.'

'When? When you say your final words? Because you know they *have* changed their minds before and not let the accused speak at the end. How is anyone going to understand then?'

'You don't know jack.'

'Then explain it to me.'

Martha shrugs and folds her arms across her chest. 'No,' she replies.

Silence falls over the room but for the clock ticking away the seconds and the minutes. Neither of the women look at each other. Martha's breathing is erratic; long and slow followed by short judders. She stares out of the window, watching the red and the orange of the leaves swirling out of control on the wind.

Finally Martha picks up the envelope, peels it open and lifts out a sheet of paper. Holding it near her lap, she reads, blinking and blinking more and more as her eyes drift down the page.

When she's finished she sniffs, wipes her hands over her face, folds the paper and places it back in the envelope again.

'Sometimes,' Martha whispers, 'by not doing anything, you're in fact doing something very big. You're a cog in a machine, going along with things because every other cog is as well and bucking against it is too hard.'

She looks at Eve.

'But, you know, there comes a point where you have to make a decision; you either keep turning, watching the machine getting bigger and more powerful, destroying things as it does, or you do the only thing you can – you make one small movement in a different direction, praying it will jam things up or make people take notice.

'I didn't mean it to happen like it did – truth should be simple, shouldn't it? Folks should know – but Paige, he . . .' She pauses, looks down to the letter and back to Eve again. 'What do you know about him?'

Eve shrugs. 'Millionaire, reality TV star, charity ambassador, beautiful ex-model wife, teenage son. The tabloids love him. The public too.'

'Your public love him, maybe. Ask the people who live near the Rises about him. Go see Gus Evans – you can trust him, he's always looked out for me – ask him what he thinks.'

'I met him yesterday when I took your note.'

'Yeah, well go back and ask him then. Or find where the old homeless people are now, ask them about the night my mum was killed. Ask them who gave them the money to *disappear* that time. Ask them when the security cameras at the underpass stopped working.'

'Gus did talk about some things . . . but what are you suggesting?'

'I'm not suggesting, I'm telling. Jackson Paige wasn't the man the public, *your* public, thought he was.'

'*Your* public? What do you mean?'

Martha laughs. 'People like you with money, from the City or the Avenues, who see the glaze on stuff but not the cracks underneath because it's easier that way.'

'I see the cracks.'

'If you see the cracks then you're worse than those who don't.'

'Why?'

'Because you do fuck all about them.'

'I do this!'

Martha laughs again. 'Yeah, right. You come down from your ivory tower to talk to us low-lives to make yourself feel better. Oh, and yeah, you plant a tree.'

'It doesn't make me feel better.'

'No, it probably doesn't.' She looks at her sideways. 'You do it to remember your husband? Because you think you owe him something because you watched him kill a man and wind up in here?'

'The man was . . . beating him . . . Jim would've died . . .'

'Is that what you told the police when they arrived? That you stood by and did nothing?' Martha huffs at her.

Eve stares at her, unable to speak.

'You don't need to explain yourself, but that's why you can't let go, isn't it? That's why you planted the tree. That's why you do this job. And that's why you won't go on *Death is Justice*, because of the guilt you feel. He lost his life and you kept yours.'

Eve's eyes fill with tears. 'I suppose you must've read the papers, watched the news reports.'

'People round where I live know what goes on, not from tabloids and stuff, but by listening and watching – ask anyone. We – me and you – we're more alike than you think.'

'I don't want to talk about this,' Eve says.

'Neither do I.'

The both fall silent again; neither looks at the other.

The clock ticks.

The wind blows at the tree and a flurry of leaves crinkle to the ground.

Martha glances to Eve and back again.

'He must've loved you very much,' she whispers, 'to do that. He must've known he'd be executed.'

Eve takes a struggled breath. '*He* must love you very much,' she says.

'Who?' Martha whispers.

Eve nods towards the envelope. 'The young man who came to my house last night. The one you wrote the note for.'

The corners of Martha's mouth tip in the vaguest smile.

'How did he know where I live?' Eve asks.

'I don't know,' Martha replies.

'Should I be worried?'

'Not at all,' she says.

Eve reaches down into her bag again. 'Your neighbour is a very kind lady,' she says. 'And she thinks a lot of you.'

Martha shrugs.

'She sent you these.' Eve places a packet of biscuits on the table.

'I didn't think . . . can I . . . am I *allowed* these?'

'No, but,' she says as she tears open the packet, 'while you're in here with me, who's going to know?'

Martha

I can taste the biscuits in my mouth all afternoon. I refuse the food they offer me later because it looks like crap and probably tastes like it too. I keep hoping I'll find bits of biscuits stuck in my teeth at the back.

Bless Mrs B.

And Eve.

We all knew what happened with her husband, Jim. Official line, what they told the police, was that some bloke jumped them on the way home one evening. Gave him a few blows to the head to knock him out and then tried to rape her. He came to pretty quick, grabbed this lump of metal and whacked the guy over the head with it a couple of times to stop him. Killed him. Always said he didn't mean to and that it was self-defence and to protect his wife, but then folks are complicated, aren't they? Yeah, I know, I should look at myself first – pot and kettle and all that.

Truth is a strange thing that's not always best to know nor to tell.

I like her though, Eve. She's nice, but she's the same as the rest of them up there.

She didn't let me keep the letter. Said they're bound to find it. It doesn't matter because I can remember every word anyway. If I lie here and close my eyes I can hear him saying the words.

My God, I miss him.

I wish I could be around to see what happens after people find out the truth. If there is a heaven, or some kind of afterlife, then maybe I could watch. Maybe I could be a ghost and come back and see it all unfold as different people find out. I wish I could be with him then. Oh, the scandal.

I wonder if he would be able to sense me with him.

If he could see me.

I wonder . . . oh God . . . I wonder if he'll find someone else.

Of course he will. How could he not?

I wonder if he'll always remember me.

What's it like to die?

Will it hurt?

Jesus Christ, girl, shut the fuck up.

Think of good times, happy times.

Think of that night in the rain with him . . .

I told myself that night, as I walked up flight after flight of stairs, the lift broken again, that there was no way I was going to meet him the next day, but there was a problem with that. I didn't want to meet him, but I went there every evening, that's what I did, and if I was going to be there anyway, then it might be nice to have someone to talk to.

Maybe.

So the next night I stood in the covered doorway of the boarded-up shop opposite the underpass, not waiting *for* him, just waiting, for something. It smelt a bit of cat piss and there were food wrappers and cigarette ends, but it was out of the rain and you could watch folks go by without them seeing you. It's where he was standing the first time I saw him.

He was coming along the other side of the road, his hood up, his hands in his pockets, dark jeans and dark trainers. Inconspicuous. He could be anyone from anywhere. But not to me.

'I wasn't sure if you'd turn up,' he said as he stepped into the doorway.

'I didn't have anything else to do,' I replied. 'So I thought I might as well.'

He turned and as the streetlight caught his face I saw him smile.

For a few minutes we just looked at each other. Outside of our doorway the rain hammered on the concrete and tarmac and above us cars rumbled, but there, in our shelter, was only us. For a few seconds, in my head, we were all there was in the world.

Suddenly self-conscious I glanced away and down to my feet scuffing through the rubbish.

'You want to go somewhere else?' I asked.

'Yeah,' he replied. 'Where's nice?'

'Only one place around here,' I said.

I hadn't been to Bracken Woods for longer than I could remember.

Was I ten when I was there last? Eight, maybe?

Going back, I realised it held some piece of my childhood in its branches. In there again I *was* eight, or ten, searching for conkers with my mum, dodging nettles threatening my bare legs, fearing eyes were watching me from the darkness.

Everything was smaller, like I was looking down on it from higher up.

The canopy of the trees was thick enough to keep most of the rain off us, and we strolled along in near darkness with the patter of water on leaves and its trickle down bark and stalks.

'What is this place?' he said. 'It's fantastic!'

I smiled at him. 'This way,' I said and I led him past the largest oak tree and down a rough path.

'How do I know I can trust you?' he whispered. 'You could be leading me into a trap.'

I stopped walking and turned to him.

'How do I know I can trust you?' I asked.

In the dark I could barely see him. I listened to the few raindrops hitting his hood and running down his jacket, and I watched the odd one catch the moonlight as it dripped down his face.

'I am sorry about your mum,' he whispered.

I shook my head and blinked the water from my eyes. 'You didn't do it,' I breathed.

'Neither did Oliver B. You know who did do it though, don't you?' he asked.

I carried on staring at him. I could feel it all welling up in me; the frustration and the anger and everything, and I didn't want it right then. 'No,' I managed to whisper. 'Why? Do you?'

I watched his dark shape in the glinting light as he pulled down his hood, and I could feel the sadness pouring from him. He looked at me for too long without saying anything.

'Was it *you*?' I asked. 'Is that why you've been going to the underpass? Cos you feel guilty? Feel like you need to do something to make it all better?'

'No,' he said. 'No, Martha, it wasn't me, I . . .'

'You're lying aren't you?' I spat. 'It *was* you. Of course, it all makes sense.'

'No, I promise it wasn't.'

'Then . . .'

'It was my dad. OK? It was Jackson. I saw the car when he came home that night – Lord knows how it was working. I know what happened, and Martha, I am so sorry. I should've . . .'

His words faded away. I had no clue what he was saying. I felt like I'd been smacked in the face or thrown down the stairs. I was numb. Empty. But hurting. Confused and disbelieving.

'What?' I said, holding my head. 'What? What the . . . ? How could you know and not *do* anything? How could you let someone else die for it? Ollie, oh God, oh for fuck's sake, Ollie *died*. They killed him. You let them kill him. Jesus Christ . . .'

I think I marched up and down through the trees; I think I punched one of them because my knuckles were bleeding and green and brown after.

'How could you? How . . . ?'

'Martha . . .'

He came towards me with his palms up in peace, but I punched at his chest and slapped at his face and he lifted his hands to protect himself but didn't try to stop me.

'Get away from me!' I shouted. 'That was my mum he killed! Ollie was my neighbour, him and Mrs B were like family. How could you? HOW COULD YOU?'

'Martha,' he said and his voice was calm and restrained. 'I'm sorry. I'm so, so sorry, there was nothing I could do . . .'

'You could've told someone! You could've stopped it!'
I picked up a tree branch from the ground, gnarled and pointed, and I held it up ready to hit him with it. 'I'll do it,' I told him.

'You'll what? Kill me? Will that make it all better?'

'An eye for an eye,' I hissed at him.

'Is that really what you believe? An eye for an eye? Like our stupid justice system that killed Ollie? That didn't ask for evidence, didn't give him a defence? That didn't find proper and fair justice for your mum?'

'*You* could've saved him!'

'Do you really think so?'

'You could've gone to the police.'

'Who wouldn't have listened.'

'Or the press . . . or . . . or gone on *Death is Justice* . . . or phoned in to it . . . or . . . or . . .'

'Oh come on! You know how things really are, don't you? You know about the corruption and the deals done. You know Jackson could just rig the phone lines. There's no real justice – it's all manipulation and lies.'

I stared at him. I knew how things were, we all did. But . . . He closed his eyes and lowered his head.

Did I want revenge? *Was* it revenge, this, threatening him? I tried to think . . . be calm . . . breathe . . .

He was right, and deep down I knew that.

What he said ate at me.

I sat in the flat watching the rain on the window while the sun went down and came up again.

I couldn't get my head round the fact that somebody knew but did nothing, and doing nothing meant that Ollie had died. Was I angrier about that or that Jackson hadn't been brought to justice for killing Mum? I didn't know.

In those hours, in my head I shouted at him, punched and kicked and screamed at him, but really all I did was cry.

In his shoes, I asked myself over and over, *what would you have done? What* could *you have done?*

By the time it started getting dark again I realised I'd never have an answer to that and even though it was still raining I knew I had to get out. I'd had enough of sulking.

He was there waiting for me again but this time with a flask of hot chocolate, a blanket and an umbrella.

'I'm sorry,' he said. 'I wish I'd done something, but at the time . . .'

I reached out and not quite believing what I was doing or how I was feeling, took his rain-soaked hands in mine. 'You're not responsible for him,' I whispered. 'It's not your fault.'

Still holding his hand I led him past the Rises and back into Bracken Woods, and we followed the path again but this time further through the trees, carrying on until we reached a clearing that I remembered from years ago.

I strolled around it like I was visiting the home of an old relative, still like my memory of it from childhood but different: the covered shelter made from branches was broken in some places but fixed with newer wood in others; the wooden bench was more worn, with more initials carved into it and the slats more splintered. A mattress stained with God-only-knows-what and probably filled with fleas was half under a large bush, a few empty bottles and beer cans next to it, yet across the other side, right where the moonlight was falling, rested a little circle of plucked flowers.

We sat down in the shelter and at the mouth of it, where it was dry, we made a fire big enough at least to warm the fronts of us if not our damp backs.

Talking was difficult at first; I didn't know what to say to him. It was strange and awkward, both of us testing the ground with observations about leaves or trees or flowers.

Mum was in my mind. Part of me wanted to know everything about that night from his point of view – what the car was like when it came back, what Jackson said about it, what he looked like. If he was upset. But part of me wanted to leave it; I knew it was no good.

He tried to apologise again and however much I wanted to be angry at him, to make him pay, for some reason I couldn't be. He felt genuine.

Slowly we edged closer to each other. Then, as the rain began to clear, he turned to me.

'I'd like to get to know you,' he said.

'Why?' I asked. 'Because you feel some obligation to look after the daughter of the woman your father murdered?'

He winced and looked away. 'No, not at all.'

'Because you feel guilty then?'

He turned back to me. 'Because I like you,' he replied.

His words made me speechless; I couldn't do anything but look up to the stars in the night sky. In my head I told myself it was no good, that I didn't need anyone. Simpler to be alone. Easier. But saying it wasn't meaning it.

'No pressure,' he said. 'At all. Ever. We could just try being friends.'

'Isaac Paige,' I said, turning to him. 'Son of celebrity millionaire Jackson Paige, friends with Martha Honeydew, orphan girl of the Rises. It could be a headline.'

'Strictly speaking I'm his adopted son.'

'Or how about if it read: "Isaac Paige, *Celebrity Chat's* Teen Bachelor of the Year and National News' Junior Crime Ambassador Seen Slumming It".' I laugh at him.

'Don't label me,' he said. 'And all that *Bachelor* and *Ambassador* crap, it doesn't mean anything.'

He drew away from me. I'd touched a nerve.

'Still,' I replied, quieter. 'In the real world, it can't have a future. It's impossible. Our lives are too different. What would your father say?'

'I don't care what my father says.'

I snorted. 'Until he cuts you out of his will and stops your allowance.'

'I'm not like that.'

'Isaac,' I breathed, 'the only thing me and you could ever share is the sky and the stars above us, not family, or friends . . .'

He turned back to me. 'Then we share the sky and the stars, and we enjoy it while we can. While it lasts, while it's simple.'

I looked into his eyes and I knew it could never last, or stay simple, and I felt the strangest sense of shift in the air, like pinpricks on the back of your neck, or static warning of a storm. Enough to make me pause and take notice but not enough to stop me from leaning forward, touching my hand against his face, and nodding my agreement.

114

* * *

I sit up and stare out of the window; the sky's getting dark already and the stars are shining.

'Our sky, Isaac,' I whisper to the air. 'We shared the sky and the stars in it for a year.'

A whole year.

Eight months before things started going wrong.

Ten before he started following us, eleven before his ultimatum.

It was only ever a matter of time.

If we wanted to be safe, we should've stuck with the sky.

But I was right, see? I knew it that first night with him, when I looked at him in the moonlight, that he meant something. I just didn't see what it was then.

This is it.

It's him, not me.

He's stronger. More intelligent. Has more money. More influence and power.

After all, who'd listen to me, an orphan girl from the Rises?

I'll play my part. I'll see people know the truth, and settle my scores, but the rest? That's not my fight.

He's the one for that.

He can change things.

6.30 p.m. *Death is Justice*

Dark blue screen, flecks of white buzz and crackle. The eye logo, 'An Eye For An Eye For' spinning.

MALE VOICEOVER: An Eye For An Eye Productions brings you . . .

The words stop spinning. The fizz of electricity, the words turn jagged, the eye reddens, blinks.

KRISTINA: Good evening, ladies and gentlemen, and welcome to this evening's *Death is Justice*!

The theme music blares with a thumping heartbeat. In a cerise dress with plunging neckline, high-heels and perfect hair, Kristina strides across the studio to the screen. The music fades, the applause dies, Kristina smiles.

KRISTINA: This evening, ladies and gentlemen, we promise you an exciting and breath-taking show as the final votes come in live for our Cell 7 prisoner, Anton Kinsella.

A photograph fills the screen on her right – a round face of a middle-aged man, dagger-blue eyes and a greying beard.

KRISTINA: Will he be facing the chair? Will that electricity
be crackling tonight or will he be heading home?
We can't wait to find out!

The audience applaud.

KRISTINA: We'll be looking at the stats, asking *your* opinions
on the crime and the perpetrator, and linking up
with our live feed from Cell 7 as his potential
final hours and minutes tick by.

A video feed from Cell 7 replaces the photo of the accused.
In the top corner a timer counts down while Anton Kinsella,
dressed in white overalls, walks back and forth past a chair
with leather straps at the ankles and feet and a metal crown
at the top.

KRISTINA: Keep voting, viewers. This is your decision. *You*,
the people, deciding the justice, and *you*, the
people, serving it.

She glances down to a monitor on her desk.

KRISTINA (frowning): He's looking worried there, I think.
But let's turn our thoughts first to the story that's
grabbing everyone's attention . . .

Her heels click as she strides to her desk.

KRISTINA (smiling): . . . the cold-hearted killing of national treasure Jackson Paige. Today is day three on death row for Martha Honeydew and as is usual for day three, now the shock has died down somewhat and the dust has settled, we have a guest who is acting as the accused's representative and speaking on her behalf.

She stops at the desk.

KRISTINA: Frankly, viewers, I'm very interested to hear what this representative will have to say on behalf of someone who has already admitted her guilt – what could anyone say? – but we are committed to bringing you a fair and balanced argument.

She pauses and a ripple of appreciation sounds over the audience.

KRISTINA: Not only that, but yet again we are bringing you an exclusive here on *Death is Justice*. *Never* before has *anyone* been a representative twice! But that is what we have here – yes, indeed, her *second* time! Can you believe it?

Her face is serious, a coldness to her eyes, yet the hint of a smile.

KRISTINA: Yes, viewers, and here's where it gets complicated – this person previously represented her son, who was executed for the brutal killing of Martha Honeydew's mother, Beth. Of course, I'm sure you remember the case. But here she is again, appearing today on prime time television on the world's leading and ground-breaking channel for justice, speaking on behalf of her son's victim's daughter!

She pauses with her mouth open in mock horror. The audience gasp.

KRISTINA: I know – what a turn of events! I am *most* intrigued to hear what she has to say and *why* she has chosen to take on this role. Ladies and gentlemen, I give you – Mrs Lydia Barkova.

The audience applaud over an electric beat of intro music as Mrs B, dressed in black and with her unruly hair tied back for the occasion, shuffles from backstage and towards Kristina at the desk. Kristina smiles and indicates to the seat on the left. As Mrs B sits, Kristina moves around and takes the seat in the centre. The music fades, the applause stops.

KRISTINA: Welcome to the show, Mrs B. I believe that's how everyone refers to you – Mrs B?

MRS B (nodding): Correct. My friends call me Mrs B.

KRISTINA: Excelle—

MRS B (interrupting): You call me Mrs Barkova.

Kristina's face tilts sideways with a half-smile.

MRS B: I don't know you. You're not my friend.

Kristina's smile slips, but only briefly.

KRISTINA: Moving on, or not quite moving on, let's talk about your previous appearance here when you were representing your only son, Oliver.

MRS B: About that I have nothing to say.

KRISTINA: You don't wish to comment on whether that is why you're defending Martha Honeydew? Do you feel you have a responsibility to her? Is it guilt that drives you?

MRS B: Guilt? Why guilt?

KRISTINA (with a laugh): Because your son killed her mother! Surely you hoped you'd brought him up better than that!

MRS B: My son did not kill Beth.

KRISTINA: You mean Mrs Honeydew?

MRS B: Yes, of course I do. We were friends, I called her Beth.

KRISTINA: So he killed your friend?

MRS B: I tell you he did not kill –

KRISTINA: Yet the public found him guilty. Are you trying
            to infer all of the . . .

She glances back to her notes.

KRISTINA: . . . six hundred thousand, four hundred and
eighty-nine people who voted him guilty were wrong?

MRS B (quietly): I know my son.

KRISTINA: Leaving that aside for one minute – let's return
            to a point you raised a moment ago – you and
            Beth Honeydew were friends?

MRS B: Yes, very good friends. We lived next door to each
        other.

KRISTINA: She helped you a great deal?

MRS B: She did, yes. She was good lady. Her daughter is good
        girl – that is why –

KRISTINA: We'll come to that, Mrs B. As I was saying –

MRS B: I said you call me my proper name – Mrs Barkova.

KRISTINA: Apologies. Again, as I was saying, Beth helped you
a great deal as your background – your origins,
shall we say – are very different, aren't they? Your
values are not traditional to this country, are they?

MRS B: I came to this country when I was three years old.

KRISTINA: Yet when we look at your history, we can start to
understand how things have gone so drastically
wrong for you.

MRS B: What went wrong?

KRISTINA: You were raised solely by your father, who, not
being able to afford child-care, took you to work
on the docks and boat yards with him.

MRS B: My father was good man.

KRISTINA: Where you learned inadequate English.

MRS B: Mrs Albright, you talk crap. I not sit here and listen –

KRISTINA: Mrs B, your culture might not allow for manners,
but mine certainly does, let me finish –

MRS B: Manners? This is manners? You invite me here to talk about Martha and you insult me? No, I not let you bloody finish, cos you talk nothing of sense. You talk shit and you tell lies. I'm not here to talk about my son or my father, God rest their souls, or the fifty-four years I have lived in this country, I'm here to talk about Miss Martha.

KRISTINA: Ladies and gentlemen, she says she has manners, yet she swears like a trooper!

The audience laugh.

MRS B: You interrupt again; you only like things your way. Now shut your face and listen.

Kristina leans back in her seat and folds her arms across her chest and raises her eyebrows.

KRISTINA: Please, go ahead, Mrs B.

MRS B: Where I come from is not of interest. Who I am is. I know difference between right and wrong. My son too. Martha too. I'm here because Martha have no one, she is lonely in world. I'm here to tell you that she does not deserve to be killed.

KRISTINA: You're saying she's lying?

MRS B: She has been through very hard times. She has no family. She had to drop out of school to work to pay rent.

KRISTINA: I'm sorry, Mrs B, but what rent? She's a minor, she should be living in a care institution and supported by the government.

MRS B (sighing): No, she not like that. She says they are shit places. She pays rent for her mother's flat and she need to earn money for food too. She works hard, long hours cleaning toilets and things. She is kind girl. Caring too. She look after me since Ollie executed. She come round every day. Some days we eat tea together and sometimes she stay with me 'til late. That way we only need pay to heat one flat.

Kristina leans forward, her hands clasped in front of her.

KRISTINA (voice low): So you cook dinner for her and let her stay with you. That's very kind of you.

MRS B: She is lovely, sweet girl. She never done nothing wrong. This, it breaks my heart. She is a baby. Her mother would be . . .

Mrs B takes a tissue from her pocket, wipes her eyes and blows her nose. Kristina nods her head and places a hand close to Mrs B.

MRS B: I try hard to help. I miss my boy and I miss my friend and now, soon . . . She is good girl, I tell you. Her mother, Beth, she brought her up well and would want people to see what a good girl she is and not remember her as a murderer. She would be better at this than me, she would make people see and understand.

She gulps tears back.

KRISTINA: I think, Mrs B, that life has been very hard for you too and I – I'm sure the audience as well – hear your plight and your worries and we wish you happiness for the future. You have done your friend proud, hasn't she, ladies and gentlemen?

Nodding, she looks to the audience and a ripple of applause sounds around the studio.

KRISTINA: You have done your duty – provided Martha with a representative, informed us about her and put her case over to us, and for that society is grateful.

MRS B: She is a clever girl. She knows what is going on, she sees the corruption and she wants to –

Mrs B's voice is suddenly cut short. Kristina ignores her and stands. The spotlight follows her towards the audience as the light around the desk and over Mrs B fades.

KRISTINA: As we bring this to a close, viewers, let's round up what we have found out this evening from Martha's representative who, by her own admission, knows her better than anyone. Mrs Barkova, an immigrant to this country who was brought up mainly within the rough boat yards and docks, who after more than fifty years is yet to learn our language properly, has stated that Martha has dropped out of school, that she is illegally paying rent on a council flat that is not in her name and is too big for her needs. She has informed us too, that Martha thought herself too good for care institutions.

A quiet scuffle in the shadows around the desk is drowned out by Kristina's voice.

KRISTINA: We have also learnt that the accused would visit Mrs Barkova every day and eat her hard-earned food, yet pay no money towards it. But despite all this, a lonely Mrs Barkova insists the girl does not deserve to die. I ask you, viewers: does this fit the description of a girl who is innocent, or does it sound to you like a lonely old lady is being tragically manipulated through her guilt? This is not my decision to make. All we can do here is provide you with the information given to us.

Behind her the lights slowly fade up and Mrs B has gone.

KRISTINA: We'll leave those questions in your mind, viewers, as you ponder on which way to vote, and we'll take ourselves back to Cell 7.

The video link of Cell 7 fills the screen behind her, the man sitting on the floor in the corner, his head in his hands.

KRISTINA: With less than two hours before voting closes, we can see the stats are . . .

Two columns appear on the screen, Guilty and Not Guilty, accompanied by a ticking noise as they move upwards. Not Guilty stops under halfway, Guilty continues, the ticking louder and louder.

It stops with a bang. '75%' flashes across it in red.

KRISTINA: And there you see it, ladies and gentlemen – 75% – there will have to be some fast fingers to get that dropping! Looks like we're in for an execution tonight. Join us after the break.

She smiles and the screen fades.

Eve

Eve throws the remote at the screen. It cracks and goes blank.

'One chance to speak for her. One. And that cow . . .'

Max steps into the room, looking at his mother and the broken television screen.

'You remember I set that camera up at the front door ages ago?' he says.

Eve closes her eyes and leans back on the kitchen cupboards. 'What about it?'

'I got it to zoom in on your visitor yesterday. You'll never guess who it was.'

She peels her eyes open. 'Show me,' she replies.

Martha

They've left the cell door open. I still can't get out though, there's bars across it instead. Never noticed them before; they must be on the outside wall.

I can't see much – the wall opposite and the door to Eve's room – but I can hear movement and voices coming from down the end of the corridor.

Think I know why.

Seven cells, you see, but not seven people, because someone isn't murdered, or caught, every day. I don't know how many other people are down here. There's not just me, but I don't think there's someone in all of them.

One thing's for certain though – seems like there's someone in 7. He'll be the one I saw on my first day, who laughed when I told him I killed Jackson Paige. I should've told him murder isn't a laughing matter and neither's death. I'd never wish anyone dead. I'd wish they'd fuck off and leave me alone, become better people or go live under a rock away from everyone, or something like that, but I'd never wish them dead.

I wonder if it was the Cell 7 man I heard crying earlier.

I wonder what his name is, what he did. Or what he didn't.

I don't know where the guard's gone. Left us, maybe. Maybe he isn't here all the time. We're all locked away, how would we even know?

For a second the thought of a fire breaking out and us all roasting like chickens fills my head, but then I think, what would it matter anyway, and then I wonder if I've already thought that before. Then I wonder if I'm going mad.

They say solitude does that to you.

Then there's lack of sleep and that bloody dripping yesterday.

It'd be no wonder if I lost it.

Seven days of hell, I'll be begging them to kill me at the end.

Somewhere there's a door opening and closing, a cold draft, loud serious voices, then someone laughing. Someone else sobbing.

'No, no, no!' I hear. A man's voice. 'Please, no!'

Is that him? The Cell 7 guy?

'Guilty!' I hear. A chorus of voices. A few cheers, some clapping.

'Kill the bastard!' someone shouts.

'An eye for an eye!' someone else says.

I wonder if he actually *did* do it. If he actually *did* kill someone. In cold blood. Eve comes to my head, and her husband – that was self-defence, well, kind of. What if you killed someone by accident?

There's so much grey.

But there isn't room for grey any more.

It's gone quiet now and a strange atmosphere fills the place. I feel overwhelmed by sadness and suddenly I'm crying. I sit down on the floor and my tears roll off my nose and drop onto the floor.

Splash, splash. Tiny drips making tiny dark marks.

I touch a hand to my cheek to wipe them and I'm thrown into the past and there you are in front of me. I close my eyes.

'We knew it could never last,' you said when Jackson first became suspicious. 'Remember that night in the woods? You told me it has no future. You said the only thing we could ever share is the sky and the stars above us, not family, or friends . . .'

'We shared Mrs B. She accepted us.' I was starting to panic.

'But nobody else. We agreed to share it while it lasted, while it was simple. It's not any more . . .'

'You're finishing it?'

'Martha, if we don't, he'll finish it for us. He'll finish us!'

'Isn't it worth fighting for?'

'If it was only my life, I'd risk everything, but how can I risk yours? You know what he'd do. I can't risk him hurting you and I can't risk someone else paying for that.'

I took his hand in mine and stared at him. 'What do you want, Isaac?' I whispered. 'What do you really want in life, for your future? What do you dream of?'

'It's different,' he whispered. 'What I wanted before I met you . . . it's changed.

'I suppose I've always known how corrupt he is, my dad, and the killings . . .' He paused and shook his head. 'But, and this sounds terrible, I had to ignore them so I could get on with living. Otherwise, I don't know, I don't think I could've coped. I watched him doing his charity work and, you know, I liked that, and I liked going in to the places with him and I thought I could do something like using his money and influence to do

131

some kind of good in the world. Try to balance things a bit . . .
But meeting you? You've opened my eyes and made me see
there is so much more to balance than I ever thought there
was.' He paused and swallowed hard.

'But you've *inspired* me too, made me see that perhaps I can
actually try to change things, on a big scale.'

I shifted uncomfortably.

He smiled. 'You are so strong. You are a tiny person in a
great big world with no money, little education, no family . . .'

'Gee, thanks.'

'Hear me out. You haven't got any of that, but you want to
keep fighting to try to show people the truth of what happened
when you don't have to.'

'I owe it to them.'

He shook his head. 'You don't really, but you're a good person
like that. But here I am with the money, and the influence and
the education, and some kind of warped family, and what do
I do? Nothing. You . . . *you* . . .' He moved forward again and
took my face in his hands. '. . . have given me this dream that
things can change and things could be better, for me, for you,
for everyone.'

'Everyone knows the justice system's corrupt,' I whispered,
'but they're all scared of being caught on the wrong side of it.
You really think you could change things?'

He shook his head. 'Not by myself,' he said.

'Together?' I asked.

He nodded.

Justice and truth for my mum and Ollie was all I dared to
hope for; what he was talking about seemed way out of my

league, but I dared to think at that moment that maybe he was right – maybe if we each played our own part, then together we *could* change things.

I drift back to the present and I stare around the cell: cold and harsh, and so lonely, yet the light different with the bars across the doorway. I never thought back then that what we did would be this big or this final, but this is my part and it's nearly played out.

I'm trying, but all I was, all I am, and all I will ever be, is an orphan girl from the Rises.

There's a shuffling outside in the corridor, or in a cell, and my stomach tips in surprise or fear.

'What's your name?' a voice says.

'What?' I reply and I sit up and wipe my face, trying to figure out where the voice came from.

'Your name?' it says again. A male voice, scratchy like there's something in his throat.

'Martha,' I reply. 'What's yours?'

'Emilio,' he says.

'You a prisoner?' I ask him. 'What cell are you in?'

'Errr, 4, I think,' he grumbles. 'Kinda lost count.'

'I'm in 3.'

'Well, I must be in 4 then, cos I'm sure as shit it ain't 5. You're a woman?'

'Ermm, girl, I suppose. I'm sixteen.'

'Sixteen? What you doing in here?'

'I killed a man.'

'You're admitting to that? I mean, I killed a man, but I'm not telling no one. Innocent, I said, try to prove otherwise. Not that they need to prove . . . Who'd you kill? Some boyfriend?'

'No. Jackson Paige.'

His laugh echoes down the corridor and through the cells.

'Jackson Paige? What, *the* Jackson Paige?'

'Yeah,' I reply.

He laughs again. 'Brilliant,' he says. ''bout time someone took him off that pedestal he put himself on. Brilliant.'

'But he's dead.'

'Girl, you probably *saved* lives getting rid of him. No probably about it, you *saved* lives; they should be giving you a medal, not sending you to the electric chair!'

'Still,' I reply, 'can't go around killing folk just because you disagree with them.'

For a moment he's quiet and I can hear his heavy breathing and his body moving. 'Yeah, well, y'know . . . complicated, ain't it? Sure it wasn't like you just killed him for fun. Must've been reason.'

'Yeah, there was a reason, but I'm still going to die,' I whisper.

Again he's quiet. On the other side of the corridor there's the noise of shuffling chairs and a door creaking.

'I'm not gonna to lie to you,' he says. 'You're going to die, probably, yeah. He had too many people in his pockets. But if I get out, girl, I'll use every last penny I can find to vote for your innocence.'

'Emilio . . .'

'But it wouldn't make no difference. He made himself the nation's sweetheart. But one day, right, one day, people will see what fools they were.'

Voices come from the other side of the corridor, some laughter too, and a clattering of wheels and metal.

'Did you really do it?' he asks.

The door at the end of the corridor smashes open and I jump.

'*Did* you do it?' he asks again.

From the bars across the door I can see a trolley coming down the corridor, the wheels spinning across the cobbles, two sets of boots pushing it. I glance up and lying on the trolley is a body dressed in the same white prison overalls as me; his arm flops sideways and dangles at his side, his fingers like sausages from the fridge, the tattoo of a rose down his hand.

The man I saw on my first day here.

I watch it swing past me on the trolley, follow it as it heads down the far end and listen as the other door bangs closed.

'We had this idea,' I whisper.

'What?'

The door flies open again and the guard appears.

'Bedtime, ladies!' he shouts. Keys jangle around him, a metallic thud sounds and the door begins to slide across.

I scurry to my knees, pressing my face against the bars as the door moves towards me.

'We had this crazy idea!' I shout to Emilio.

A baton slams between the bars and down on my fingers. I scream but I don't move. 'That we could actually make things better!' I shout again but everything turns black.

Something wakes me. A hissing noise. Like a can of deodorant being sprayed, or air freshner. Then it stops.

135

I'm lying on the floor near the door. It's dark. So dark I could be floating in space. No, darker than that because there's no stars. It's cold too. And now, completely, absolutely silent.

The skin on my forehead feels weird and I lift a hand and touch it and something flakes off on my fingertip.

Dried blood? I wonder. *Did he knock me out?*

My eyes are getting used to the dark, shapes are looming out – the bed, the toilet, the sink – yeah, the usual.

And the window up there. The sky draws me to it. I love it. I wonder what's out there, what it's like to be up there and feel so alone.

Like this? I ask myself. No, it'd be peaceful, calm. Free. And devoid of all the shit that's on earth.

I should go live up there. Create a colony.

Yeah right, in your dreams.

Dreams are all I have in here. And memories.

I shuffle across the floor and lie in the bed.

This cell's been simple, I think. But then I blink, blink again, and I see something coming towards me out of the shadows.

Someone coming towards me.

Dark at first, then lightening, shape forming. Female, shoulder-length hair, shorter than me, slender but a round face. Dark eyes, a wide smile, arms outstretching towards me.

I blink, blink. Close my eyes, screw them up.

No, no, no, no, no, I say in my head. Don't let it trick you.

I open my eyes again.

She's in front of me. Bending towards me. Smiling at me, her arms reaching to me.

'Mum?' I whisper.

'Martha,' she replies. 'It's so good to see you.'

'But . . . but . . . Mum, aren't you . . . aren't you . . . ?'

'I had to come and see you,' she says.

Her voice so warm, so kind and comforting. So good to hear it again. And see her again.

I sit up. 'I've missed you so much,' I say. 'It's so good to see you.'

'I had to come and see you to tell you –' she pauses, staring down at me, something's changed, something's wrong, her face, she looks – 'to tell you how *disappointed* I am with you.'

'W . . . what?'

She leans right in to me, her face so close to mine. 'How could you? How *could* you? My daughter a killer, a murderer. How do you think that makes me feel?'

'But . . .'

She stands up and starts pacing up and down.

'I didn't bring you up to become *this!* You . . . you . . . cold-hearted . . .' She stops walking and lurches towards me. '. . . cold-hearted BITCH!'

'What? But, Mum, you've got to understand.'

'I understand; don't think I don't.' Her voice is louder and louder, filling the cell and vibrating off the walls. 'You blew holes in the nation's sweetheart! You riddled the people's icon with bullets! You blasted the body of our hero to PIECES! For what?'

'No.' I put my head in my hands and rock back and forth. 'No, Mum, no, it wasn't like that. It was one bullet, one, just one, and he –'

'You got it WRONG! You know that?'

'What?'

'Jackson Paige didn't kill me!' she shouts. 'Isaac was LYING to you. He's a LIAR and he HATES you!'

'No, he wouldn't . . .'

'You're a murderer and I HATE you! I'm turning in my grave because of you!'

'No, please, no, don't! Mum, Mum, I love you, don't do this, please! It wasn't like that, it wasn't, it wasn't. Please.' I pull the sheets around me and collapse onto the mattress. 'I'm sorry, I'm sorry. Mum, please, please, forgive me.' I sob and sob, and her footsteps fade away.

'Martha?' Another voice.

'Leave me alone,' I reply. 'Please, just go away.'

'You've told me that before and not meant it.' I know this voice. 'Actually you told me to fuck off, remember? The first time we met? Outside the flats?'

'I remember,' I whisper. *Of course I remember*, I think.

'Don't you want to see me? I snuck in. Stole the guard's keys.'

'I'd love to see you,' I say.

I think I hear footsteps move across the floor. I turn around.

The moonlight from outside the window glimpses on his skin and twinkles in his eyes. He smiles and my body warms and my heart melts.

'Isaac,' I breathe and I feel myself relax. 'Oh God, it's so good to see you. I thought I'd never see you again. I thought . . .' I'm crying again now, but with relief. 'How did you get here? Are you going to take me with you?'

I can't look away from him. His whole being gives me relief and comfort.

138

'Would you like that?' he asks. 'Run away, just me and you. Start a life together somewhere safe where we can be together?'

I nod. 'Yes, yes, oh that'd be great. That'd be so good. Yes, Isaac, yes, let's, please.'

'Well tough SHIT!' He lurches towards me, the words screaming in my face. 'Why would I want to be with a KILLER? That's all you are. A MURDERER!'

I can't move. My mouth's open but I can't say a word.

'You think I loved you? Hey? You really think that someone like me would *ever* love someone like you?' he spits the words at me.

'I . . . I . . .' I can't speak.

'I never loved you. NEVER! You're nothing but a dirty whore. A slag. Just like my father said. I *used* you!'

'Isaac, please, no!' Tears come now and I can't stop them. My world is falling apart. I'm being torn to pieces. I'm going down. I can't . . . can't . . .

'Go to your death, you slag, with these words ringing in your ears: I . . . never . . . loved . . . you! Got it?' he shouts.

I stare into those eyes that I know I'd seen with love in for me.

'Got it?' he shouts again.

I nod because I have to.

As he turns away from me I reach a hand out to grab his, but I miss.

I close my eyes, pull the sheets over my head and collapse back down.

My heart's been ripped out. My soul is burning. I am empty.

I cry. Sob. Until my head is pounding and I am drained. Only then do I peer out from under the sheet. I half expect to see them both, but of course, they're not there. Even in this dull light and with blurry eyes I can see the door is still closed and see how small the window is.

You know they weren't real, don't you? They were holograms or hallucinations or some other weird shit.

My head's heavy. There's a weird taste in my mouth. I feel crap.

I roll onto my back, stare across the cell.

There's that hissing noise again.

What is that?

I blink some more and sit up. My eyes are blurry from crying, and they're heavy, but I can see something near the door . . . something coming from under it that the moonlight's struggling to get through.

Like fog . . . or mist . . . or . . . gas . . .

They're *gassing* me? What? Why?

'Because they can!' I turn my head around and Ollie is standing next to the bed, spinning his car keys around a finger, his curly hair tumbling around his head. 'Because they hate you, because they *control* you, control everything . . .'

'No, no, no.' I struggle out of bed, pulling the sheet with me. 'You're not real. I'm not listening.'

'You're weak and you're useless and you could never achieve anything . . .'

'I'm not listening, not listening . . .' I drop to the floor.

'You didn't save me, did you? Didn't vote enough. And I loved you. You were like a little sister to me.'

I crawl to the door and I can feel it on my hands now, the vapour, gas, whatever it is. *This isn't right*, I think, *how can they do this? How . . .*

'Do you want to know what it feels like to die?' His voice is so harsh.

I push the sheet into the gap under the door, ramming it in with my fingertips as much as I can.

'Want to know what the pain is like?'

I try not to listen.

'You know nobody likes you. Nobody but me ever did, and you let me die. Isaac was just using you. How could you ever think –'

I stand up and stare at this apparition of Ollie. The room's turning around me, my head feels thick but I will not be beaten like this.

'Shut the fuck up,' I slur. 'You're not real and I'm not listening.'

My legs buckle beneath me and suddenly I'm on the floor and I lie there as if I've been in a fight, emotion draining from me like blood.

CELL 4

Eve

The woman at the desk flicks a pen between her fingers as she stares at the computer screen.

Eve stands in front of her.

'What did you say your name is again?' she asks without moving her eyes.

'Eve Stanton.'

'We don't just let anyone on, you know, Mrs Stanton,' she replies. 'It's a very important and well-respected television news show. It's vital to our integrity that we uphold the strictest of policies. Our guests are usually by invitation only, and only the most knowledgeable in their field are invited to share their opinions as it can sway the audience vote and thus alter the course of justice.'

'Are you reading that?' Eve asks.

She looks up. 'No.'

Eve turns away. On the opposite wall is a bank of seven television screens; above them, the numbers of each of the cells.

She turns back. 'They're . . . are they . . . ?'

'It's something we're trialling within our office environment and hoping to introduce across the market, available in all homes, businesses and offices at a premium rate for twenty-four-hour constant coverage.'

'Of the cells?'

'Yes, ma'am. Of the cells. We have zoom capability, night vision, sound capture . . .'

'You're *watching* them?'

'And you can soon, too, with our very own subscription-only channel dedicated to the deliverance of a premium justice service.'

'But that's a violation of privacy.'

'By violating our laws,' her eyes are down again, 'the prisoners have forfeited their claim to any such privacy.'

'That's against human rights.'

'According the terms of the contract they sign upon entrance to death row, they forgo their human rights.'

'Do they know they're being watched?'

'All information relating to the usage of any data was contained within the small print of the contract and available for each prisoner to see when they were requested to sign.'

Eve frowns and looks back to the screens, and taking a step towards them, she focuses on Cell 4 – Martha lying on the bed, her head hidden by the sheet.

Eve lifts a finger and touches the screen.

'When did the windows get smaller?' she asks.

'We're not at liberty to discuss the architecture of the cells, but we are in constant talks to assure the quality of your viewing pleasure.'

Eve glances over the wall. 'There's another socket here,' she says. 'Seven screens for seven cells, but a spare socket. What's that for?'

The woman's face lights up in smile and she looks to Eve. 'That's for our latest innovation,' she says. 'And our eighth interface. A computer screen is to be fitted there that will provide a live feed to our new, state-of-the-art VC.'

Eve strolls back to the desk. 'VC? Video conference?'

'Virtual counsellor,' she says with glee.

'Pardon?'

'After conducting research across the viewing public it was found that the vast majority felt their viewing experience was diminished by a lack of accessibility to the accused, in particular to the thoughts that may have led them to committing the crime. As I'm sure you, a viewer, will appreciate this can unjustly sway the audience vote and thus –'

'Alter the course of justice.'

The receptionist lifts her head and smiles wide.

'Actually,' Eve continues. 'I'm not a viewer.'

The smile falls and her mouth opens. 'Oh.'

'I don't watch. I feel the course of justice has already been unjustly swayed by the introduction of a system that relies on money.'

'Oh, but –'

Eve raises a hand. 'No. In fact . . .' She stops and looks around her. 'Sometimes, Miss . . . I'm sorry, I don't know your name . . . sometimes don't you find yourself in a situation and wonder how the hell you got there?'

She looks at the screens again.

'I can't help but wonder if at some point in our history we've taken a wrong turn; that at some point somebody must've had the power to stand up and say no, but for whatever reason they didn't. It's as if they pushed a ball down a hill to see what would happen but now they can't stop it.'

'What ball?' the woman asks.

'And now,' Eve's voice is rising, '. . . now it's so big and powerful that . . . that . . . and all these people, who could be innocent . . . are . . . and we're stuck in this hellish place.'

'What did you say your name is?' the woman asks, the phone in her hand.

'Are you calling security?' Eve asks. 'I'll save you the bother.' She turns and strides away. 'Eve Stanton!' she shouts behind her. 'Designated counsellor to the accused!'

She slams through the glass doors and out into the street.

Martha

My head's banging. My face is swollen. I think my fingers are broken.

I don't want to move off the bed and I don't think I can anyway.

I don't care any more. I'm drained. Empty. Done.

I don't want any more time or days, I want you to kill me now.

I don't want to be your plaything that you torture. Giving me hallucinations to watch me lose it. Or to break me.

If I wasn't already telling you I'm guilty I sure as hell would be now just to make it stop.

Wonder what time Eve will be here.

What will she say?

Will she do anything?

What's it matter anyway?

I'm in Cell 4 but I don't know how I got here. Last thing I remember was collapsing on the floor, thinking how crap everything is. Wondering if that's really what my mum and Isaac and Ollie believe and then thinking it must be and then trying to work out how I could turn the bed sheets into some kind of noose and just do away with it all now.

Next thing I know, I wake here, feeling half dead already.

I know I'm in 4 because someone has written '3 MORE DAYS' on the wall in big brown-red letters.

I'm staring at it, wondering what they've written it in when there are no pens or anything.

There's something else on the wall above it, right at the top where it joins the ceiling, like a box or something. I don't know. I roll over and face the wall.

Three days.

Three more sleeps.

Three more sunrises through windows that are getting smaller and smaller with each cell. If the next cells have windows, that is.

Three more sunsets.

Can we skip a few, please? Can we do it now and get it over with?

No, hang on, four more sunsets. Of course, execution is after everyone's had time to eat their dinner and walk the dog and settle down for an evening's entertainment in front of the telly with a cup of tea or a glass of wine, depending on the day.

Bliss.

I don't know what time it is. I don't want to look at the clock. I'm going to stay here all day. Lie and sleep. Sleep and lie.

Or die, please.

God, my head hurts.

I yank at the sheet, thinking the cool of it will be nice on my eyes, and the bed shifts away from the wall.

Something there catches my eye. The edge of a word or a pattern. I stare at it for a while. I don't want to be curious. Can't be bothered. Don't want to know what it is.

But . . .

No, Martha, just go to sleep, leave it be, ignore it.

But . . . I summon energy from somewhere, push the bed further away and I can see more.

Push it further and –

The wall hidden behind the bed is covered in red writing.

I sit up – I can't help myself – and I peer closer.

Ted McNally. Thomas Redfearn. Alison Holmes. Craig Stiller. Marcus Allcock. Ahmed Johnson. John Reinbeck. Oscar DeVillo. Clarice Netenberg.

The names are written awkward. Blurry. Some smeared, some with drips and runs.

They're written in blood.

They go on and on and on. Hundreds of them.

Suddenly I'm awake again, and alive, and caring.

That was not your mum and that was not Isaac, that bit of me inside says, stronger now, and I'm listening. *They gassed you, made you see your own worries, but your mum and Isaac didn't think that, they never did and never would. And you* know *that. Don't let the bastards win.*

I nod. *I know*, I think to myself.

Be strong. Keep strong.

I look back to the names. A shiver runs down my spine.

How many people have been in this cell, facing only three more days of life with so much left to do or say? To apologise, explain, beg for understanding or for right and proper justice?

I read the names like I've got an obligation to their souls.

Boris Axenborough. Corrine Hamah. Edith Chalabi. Oliver Barkova.

Ollie. My neighbour, my babysitter, my friend. Confidante and guilt.

I lean forward and catch my finger on a bed spring, it digs into my skin and red blood oozes out. I squeeze it and more comes up like an inky bubble.

As I stand up there's a whirring sound on the wall behind me. I look around, I'm sure the box near the ceiling is moving.

I watch it.

6.30 p.m. *Death is Justice*

Dark blue screen, flecks of white buzz and crackle. The eye logo spins.

The caption – 'Sofa on Saturday' – drifts across as the theme tune begins, slower and sweeter than on weekdays, the backing heartbeat quieter. The caption disappears in a muted flash and lights come up on a more intimate studio. Kristina, dressed in fitted grey trousers and a pink blouse tight across her chest, is seated on a bank of slouched leather sofas, a low wooden coffee table in front of her splayed with magazines and newspapers. Next to her is Joshua Decker, fitted trousers and a shirt open a little too much.

The theme tune fades out.

KRISTINA (smiling): Good evening, viewers, and welcome to your very special Saturday edition of *Death is Justice*.

A gentle applause from the audience.

KRISTINA: Joining us today is our usually roving reporter, Joshua Decker, allowed inside from the winter weather.

The audience applause is louder, a gentle ripple of female voices.

JOSHUA: Thank you, Kristina, it's a pleasure to be here.

KRISTINA: Indeed. Well, as always on Saturdays, viewers, we aim to bring you something special, and this week is no exception as we have *two* guests joining myself and Joshua today! Firstly we have none other than Rafi Mannan, CEO of the media corporation Life Visions, the company that has taken our justice system and turned it into the world-leading, innovative system it is today. The fairest, many say, in the world, where each and every one of you, our public, is juror and decision maker. Good evening, Rafi.

The camera pans out to show Rafi at the other sofa: loose, floppy hair, jeans and a sweater.

RAFI: Good evening, Kristina, Joshua.

JOSHUA: And secondly we have editor-in-chief of the National News, Albert DeLonzo.

A slender man in a white shirt and grey waistcoat leans in from the other end of the sofa, raises a hand and smiles.

ALBERT: Pleasure to be here.

KRISTINA: Thank you both for joining us. Rafi, if I can turn to you first, I believe you have some exciting news to deliver to our viewers.

RAFI: Some very exciting news, yes. As you may be aware, Life Visions are constantly examining ways to enhance the viewing experience of the cells, looking at how to bring voters closer to the accused and to death row and thus enabling them to make informed choices upon their votes. Collating and analysing results of viewer feedback, it became evident that viewers weren't engaging completely with the experience and thus to ameliorate this I am very pleased to announce that we are now able to offer an innovative and far more inclusive system, allowing for intimate involvement from viewers wherever they are.

JOSHUA: You're keeping us in suspense . . .

RAFI: From this very moment, we are launching the start of *twenty-four-hour viewing* of all of the seven cells!

The audience applaud. Rafi grins and bows his head. On the other side of the sofa DeLonzo nods.

RAFI: For a monthly premium, viewers will be able to connect via their televisions, computers, phones, whatever system they use, getting up close and personal with our accused as they languish in their cells. *Never before in history* has this been seen. You'll be able to watch every movement, every facial expression, see every chink and flaw in their characters and any defence, excuse, reason, or *innocence* you think they may have.

KRISTINA: Rafi, this is something I've been suggesting for a long time. I'm so pleased to see it finally come to fruition.

RAFI: At Life Visions, we've always taken our responsibility to the viewers, and the accused, seriously. We understand the devastation a voter could feel if they, at some future point and for whatever reason, discovered they had voted incorrectly, and of course, the implication of that upon the accused. This is akin to putting the accused in your homes but, of course, without the danger!

JOSHUA: And I believe you have an exclusive offer for us right now, Rafi.

RAFI: That we do. To launch this exciting development, we are offering this service free for the next seventy-two hours. That is to say that you can tune in now, choose whichever cell you wish to view by pressing the red button, change cells as many times as you wish, and continue watching non-stop until Tuesday evening, at which time you can choose to take the package at a reduced introductory rate, available for subscription today. Taking advantage of this offer will, of course, enable you to watch Martha Honeydew's time in Cell 7 – the last cell.

KRISTINA: Watching her as time leads up to that all-important decision. Watching what could to all intents and purposes be her final hours. And what excellent timing – introducing this during the landmark case of the first female teenager ever on death row.

RAFI: We are blessed with having the opportunity to be an active part of the whole justice system, especially in such a case. It truly is democracy in action. We demanded a safer world, we were presented with one, but with the added responsibility of ensuring we consider not only the lost life of the victim, but also the threatened life of the accused.

JOSHUA: Well, viewers, before the end of the programme we'll be having an exclusive *sneak peek* of this new system and tuning in directly to Cell 4 with Martha Honeydew, so do stay tuned. But before we go to that, let's turn to our second guest, editor-in-chief of the National News, Albert DeLonzo. It's a pleasure to have you here, Albert.

ALBERT: The pleasure's all mine and I must say I am *massively* excited about this new project from Life Visions! Wow, is that going to be good, and I just know my readers are going to be chomping at the bit to sign up. There's nothing quite like people watching, is there?

JOSHUA (smiling): Oh, I *love* it!

KRISTINA: Albert, you have your finger on the pulse of society; tell me, what are the people thinking about this now? How are they *feeling*?

ALBERT: That's an interesting question, Kristina, and this is a *fascinating* case.

JOSHUA: Yet open and closed, surely?

ALBERT: You would think so. There is a great deal of anger and resentment towards Honeydew. We've witnessed public outpourings of grief. There has, for example, been a candlelit parade through the streets, culminating in the gathering of approximately five thousand people at the gates of Jackson's mansion, a book of condolences has been opened at the cathedral with a queue of people stretching over a mile waiting to sign it, and there has been – perhaps the most striking thing of all – an *ever-growing* collection of flowers and gifts left at the murder site that is becoming a veritable *carpet* of grief.

KRISTINA: I believe we have a photograph of that coming up on your screens now.

The camera pans out. In the smaller weekend studio the screen to the right seems larger. A photograph of the murder scene fills it – in the background the hard, bland concrete of the High Rises, a dull, grey sky, and a tarmac road; in the foreground an explosion of colour. Flowers, soft toys, hand-painted banners with Paige's name emblazoned on, potted plants, shining crosses, photographs of his smiling face, candlelight flickering on all of them.

A police officer stands vigil near a group of people with their hands in prayer.

ALBERT (whispered): Would you look at that! There is no truer marker of a man than how one thinks of him upon death. Hundreds and thousands of people are making the pilgrimage to the Rises, an area where before they would probably have feared to tread. And look at them now.

On the screen the camera zooms in on a small child holding a red rose, a tear leaking from under her closed eyelids and down her cheek.

The studio is silent. The picture fades. The camera turns back to the sofa, Kristina dabbing her eyes and Albert replacing a tissue in his pocket while the other two men shake their heads in shared exasperation.

ALBERT: A hero of our time has been stolen from us.

JOSHUA: A tragedy affecting so many lives.

RAFI: We can only be thankful that due to our system, acts like these are relatively rare and most heavily punished.

KRISTINA: I believe you have some gossip for us though, Albert – something you've picked up on the grapevine.

ALBERT: Well, Kristina, not exactly picked up on the grapevine, but something I've seen myself.

KRISTINA: Do tell!

He leans forward; the camera zooms in on him.

ALBERT: Yesterday I believe I witnessed a meeting of important minds who've spoken out in the past against our current system. None other than Justice Cicero.

KRISTINA: *Mr* Cicero.

ALBERT (laughing): Of course, *Mr* Cicero sharing coffee with designated counsellor to the accused, Mrs Eve Stanton. One of my photographers managed to take this photograph.

The camera pans out again and the screen on the right is filled with the image of Cicero and Eve in the coffee shop. He's leaning towards her, eyes peering over his glasses, while she rests her head in her hands looking down.

JOSHUA: A sad photograph.

ALBERT: I wonder what they're talking about. Martha's crime, the justice system, the unavoidable fact that she is likely to be the first teenage female executed on death row? Or how they could get her off?

KRISTINA: That is quite a scoop you managed there, Albert. Mr Cicero was quite clear in his views when he appeared here on the show.

ALBERT: Yet Eve Stanton is somewhat of an enigma. Famously, her husband was executed following killing a man he claimed to be attacking them. She petitioned for the role of Counsellor to be introduced citing humanity laws.

KRISTINA: Prisoners aren't allowed visitors.

ALBERT: Precisely her argument, that it was inhumane to disallow human contact.

RAFI: Yet they've killed someone – what do they expect?

ALBERT: To speak with her, now that would be a scoop.

KRISTINA: Something I do find puzzling in all this, is the lack of comment from Paige's family. The morning following the murder, a brief statement was released from his publicist, but we've heard nothing from his wife or his son.

JOSHUA: Perhaps they are literally overwhelmed with grief.

ALBERT: Yes, I agree with you, Josh. That their grief is most probably stifling them and rendering them incapable of comment. We, as the public, must respect their privacy in this, the most terrible of times for them, and we must wait patiently in the wings for their comment. Presently, I have a number of journalists camped outside their mansion, waiting for that moment when they *are* ready to talk. Yet what comment can they give except to express their shock, horror and feelings of interminable loss at this tragic killing. A senseless killing by a *child*, no less – a *girl*, who, by society's expectations, should be in the prime of her innocence.

On the screen two photographs appear. On the left, Martha in her school uniform: freckles, a smile and her long hair tied back. On the right, a police mug-shot of her: white prison overalls, a tear-streaked face and a newly-shaved head.

ALBERT: I raise a few questions to finish on, Kristina: is this typical of a single-parent family; is this what happens when only one role model is present in the home, and if so, what does the future hold for us? And, looking at our two photographs of her, school-girl Martha and Murderer Martha, how could the mother fail so badly to allow her to become that girl on the right?

KRISTINA: A truly fascinating insight there, Albert, thank you.

She turns back to the camera.

KRISTINA: And now as promised we have that exclusive for you. Rafi, isn't this exciting?

RAFI: I've been waiting for this moment for so long, Kristina.

KRISTINA: And I'm sure our viewers and our audience are *just* as excited as we are.

A murmur sounds over the audience. Kristina places a hand to her ear.

KRISTINA: Yes, we're able to go live to Cell 4 right now, and discover, with potentially only seventy-eight hours of her life remaining, what Honeydew is doing.

The screen fills with something off-white – darker in places, crumpled and creased in others.

KRISTINA: We seem to have a technical issue, ladies and gentlemen. If you could bear with us . . .

She puts a finger to her ear again, listening, and frowns.

KRISTINA: We don't appear to have . . .

The off-white moves, shuffles, sweeps across the screen and is taken away. What is revealed behind it blurs then re-focuses. Standing in the middle of Cell 4 is Martha, bloodied fingers and hands holding the off-white bed sheet she's just pulled from the camera.

Kristina's hand slaps over her mouth.

JOSHUA: Oh my . . .

RAFI: Shit.

ALBERT: Whoa!

Martha's bed is turned over and thrown against the door. Clearly visible are all the names previously hidden, and above them, in blurry, blotched, greasy red, with a few runs and drips are the words 'HOW MANY INNOCENT?'

The camera zooms to the names, to Martha's face, then to her hands and fingers covered in blood. She drops the sheet and collapses on the floor. The camera freeze-frames on her closed eyes.

JOSHUA: Someone get her a medic.

Within minutes the switchboard for cell viewing subscription is jammed.

Martha

He woke me from a sleep I didn't even know I was in.

He gave me back a reason to get up every morning and reminded me why I should breathe in and out.

He lit me.

I smiled for the first time I could remember.

He made it possible for me to save myself.

If only it could've stayed that way.

For eight months life was good.

You'd leave your car at the boundary and walk down. You'd bring cakes or takeaway with you sometimes and we'd sit on the floor in my flat and eat them like having a picnic. Or we'd walk, explore through the woods, which became our place, a deer once passing in front of us while on the horizon the sun was rising and a beautiful orange-pink light warmed our faces as we watched in awe.

Spring came and I finally felt strong enough to sort through Mum's things. But warm memories stirred by photographs and cards disappeared when I found those letters. Meeting you that night I could barely speak.

'What's wrong?' you asked and I passed you what I'd found.

My fingers and wrists are bandaged. The words I wrote, and the names that were hidden, are scrubbed clean. Is that a camera up on the wall? If it is, who's watching it and who saw what I did?

I could ask Eve, if they'd let me see her.

I heard her shouting on the other side of the door when some medic was wrapping bandages around me. I was hoping she'd have another message for me. I still see the words of the other when I close my eyes – *Please don't do this. Tell Eve you want to change your plea. Tell her the truth. I love you. I want to be with you. I xx*

What good did the truth ever do?

Ollie told the truth.

This is the way.

Some things are more important than being together, and we could never stay together. We had our time and now it's gone. Nothing but memories.

My fingers hurt. My wrists. My head.

My soul is too tired for anyone to bear.

When I'm sitting in that chair, the straps around me, waiting for the electricity to hit me, it's your face I'll see.

In this life we can't be together, but I'll wait for you in the next.

Eve

Eve pours a large glass of red wine and slumps down on the sofa. Max has lit the fire, made dinner and tidied up.

I'm blessed with a son like him, she thinks.

There's a soft knock at the living-room door and he peers around.

'Mum, he's back again.'

Eve takes a glug of wine and sits up. 'Show him in, Max.'

'You know what this could look like? It's not a good idea.'

She places the glass on the table. 'Thank you,' she says, her tone clipped. 'I understand, but –'

'And that guy from the newspaper has got someone following you. They had a photo of you on the TV. If they get a photo of you and –'

'Thanks, Max, but you can show him in.'

She hears his tutting and his mumbling and muttering under his breath as he disappears again, and she hears his gruff voice at the door, and his words telling the visitor to take off his shoes.

There's another gentle tap at the door and Eve stands up.

A young man in a hooded jacket steps inside. His shoes are off. As he extends one hand to her, he pulls down his hood with the other.

'Thank you, Mrs Stanton,' he says, and bows his head a little.

She shakes his hand. 'Sit down, Mr Paige.'

'Please.' He gives an awkward laugh. 'It sounds like you're talking to my father.'

'I'm sorry,' she replies as she sits. 'That must still be very painful.'

He looks to her with eyes full of confusion, and they hold each other's gaze for a fraction too long before he looks away and sits down on the sofa opposite her.

'Call me Isaac,' he says.

'Would you like a glass of wine, Isaac?'

'No, thank you, Mrs Stanton.'

'Eve.'

He nods.

'It's been a shit day, Isaac,' she says, lifting the glass to her mouth again.

'I saw the show earlier, with Martha. She . . .' He stops, his words lost.

'What they do to the prisoners in the cells is shocking. It's no form of justice or entertainment I want to be associated with but I'm scared for the future and I can't walk away.' Half a bottle of wine has made her talkative. 'This government pretends to be acting on behalf of its people but it's lies. The PM and his cronies manipulate us to behave just how they want us to.' She downs the rest of the glass and pours another.

'And anyone says something against it, you know what happens?'

She doesn't wait for Isaac to reply.

'Of course you do. They rule by fear and our fear gives them *ever more* power. And I'm sorry for your father, because whoever did kill him, and I'm certain it wasn't Martha, will no doubt never be found. And that, Mr Paige, *Isaac*, is a tragedy for both of them. But we both know there's no justice here any more.'

He says nothing.

They sit in silence. The light from the open fire flickers around the room and on their faces, everything obscured by shadows and half-light.

'I'm glad you came back,' she says. 'Though Max – he's not so glad.'

'Sounds like he worries about you.'

Eve takes another mouthful of wine and looks into the fire, feeling the heat on her face and skin and blanching from the white of the flame at the base of the coal. 'Have you seen Mrs B since she was on the programme?' she asks quietly.

'Yes,' he replies.

'I feel bad for encouraging her to do it.'

'Don't. She's glad she did it. She had to try.'

She nods as she turns from the fire and catches his eye.

'How did you find out where I live?'

'That isn't difficult to find out, Mrs . . . *Eve* . . .'

'For someone with your money and influence?'

'No,' he replies, staring straight at her. 'For anybody who has a phone or a computer and the internet.'

'That's not everyone.'

He shuffles forward in his seat. 'I *know* that,' he says. 'Just because I share a surname with my father, doesn't mean I share the same ethics.'

'Like father like son . . .' She takes another sip of wine.

'If that is what you truly believe then you're not the person I thought you were. Or you've had too much to drink.'

'I can't be the person I want to be, Isaac.' She puts the glass on the table. 'I don't think I ever will be and I'm sorry for that, I really am, but I'm done with all this. You're wasting your time coming here. I've been fooling myself. I don't make any difference to any of those prisoners on death row. I'm sick of seeing people dying. People who could be innocent but nobody cares as long as it's entertaining and the crime figures are low. Oh, and as long as someone is making money out of it.'

'You're wrong. You do make a difference.'

'I don't know about that, but it doesn't matter anyway. Martha is my last case whether I like it or not. I'm being replaced. By a *virtual counsellor*.'

'A what?'

'It's unbelievable, isn't it? I'm being replaced by a computer program. A screen that talks to the prisoners. Searches its database for answers. *Computer generated empathy*.'

'When does this happen?'

'Tomorrow. Or the day after. I'm not sure. Apparently it keeps crashing. Sometime this week anyway.'

'Then you have to make Martha count.'

Slowly Eve leans towards Isaac, her brow furrowing as she focuses tight on his face and stares into his eyes.

'Why are you here?' she whispers. 'Why did she send you a letter? How did Mrs B know your phone number?'

Isaac lowers his head and stares at his shoes.

'Martha didn't kill my father,' he whispers.

'Then who did?'

He props his elbows on the coffee table and rests his head in his hands.

Eve walks across the room, closes the door and sits back down on the sofa next to him.

'Tell me who did it,' she breathes. 'And why she's taking the blame.'

His face is pale and blotchy as he looks up to her. 'Do you believe in promises, Eve?' he says. 'That if you make a promise to someone you love, and who loves you back, that you have to uphold it, even if doing so means they will die?'

She stares at him, memories of Jim, that night and the promise she made to him flitting through her head. 'You and Martha Honeydew . . .'

'Even if that promise was their idea, and they knew when they asked you to keep it what it would mean?'

'Tell me,' she says. 'Share it with me. Let me help you.'

'I can't,' he breathes. 'I can't betray her trust.'

'You know who killed your father?'

He nods.

'You know for certain that it wasn't her?'

Again he nods.

'Can you prove it?'

He snorts with derision. 'What does *prove* matter any more? Who cares about evidence?' He pulls in a staggered breath. 'I've said too much. I didn't come here for this. I was hoping she'd replied to my letter.' His tone is abrupt, final.

'I'm sorry,' Eve mumbles.

'Get her to ring me from your phone.' As he stands to leave, he passes her a piece of paper with his number on.

'If they let me see her . . .'

'Five minutes ago you said you couldn't make a difference; this is your chance to. Your last chance ever. You have to see her.' He turns away.

'Why is she covering for someone else?' Eve says after him. He stops.

'We had this idea, a plan of sorts, but things changed quickly. My father, he . . .' He pauses. 'I need to tell her I've had time to think and it doesn't have to be this way – I don't want it to be – we were too hasty. And you need to find Gus too. Ask him for the papers Isaac and Martha left. And when you go there, when you leave, make sure you're not being followed or all this will be for nothing.'

Martha

My mum would've liked you. My proper mum, not that hallucination-weirdo from last night. Mrs B liked you. After she got over the shock of who you were.

'What the fuck you doing with a Paige? They no good,' she said, her language bluer than the sky, picked up from her father who learnt English from dockers and fishermen. 'Pretend they are, like painted faces, but bad people. You bloody know.'

'He's different,' I told her. 'He's adopted anyway, he's not a real Paige.'

'Ach . . . makes no odds . . . Born naked in body and mind,' she says. 'Situation, bringing-up, you know – pears and trees.'

'You mean apples,' I chuckle. 'Apples don't fall far from the tree.'

In two weeks she was asking you over for dinner.

'That bloody pear sprout legs and run away from tree,' she said after you'd gone home.

I laughed at her. 'Apples, Mrs B.'

Not long after, I found her sitting in the middle of her living room floor surrounded by old newspapers. She tapped the one closest to her.

'Took long time to find,' she said. 'But I remember now.'

I crouched next to her and took the paper, the smiling photo of a dark-haired man.

'God, he looks just like –'

'Because he is Isaac's father,' she said. 'Died when boy was only baby. Cancer.'

The man's deep eyes drew me to him.

'Handsome, hey?' she said with a nudge of her elbow. 'Like Isaac.'

Heat spread through my face. 'I . . . d–don't . . . know,' I stammered.

Mrs B's laugh filled the room and the walls seemed to vibrate with it. 'You never have no words!' she said. 'Yes, handsome, isn't he?' Her huge hands slapped me on the back and her wide eyes twinkled. 'Watch yourself, girl: boys like that make your knickers fall off.'

I ducked my head down, hotness in my cheeks. 'Mrs B! I don't know what you mean!'

'I think you do.' She nodded, her narrow eyes peering at me through her glasses. 'Make sure you keep your hand over your tuppence!'

'What?' I sniggered. 'My *tuppence*? What's that?'

'Your moneybox, your privates, minnie, honeypot. I hear all kinds of words for it. You know what I'm saying. No mother here to tell you so I do. Keep you safe.'

My cheeks burnt red.

'Mrs B, you really don't need to worry, I can take care of my . . . my . . . *tuppence* . . .'

Her elbow nudged me again. 'Funny when you embarrassed,' she said. She put her arm around me, hugged me tight and the air in her lungs bellowed a hearty laugh.

I laughed back with her.

It's nice to feel a smile in my chest. Those memories of you are good. In here, memories are all I have to pass the time. And visions of hope for a fairer place. A better one you can fight for when I'm gone . . .

When I met you off the train at the underpass a few days after, you were an hour late; you had a different jacket on, bigger and with a large hood pulled over your head.

'I tried to ring you,' I said. 'What's wrong?'

'I think he's done something to my phone,' you replied. 'He knows everywhere I'm going. I think he suspects something. He keeps making jibes about girlfriends. Saying things like me bringing home a nice girl who lives in the Avenues.'

'What?'

You shook your head. 'Forget it, it's not important. But . . .' You held my arm and ushered me into the shadows. 'There's something else. Where can we go to talk?' you whispered. 'Not your flat, they could find us there. Somewhere safe. I've found some things.' You eased open the front of your jacket and in the orange of the street lights I could see rolled-up documents and papers stuffed wherever they'd fit. 'I photocopied them.'

I stared at them. 'I know someone,' I said. 'We can trust him.'

Your face was a picture when Gus answered the door to his flat. 'Untidiness doesn't make you untrustworthy,' I whispered to you as we stepped inside.

Between discarded clothes, chip wrappers, empty drink cans and dirty plates, we pored over the documents you'd gathered from your father's office: hand-scrawled letters, accounts in different names, bank details in different countries.

'I don't understand all this,' I said.

'Me neither,' you replied.

Then we found a list – names of police officers, high-powered officials, journalists, TV personalities, executives of multi-national companies . . . all with large figures next to them, some with details of crimes and misdemeanours nobody would want made public.

'They were all in his pocket? He could do whatever he wanted and hold this over their heads until it all went away?' I asked.

'It looks like it,' you said.

I held the list in my hand, scanning over the names.

'This is crazy,' I said. 'This is huge. How could nobody have been punished for these crimes? These . . . *murders* and *rapes* and . . . *Jesus* . . .'

'Somebody would've been,' you replied.

'Yeah maybe, but someone who was innocent!'

'What I don't understand,' you said, 'is how he organised this. How he thought it up. He's a straightforward man. This is cunning and sly. He's not that intelligent.'

'You think someone else . . . ?'

'I don't know. I really don't know.'

Neither of us dare say the names or the crimes out loud but in our heads we read down the list. I couldn't swear or shout. Couldn't even cry for the shame I felt for being part of a society where this could happen.

'This isn't just about me and you any more and whether we can see each other or not,' I said. 'This is about everyone. My mum, yours, Ollie, Mrs B, Gus, all the victims who've never had proper justice, the people on death row with no defence . . . everyone.

'Everyone knows the system's become corrupt, just nobody says it. Nobody dare. But they don't know it's as bad as this.' I waved a hand over the documents in front of us. 'Do you reckon . . .' Thoughts whirled around my head. '. . . reckon we could use this somehow?'

'And do what with it?' you asked.

'We could hide it here, with the letter I found too, and we could get someone to listen. Show it all to them.'

'Who? You know what will happen – mention it to anyone who could do anything, like a journalist or the police, and somehow either this will all go missing, or we will. That's if they'd listen in the first place.'

'Maybe they wouldn't listen to an orphan from the Rises,' I said, 'but they would to the son of Jackson Paige.'

'But . . .'

'Just imagine – if we could bring *him* down, we could bring down all those connected to him. Think how many lives that could save, and if we could prove the corruption, maybe that could change the justice system, bring fairness back to it. It's too late for Ollie and my mum and yours, but for others . . . This is what you wanted.'

When I got home that night my flat had been broken into and trashed. Cupboards were emptied, sofas and chairs ripped apart, wardrobes pulled over, photos torn from frames and the glass shattered.

You remember that? You remember how speechless you were when I told you about the threat painted on my living-room wall? Was that the tipping point for you? Knowing that your so-called father had threatened my life if I ever saw you again?

And they didn't even know about the documents then. Was that in your head the night Jackson Paige was shot? Because it sure as hell was in mine.

'I can be the martyr,' I had said to you that night, the gun in my hand, Jackson on the floor. 'But the fighter has to be you.'

Blue of police lights flashed on your face and in your eyes. My God, did I love you, still do.

'No,' you replied.

I wanted to tell you we could run away and always be together, but that was selfish. We were staring at possibility of change, proper justice and for the truth to finally be out; I could *not* turn from it.

'It has to be,' I said. 'You have the influence and the money. People will listen to you. You can do that. I can't. But I can do this.'

If I close my eyes now, here in this cell, I can remember the feel of his last kiss touching my lips, and if I imagine hard enough I can smell him close and sense him with me. And I can hear the last words I'll ever hear from him as he said I love you.

'Go!' I shouted to him on that night, and I watched his shadow disappear into the darkness, knowing it was the last time I'd ever see him.

CELL 5

Eve

Eve's car rolls down Crocus Street. Her dark glasses cover her bloodshot eyes but as she peers and squints through the windscreen at something in front of her she pulls them off and her eyebrows lift in surprise at the expanse of flowers and tributes to Jackson now stretching the whole length of the path and into the road. Grey and cracked pavement and tarmac covered in soft petals and beautiful colours.

'How many now?' she says to herself.

With a sigh and a shake of her head she turns the car the other way and sees what she was looking for. Slowing down, she pulls up next to young man in baggy jeans and a sweatshirt, a hood pulled up hiding his face. She winds the window down and he glances sideways.

'You again,' he says.

'Get in the car, Gus,' she tells him.

He carries on walking. 'What?'

'Get in the car!'

'Hell, no. I was told about getting in cars with strangers,' he says. 'And you about as strange as they come.'

'Get in the bloody car before I ring the police and have you arrested for something I make up!'

He stops. 'Jesus, you crazy woman! All right, all right.'

He climbs into the car and she drives away.

183

Martha

Two more sleeps.

Two more sunrises through smaller and smaller windows.

Two more breakfasts of cold toast and orange juice.

Three more lunches.

Three more dinners 'til I die.

I stare around the cell. It's soul-destroying. Brain-numbing. Hope-eating. Madness-inducing and all those other things that bring you down.

I feel drained.

The days revolve around food and sleep and the rise and fall of the sun.

Will I get to choose what food I have on my last day?

My last supper, but there won't be wine or friends around a table. I don't have enough friends to fill a table anyway and there's only one person I'd want to share my last hours with.

We could never socialise like normal people. In his part of the City the paparazzi followed him around like wasps to jam; if he'd been seen with me, a girl from the Rises, it would've been splashed over every tabloid in town.

He said he didn't care, but I did.

They'd dig up stuff on me too. Go on about Mum being killed. 'Daughter of Hit and Run Mum,' it'd read, or 'Orphaned by Killer Neighbour'. All that crap and all those lies.

World's made up of lies and half-truths.

I didn't want whatever me and Isaac had shadowed by that and reminding us both that it was his dad who killed my mum.

But hey, I suppose that was what brought us together.

If I could pick a last supper, it would be him and me. An evening in the woods, orange sunset through branches, quiet but for birdsong. I don't care what the food is – something that doesn't make my breath smell or make me burp – sticky toffee pudding like my mum used to make, or Mrs B's honey cake. I'd eat it slowly, enjoying every mouthful and every second with him.

One summer's night, we sat together in the park on the two remaining swings. It was about a month since his father had started asking questions about where he was spending his time and who with, and our conversations had become more serious. Our time felt threatened. We sucked up every second we could before the inevitable end came.

'The evening of the crash,' he told me, our swings creaking as loud as the traffic in the distance, 'he came home ranting and raving. It was late. Eleven o'clock maybe, or midnight. I heard him talking on the phone. He'd been drinking. My mother was shouting at him, she was hysterical. "*You been seeing that bitch again*," she said.'

'He was having an affair?'

'He'd had quite a few, all with women from the High Rises, but my mother, *adoptive* mother, looked good on his arm and her family had money; he'd never leave her . . . she's a powerful woman in her own way. Anyway, they were outside the back of the house shouting and screaming at each other, so I climbed out of bed and went to see what the fuss was about. You couldn't miss the car, it was . . .'

'A homeless guy told me it was a 4x4 that hit her,' I said.

He nodded, looking sideways as we swung past each other.

'Ollie's car was only some tiny thing. Rattled if it did over forty. We used to joke that he better avoid foxes cos hitting one would write it off.'

'The car was wrecked,' he said, scuffing his feet on the ground under the swing and coming to a halt. 'It was . . . the front was . . . well, you don't need to know.'

I stopped next to him. The bulbs on the streetlights near the park had blown ages ago and nobody had replaced them. It was dark. I could see his outline against the lights from the main road in the distance but not much more.

'Half an hour later some men turned up in a truck. My father let them in and I saw him give them cash and shake their hands. Two of them set to work on the 4x4.'

'Doing what?'

'Fixing it. It looked hopeless to me, but they'd brought a new bonnet and paint . . .' He sighed, took my hands and pulled our swings together. 'I'd already taken photos though,' he whispered. 'And I tried to record the other men talking to my father on my phone, but the quality wasn't too good. I snuck out of the house and followed them when they left. I don't know why; it would've been easier to head back to bed, pull the duvet over my head and be ignorant, but something

186

stopped me. I parked over there in an old car park,' he pointed past Crocus Street and towards a closed-up bar, 'and I dodged through the shadows and hid in the doorway of the shops.'

He squeezed my hand.

'I listened to them talking as they stood over her, then I followed them towards the High Rises, and while they were smashing up Oliver B's car to make it look legitimate, I was hiding among the bins. I can't imagine, with the noise they were making, that I was the only one who saw them.'

'Then why didn't you do anything?'

I felt his hand run down my hair and rest on my cheek. 'I phoned for the police and an ambulance,' he said, 'but what else could I have done?'

'Told someone who could do something?'

'Like who, Martha?'

'The police? Newspapers? A journalist? Someone . . .'

'Nobody would've believed –'

'You had proof! It could've been a scoop for them. You could've told them what your father did, shown them the photos, the video. They would've loved it, put it on the front page as a scandal.'

He lifted my hands to his face and kissed them. 'I wish,' he whispered. 'I really do wish that could've happened. But you know it wouldn't have worked. The story would barely have got from anyone's mouths before it disappeared, and all evidence with it. You know that, Martha. Have you ever wondered what the most powerful thing in the world is?

'Some person?' I said. 'Someone with the interests of the people at heart. Or it should be.'

'It should be, but it isn't. Power is the most powerful thing in the world. Whoever has it can do whatever they like. How they get it might be legitimate, but how they keep it, grow it or exert it, that's the worrying thing.'

'This is wrong. Even with all that evidence we can't do anything. What's the point of trying? How can we ever get anyone to listen or show anyone?'

He pulled me towards him and I felt his warmth on my face as we kissed.

'We don't give up,' he breathed. 'Here – now – you and me – together we'll find a way.'

He let go of my hands and stood up. 'Enough doom and gloom,' he said, and he twisted the swing I was sitting on around and around, the chains it hung by wrapping around each other as my seat squeezed and lifted a bit.

'Hold on,' he said, 'and look up.'

I did as he said and he let go, and I watched the pinpricks of stars in the sky above me as the world spun and tipped around me first one way, then the other, over again, 'til all the twisting of the chains ran out of energy and the swing stopped.

'That's mad,' I said, and on wobbly legs I stood and with my head still spinning, I kissed him again.

The whirr of the camera on the wall brings me back and takes away the smile my memory gave me.

Seems a way found us, Isaac.

I lift my head and look at the camera. How many people are watching me?

All the people from the Avenues and the City who've got Jackson Paige on a pedestal?

How many more will be watching in two days' time?

They'll know the truth soon enough.

Eve

Eve parks her car at the underpass within sight of the mountain of tributes to Paige.

Gus tuts.

'What?' she asks.

'This crap,' he says. 'People are so stupid.'

'You know the truth then?'

'I'm probably the only one who knows *all* of the truth, but it don't mean I'm going to tell you.'

'Because I won't pay you for it?'

'That, yeah, and because of honour,' he says.

'Oh don't give me that.'

'What, you think cos I'm from the Rises and I haven't got no money, and cos of them owning me like they do, the authorities and that, that I haven't got no principles neither?'

'I didn't say –'

'You didn't need to, woman. You're the one with no principles, forcing me to get in the car with you. Threatening me.'

'I didn't threaten you. Anyway, why don't the authorities know? Why haven't you told them?'

'They haven't asked. They don't want to know. And like I said to you, cos of honour.'

Eve drums her fingers on the steering wheel.

190

'Where do you live?' she asks.

He spins around to her. 'What? Why?'

'Because there are some papers and letters you need to give to me.'

'I haven't got no papers and shit.'

'Yes you do. Isaac told me.'

'I'm not taking you to my house. What if folks see?'

'That's why I came at night time.'

'Don't make no odds. I'm not taking you to my house, full stop. And anyway, even if I gave you all that crap, it don't say who killed him or why.'

'You've read everything?'

He shrugs.

'Then what about Martha's letter?'

He stares at her. 'Well . . . Still don't say who killed him.'

'But it's all evidence.'

'What's the use in that? Can't do nothing with it. Who's going to listen? Who's going to print it? Pointless.' He turns and stares out of the window, watching the police officer pace back and forth in front of the tributes to Jackson.

'You know, I'm sick of this,' Eve says. 'I'm trying to do the right thing and people are difficult. Martha didn't do it, I'm certain of it, but she won't say so. Isaac more or less said it, but won't tell me anything else because of some promise, even though that means she'll die.

'You say you know everything but won't tell me. And all this time, it's getting closer and closer to that innocent girl being killed and I can't do anything about it.

'Just give me the papers,' she says.

'What if you tell someone it's me who gave you them or that I'd been hiding them? Hey? What d'you think's going to happen to me then? They'll have me. You won't see me for dust and no bugger will know or care.'

'I'm not going to tell anyone.'

'Correction,' he says. 'You don't *want* to tell no one, but sometimes you don't have no choice.'

She drops her head in her hands. 'Nobody is going to do anything to you just for looking after some papers.'

'Don't you bloody believe it, woman!'

She starts the car engine, fastens her seatbelt again and locks the doors.

'What you doing? Let me out!'

She revs the engine and the police officer guarding the flowers stops walking.

'Do you think that police officer would be interested in knowing how you jumped into my car and demanded money off me?'

'You wouldn't.'

'What about if I gave him an excuse to search your house?' She revs the engine more and the police officer stares at them. 'What if he found the documents? He'd think you broke into Jackson's house and stole them. What would happen then?'

She lets the car roll forward. The police officer's hand goes to his radio.

'Don't . . .'

'We both know what would happen, don't we? You spelt it out before. What did you say a minute ago? *They'll have me. You won't see me for dust and no bugger will know or care* – something like that, was it?'

'Y'know, I thought you was decent.'

'They were seeing each other, weren't they? Martha and Isaac Paige?'

'What?'

'Weren't they?'

'Yeah, yeah, all right, they was seeing each other.'

The car rolls a little closer.

'How did they meet?'

'I ain't saying . . .' He pulls at the door handle but it doesn't budge. 'Shit, woman! Shit! All right . . . all right . . . they met after her mum died. Isaac started hanging around down here.'

'Why?'

'Oh, Jesus, are you stupid? Guilt, of course. Cos of her mum.'

'Why did he feel guilty? He didn't have anything to do with it, did he?'

Gus lifts his hands in desperation. 'He didn't kill her mum if that's what you're asking. He's a decent guy . . .'

'What about Jackson? Did he know they were seeing each other?'

The car continues to roll and the police officer unclips his gun.

'Jackson? Shit, he *forbid* them to see each other, and her flat was trashed, said he'd kill her if they didn't stop seeing each other and he meant it.'

'So he came and found her that night?'

The police officer starts walking towards the car.

'Shit, please, let me go now!'

'Who shot Jackson? Whose gun was it?'

'I can't tell you.'

She pulls the handbrake on and the police officer shines his torch through the windscreen.

'Jackson's gun. It was Jackson's. Said he was going to shoot her, said some shit about her mum, some real nasty shit . . .'

The police officer steps closer.

'Who shot him?'

'I can't!' he says. 'It can't come from me!'

'Who was there? Who saw it happen?'

'I . . . he . . . Jesus, woman, let me go! I'm stuck here. I'm caught in some bloody triangle with the authorities, Martha and Isaac – and now *you*, and I didn't do nothing!'

The police officer knocks on the driver's window.

'What's the name of your street?'

'What?'

'Quickly, what's the name of your street?'

'Snowdrop Close, Jesus fucking Christ, Snowdrop Close!'

She presses the button, the window whirrs down and cold air blasts in.

Gus lowers his head.

'Good evening, madam, can I ask what you're doing down here this evening?'

Eve smiles at the officer. 'I'm sorry, officer,' she said. 'We'd come to look at the tributes.'

'And you?' he asks, shining the torch in Gus's face.

'Yeah, me too,' Gus mutters.

He looks back to Eve. 'No problems, madam?'

'None, thank you.'

'Well, I'll leave you to your business then.'

He starts to walk away. Gus breathes a sigh of relief.

'Oh,' Eve says out of the window, 'sorry, officer, one thing, could you give me directions to Snowdrop Place?'

He wanders back to the car. 'Snowdrop Place? Why does someone like you want to go there?'

'I'm a solicitor,' she lies. 'I have some files to drop off for a client.'

'I see. What number?'

'I'll take you,' Gus interrupts. 'It don't matter, officer, I'll show her.'

'That's very kind of you,' Eve says with a smile.

The police officer moves away. Eve closes the window, starts the engine again and pulls off.

'Y'know, you lot from the Avenues come here to do your dirty business, get us wrapped up in your crap and we have to take the blame cos you've got the money to get out of it. Shit falls downwards, woman. 'bout time it stopped. I'll give you the stuff, the letters and that, I promise, but I'll tell you what else too – stop the car.'

'Pardon?'

'Stop the car near the underpass. Here, stop here.'

She pulls to the side.

'See that on the wall?' He leans forward and points through the windscreen. 'CCTV. Been there years. Said it was to protect us. But when we needed it, said it don't work.'

'But . . . ?'

'Unlock the door.'

'Do you think I'm stupid? You'll run away.'

'Nah,' he says. 'I told you I promise and I meant it. Now, watch the camera.'

As he strolls away from the car and across the road, Eve watches the camera turn and follow him.

Counselling

'I didn't think they'd let us meet again,' Martha says, looking up to Eve with her wrists and hands bandaged.

'It took a bit of convincing,' Eve replies. 'How are you? You look tired.'

'I am,' Martha replies. 'It's . . .' She trails off

'You want to talk about it?'

Martha stares at her, her chest moving up and down as she breathes, her fingers fiddling as they rest in her lap. She wipes a hand over her shaved head. 'No,' she whispers.

Eve nods.

Martha takes a deep breath and leans forward. 'In some ways,' she whispers, 'it'll be a release when it comes. I didn't think . . . it'd . . . it'd be . . .' She folds her arms across her chest. '. . . I don't know . . .' she mumbles. 'Will I see you tomorrow?' she asks.

'I hope so,' Eve replies.

Martha hugs her arms around her body.

'The guard said there won't be any more designated counsellors, said there are these virtual ones now in a room where a voice talks to you.'

'I know – I only found out yesterday. Have they taken you to one already?'

'No.' She stares over Eve's shoulder to the window. 'Y'know,

I'm glad you planted the tree. It's nice to see something green. Something proper.'

'If they do take you to one, you don't have to say anything.'

Martha looks back to Eve.

'It's live-streamed to the outside,' Eve says.

'What about the cameras in the cells?'

'Those too now.'

'They're watching me all the time?'

'Didn't you realise that yesterday when you pulled your stunt with the message on the wall?'

'Not really. I just thought people in the offices might see it or . . . I don't know . . . What? Streamed onto the television?'

'Television, internet . . . It's free. Well, it's free up until about six o'clock on your day seven.'

'Then they have to pay for it?'

Eve nods her head.

'Could you see all those names on the wall?'

She nods again.

'Good,' Martha whispers. 'And my message?'

'Oh yes.'

Martha gives a hint of a smile. 'You've been watching it then?' she asks.

Eve shuffles in her seat. 'Just some last night,' she replies.

'Huh, I'm glad you couldn't watch the other night.'

'Which one?'

Martha shrugs. 'Cell 3, I think. They all kind of blend into each other.'

Eve crosses her hands in front of her. 'A prisoner once told me he thought that in one of the cells they gave you some sort of gas that made you hallucinate.'

'That'd be the one. Crazy fucking shit.'

Martha pulls her hands up the sleeves of her overalls and folds her arms across her chest. She shuffles further down in her seat. 'Some folks must find it funny.'

'Some crueller people perhaps.'

'Yeah and now they can watch. Like it's all part of the fun, the entertainment, y'know, like some bizarre zoo or something.' She rubs her hands over her face and exhales loudly. 'If they couldn't see the gas then it'd be hilarious, wouldn't it? I would've looked like some deranged mad girl. You never know, perhaps some decent folks won't like it, maybe there might even be some kind of public outcry, saying it's . . . I don't know . . . against your human rights or something. You'd think it would be. Being gassed and all.'

She pauses, thinking.

'What time were you watching?'

'Around four or five this morning,' Eve says. 'I woke and couldn't get back to sleep.'

'So you watched me sleeping?'

'I was concerned about you. It . . . was . . . the only way I could see how you were. Are you upset by that? Would you prefer it if I didn't?'

'Why were you concerned about me? Because it's your job?'

Eve thinks a moment. 'I suppose I was worried about what they were doing to you. How you were feeling. Not because you're my client, but because . . . because you're vulnerable. And alone.'

'Because I'm a teenager?'

'No, not really. Because you're human. Because I don't like suffering. Or pain. Because I worry about you. Because I feel useless. Because I don't want you to die.'

Eve watches as Martha wipes the back of her hand over her eyes.

'Because I think you're scared.'

Martha's breathing stutters through her chest.

'I won't watch again,' Eve says.

'Doesn't matter,' Martha replies. 'Just feels a bit weird, that's all.'

'You want to talk about it?'

'Huh, you sound like a counsellor saying *"you want to talk about it?"* all the time.'

'Now that's weird,' Eve says with a smile.

Outside the tree bends in the high wind and the birds are buffeted back and forth.

Martha looks to the side of the room. 'There's a clock in every cell, you know, and they all tick as loud as that one. I thought I'd get used to it, but you don't.'

'I remember one of the prisoners,' Eve says, 'his name was Jorge, managed to climb onto the door frame and pull the clock off the wall. He smashed it to pieces.'

'They've got metal cages around them.'

'Since then they have.'

Martha grins at her. 'Are you supposed to tell me stuff like that?'

Eve's shoulders lift.

'What will happen to your job with these new virtual counsellors?'

'You're my last client,' she says.

Martha shuffles in her seat. 'You won't forget me then?'

'I wouldn't anyway,' Eve replies. She reaches into her bag and takes out another packet of biscuits, custard creams this time.

'Thanks,' Martha says. 'They're my favourite but I don't want to ruin my figure.' She tries to smile again.

Eve pushes them across the table. 'Eat the whole damn lot,' she replies.

With incredible care Martha peels away the end of the packaging, takes out one biscuit and nibbles the edge.

Eve watches her eat. 'How long had you been in a relationship with Isaac Paige?' she asks.

For a second Martha's mouth stops moving. As she watches Eve her whole body seems to tense.

'Who've you been talking to?'

'Isaac, Mrs B, Gus from the High Rises. Did you know there was CCTV pointing to the exact point where you claim to have shot Jackson?'

Martha puts the rest of the biscuit in her mouth. 'If you know that, then you know it's pointless,' she mumbles through crumbs.

'They keep backup files of all the CCTV cameras.'

She swallows. 'Makes no odds. I don't want to go through all this. I don't want to think about it, talk about it or anything. Nothing. It's done.'

She takes another biscuit and bites it in two, watching as Eve pulls a mobile phone from her pocket and taps at the screen.

'You're not allowed . . .' Martha says.

Eve lifts a finger to her lips to quieten her, and as she holds the phone to her ear, she and Martha watch each other.

'Hello, yes, it's me. I'm here,' Eve says into the mouthpiece. 'Uh-huh. Yes, she's in front of me. Eating the biscuits you sent. You were right, they are her favourite.'

Martha's face drops. Her eyes blink and blink.

'I'll pass the phone over. No, it's fine, there aren't any cameras in here, we're OK.'

She holds out the phone. 'He wants to talk to you.'

Martha stares, her mouth open.

'Take it.'

Martha shakes her head.

'Take it,' Eve hisses. 'It's Isaac.' She pushes the phone across the table.

With a trembling hand Martha reaches slowly out, touching the phone with tentative fingers, and with her eyes focused on Eve she grasps it and lifts it to her ear.

'Hello,' she whispers.

She looks away from Eve, her shoulders hunching as she lifts her knees and hugs them to her chest with one arm, perching on the edge of her seat while she rocks back and forth.

'I miss you too,' she breathes.

She nods her head and through her tears a smile cracks. 'Did you see it? Did Mrs B? Yeah? Did she see his name?'

A second longer and the smile fades.

'I can't. I'm not . . .'

She rests her head on her knees.

'I can't,' she says into the phone. 'No . . . I can't tell them that . . . I'm not going to . . .'

She wipes a hand over her eyes.

202

'Who'd believe me?' she whispers. 'I know . . . but evidence . . . the camera . . .' She shakes her head again as Isaac speaks. 'No, we talked about this . . . even with that . . . no, Isaac, please . . . I'm not going to change my mind . . .'

For a second she glances to Eve, but her face crumples and her eyes fill with tears and she cowers into her seat with her head down low.

Her breath comes in stifled sobs. 'I love you too,' she breathes.

She turns off the phone and drops it to the floor. Eve walks around the table, and as Martha's body trembles and her tears fall, she takes her in her arms and holds her tight.

6.30 p.m. *Death is Justice*

High-pitched theme music pounds with a rhythmic heartbeat thud. Dark blue screen, flecks of white buzz and crackle. The eye logo, the words 'An Eye For An Eye For', spinning around the iris.

The music fades. The logo moves to the edge of the screen where the words stop spinning and the lights come up on a different studio – an old court room with oak panel walls, a raised wooden jury area crammed with the audience, large wooden tables and five ornate oak lecterns.

Standing to the side of a table, flanked by upright wooden chairs and backed by engraved panels is Kristina dressed in an electric-blue trouser suit with a deep neckline and pinched-in waist. Mock glasses perch on the end of her nose and on her head she wears a long judge's wig.

KRISTINA: Good evening and welcome to *Judge Sunday*!

The audience applaud.

KRISTINA: As always on *Judge Sunday* we're coming to you live from this historic building in central

London – the Old Bailey – which has stood on this spot since the late seventeenth century, and has seen the likes of the Kray brothers and Oscar Wilde on trial. Following the phasing out of courts, it's been saved from closure by being transformed into television studios for our very own show *Judge Sunday* and now also playing regular host to the brand new show – *Buzz for Justice* – on air twice daily, seven times a week.

She pauses to smile at the camera.

KRISTINA: Here at An Eye for An Eye Productions we are so excited to bring this new concept to you. If you've yet to see the trailer or tune in, you will *not* be disappointed. This is an opportunity for you, ordinary members of the public, to be part of a panel seated in front of the accused as they tell you their stories. Think they're guilty? Press the buzzer! With three of you on the panel, only a majority is needed to send them to prison. Want to be on the panel? Then go to their link on our website for details on how to purchase tickets. This is bound to be over-subscribed so hop on over as soon as you can!

The audience applaud. Kristina's teeth and her diamond necklace glint in the studio lights.

KRISTINA: Joining us again on tonight's programme is our
lovely roving reporter, Joshua Decker.

Wearing a blue designer suit with waistcoat and tie, Joshua
bounces into the room, his hand up to wave to the audience
as they clap and whistle him. He winks at a few as he passes,
takes the hand of one and kisses it with a smile.

KRISTINA: Thank you for joining us, Joshua. Not too much
roving today, I take it?

JOSHUA: Roving only from your side to our lovely audience!

A murmur echoes amongst the women.

KRISTINA: Of course, Joshua, in our court on *Judge Sunday*,
you must wear the wig.

She passes him a white judge's wig – shorter than her own.
He smiles, puts it on his head and turns to the camera.

JOSHUA: What do you think, viewers? Does it make me
look dapper?

Wolf whistles sound. Joshua strikes poses for them.

KRISTINA (loudly over the whistles): On a serious note,
viewers . . .

Joshua raises a hand to calm the audience.

KRISTINA: Tonight, exclusive to our channel, we are bringing you a panel of experts discussing teen killer Martha Honeydew's case, and helping you to make an informed decision on how to cast your votes. Is she truly guilty as she claims she is? Did she truly steal one of our national treasures from us?

The studio falls quiet. The camera zooms in on Kristina's face – wetness to her eyes, a tremble to her mouth.

JOSHUA: Let's get them on!

Joshua and Kristina step towards the empty lecterns.

KRISTINA: At lectern number one we have psychologist to the stars, Penny Drayton!

The audience clap as a stocky woman steps out from backstage, waving to the camera as she takes her place at the far lectern.

KRISTINA: From the City's serious crime squad – Detective Inspector Hart is at lectern number two.

A broad man in a crisp, blue uniform, shiny epaulettes and a row of medals strides out and takes his place. His expression is blank. His eyes are cold. The applause from the studio audience quietens slightly.

JOSHUA: Bestselling author of *Why Teens Kill*, at lectern number three is Ian Chobury.

Applause picks up slightly as a middle-aged man steps out, the lights reflecting off his bald head and his thick glasses as he briefly nods and waves and stands at the next lectern.

KRISTINA: And finally, at lectern number four, is a face already known to our viewers, and a last minute addition to our panel today, *ex* Supreme Court Judge, Mr Cicero.

Cicero pushes his glasses up his nose as he shuffles out and takes his place, his moustache twitches as he tries to smile. His hands rest on the lectern, his fingers clasped together. If the camera zoomed in on him, it'd see the beads of sweat gathering around his shirt collar.

The applause dies. At either side of the lecterns, Kristina and Joshua take their places at what were once raised witness stands. Each holds a gavel in their hands.

KRISTINA: Cicero, if we could come to you first. This is your second time visiting to discuss the case of Martha Honeydew. Why the interest?

Cicero wipes a hand through his greying hair.

CICERO: I am interested in justice for all. For the victims, yes. The families left behind, but also the accused.

DI HART: The accused? The *accused* forfeited their right to justice when they committed their crime!

CICERO: You're assuming she's guilty when all she is, is *accused*. What happened to innocent until PROVEN guilty?

DI HART: She as guilty as they come. My men caught her. She's admitted it. What more do you want?

CICERO (shouting): EVIDENCE! I want EVIDENCE! Proof, for God's sake!

Joshua taps his gavel gently on the wood. The guests stop and turn. He smiles.

JOSHUA: I think our panel are getting a little over excited there, don't you, Kristina?

KRISTINA: Indeed. Perhaps if we could bring the focus to our guest at lectern number three, Ian Chobury. Ian is the author of several best-selling crime novels, writing from the perspective of both killer and detective and so is well placed to offer insight into the minds of both . . .

CICERO (interrupting): It's fiction!

KRISTINA: . . . both our accused and our victim, Jackson Paige. Tell us, Ian, how important is this notion of evidence?

CHOBURY (quietly): Thank you, Kristina. I do believe it's important to remember what in fact evidence is, why it would be necessary, and what it would be used for. In cases our learned friend here, Mr Cicero, presided over during his career, evidence would indeed have been paramount, as it was for him to instruct on what the jury would see in order to aid their understanding of the crime and their subsequent decision. However, our justice system has evolved from this to a far superior, fairer and more democratic system. We are *all* judge and juror. We all have equal voice –

CICERO: No we don't!

CHOBURY: Your respect, please, Mr Cicero, to allow me to share my opinion.

JOSHUA (interrupting): Outspoken as always, Mr Cicero, but let's turn now to our resident expert, psychologist Penny Drayton. Nice to see you again, Penny.

He winks at Penny and she giggles back.

JOSHUA: What do you think could be this young lady's motivation to kill Jackson Paige?

DRAYTON: One does not need to reach far back in time to discover what is most likely Miss Honeydew's motivation for such an act. If we examine her childhood we can see the chaos she has had to endure. A father who disappeared before her birth, a mother who left her to fend for herself day after day, night after night, claiming to be working when in fact she was out meeting men.

CICERO: That's bullcrap! And you know it is!

DRAYTON: All leading to a tremendously unstable young lady. Let's not forget the death of her mother, too. How all these events must have affected her personality is fascinating. I believe her motivation was jealousy and envy. There is no disputing that she has had a hard life – no money, no love, no attention or compassion – she saw the lifestyle of the rich and the famous and focused her attention on them. She lured Jackson Paige there to his death.

CICERO (shouting): WHY? WHY would she lure one of the *richest* and most *famous* men in the world to kill him, and then *admit* to it? WHY would she do that?

Cicero slams his fists onto the lectern.

CICERO (shouting): This makes no sense at all and you are not trying to find out!

Kristina thunders her gavel against the wooden post.

KRISTINA: Order, Mr Cicero, please, order! Or I'll have you ousted from the court!

DI Hart laughs at Cicero.

DI HART: She said she was guilty, Cicero, you dumb ass. Why would she say that if it wasn't true?

CICERO: Well as you're an inspector you could do something radical such as going and inspecting! Ask questions! If you're so convinced she did it, find out why! DO YOUR BLOODY JOB!

DI Hart turns towards Cicero, finger raised, jabbing at the air.

DI HART (shouting): I've done my job, you moron! I've arrested a killer! I've got the gun she used and a signed confession. I've got her on death row where she belongs and I'll be there in two days' time watching the electricity ripping through her and frying her brain like she *deserves*. If you had done *your* job properly all those years ago then we wouldn't have killers on the streets now. *You* let killers go; *we* don't do that. We make the streets safe.

He takes a step from behind the lectern and towards Cicero.

DI HART (voice hissing with anger): Martha Honeydew is as cold-hearted as they come and she deserves to die!

Cicero leaps from behind his lectern, storms across to Hart and grounds him with one punch. Security men rush past. Chairs fall. People scream. The camera turns back to Kristina and Joshua now standing together, wigs askew.

JOSHUA (low voice): Some strong emotions for a very delicate case.

Kristina, mouth open, frowns at him.

JOSHUA: And never a dull moment here on *Judge Sunday*, viewers!

KRISTINA: Absolutely, Joshua! Always excitement, and often some scandal! Join us again after this short message from our sponsors – Cyber Secure – with those all-important voting numbers.

The screen fills with blue, the sounds diminish. A fluffy white cloud appears; strings of blurred text run through it. As a padlock clamps onto its corner, the text disappears and instead, underneath it runs a list of all the accused and their voting numbers.

Eve

The open fire crackles and spits, and the orange light reflects on the faces of Eve and Isaac sitting opposite each other with their heads deep in concentration.

On the coffee table are the files and documents Gus had hidden, alongside notebooks scrawled with information taken from them, and empty coffee mugs and plates with left-over sandwich crusts and food wrappers.

Max sits in the corner of the room with his laptop across his knees, looking from his mother to Isaac and back, tutting from time to time and glancing at his watch.

'Are you going to tell me what's happening?' he says.

Eve runs her fingers through her hair but doesn't look up. 'No,' she says. 'It's better if you don't know.'

'You're treating me like a child.'

The doorbell rings.

'You'll be expecting me to answer that, though?'

As he stands and leaves the room, Isaac turns to Eve.

'You should tell him,' he says.

'I'm trying to protect him.'

'Because of what happened to your husband?'

'You don't understand.'

'I understand you're putting him in more danger by not telling him.'

Cicero wanders into the room and slumps down next to Eve. He reaches into his jacket pocket, pulls out a set of keys and throws them on the coffee table. Eve, Isaac and Max stare at them.

'That's what you wanted, isn't it?' he asks, rubbing the cuts and bruises on his knuckles.

'Yes, but . . .' Eve whispers.

'You were great on the TV today, Justice,' Max says. 'When you slugged that police officer . . . that was . . . wow!'

Cicero turns to him, his moustache stretching in a bleak smile. 'Thanks, it wasn't the thing to do in normal circumstances.'

'It was,' Max replies and he takes a few steps forward, focussing on the keys. 'Is that . . . ?' His eyes fall on a security fob, a familiar crest. 'You took his keys?'

Cicero looks to Eve and back to Max. 'Well . . .' He shrugs. 'They fell out of his pocket.'

'Did they hell,' Max replies, picking them up. 'Did you start that fight on purpose to get these?'

'I can't condone violence, Max, but sometimes things are necessary.'

'You did, didn't you? What exactly are you planning?'

Eve stands up and looks at her son. 'You mustn't tell anyone . . .'

'Trust me, Mum.'

For a moment she pauses, watching him. 'The camera,' she says. 'At the underpass. It was working that night, and the night her mother was killed. All the camera feeds are backed-up.'

Max turns the key fob over in his hands. 'You know, you don't have to go to the police station to get to the computer files. You didn't need to steal his keys.'

215

Martha

This window in the cell is so small I reckon I could cover it with my hand if I could reach up there. There's no glass and the wind howls through like some wolf or crazed beast trying to get free from something. There's no light switch in here. No light bulb, just like the others, but it's so much darker. I checked for one when the sun started to set and then I just watched as everything got blurrier and the edges of everything melted into each other.

Is that what dying will be like? Will everything fade away? Will my eyes get heavy and it'll be like falling asleep? Will it hurt? It's electricity, it's going to hurt. How long will it take before I pass out? Will I pass out and *then* die or will the passing out bit be the dying bit too?

God, it's cold in here. That wind's biting.

I wish I could die by chocolate cake instead. Eat it and fall asleep. Drift off. Not poisoned because that would be painful. Drugged, maybe.

I can't remember the last time I had chocolate cake. Probably at Mrs B's. She bakes a good cake.

Mrs B believes in God. She prayed to Him after Ollie was arrested, asking for his release, but it didn't do any good. She said so. She said God had lost the round but not the fight, but she knew that he'd look after Ollie well until she saw him again.

It gave her a lot of comfort thinking she'd see him again.

I reminded her about my mum and said God was losing a lot of rounds but she had no answer for that.

I always thought that when someone close to me died, that I'd somehow *know* they were all right. That sounds stupid, because they're not, they're dead, but I thought I'd get some kind of sense that they were at peace or something, but I never did with Mum.

She was gone. Full stop.

In two days I'll be gone. Full stop.

It'd be easier if I believed.

All my thoughts and memories of you will be gone, Isaac. You'll have to carry the time we met, our evenings in the park, our walks in the woods, when you met Mrs B, the first time we held hands, the first time we kissed, made love – you'll have to carry them all, but when you die it'll be like it never happened.

We never were.

Nothing to show, no mark, no record.

My God. Who'll remember Mum when I'm gone?

Jesus. God. Shit, Mum, I'm sorry.

I remember your hand squeezing mine at the school gate, your arms around me at bedtime, your voice shouting me for tea, but I can't see your face any more.

With my eyes closed I see it in photos, in a park, at a wedding, raising a glass, frozen at that moment, but you're not in front of me now.

I hear you crying, arguing down the phone with people you can't pay.

You had a hard life. Always trying to do the best for me.

I think back. I push away thoughts of your sadness and remember. I hear your laugh.

It's Christmas. We're at Mrs B's, around the table with her and Ollie. We saved money by not buying crackers so me and Ollie made them instead. We didn't have the bang, but it didn't matter. We wrote ridiculous jokes that weren't even funny and used them instead.

You're reading one out . . . I remember it . . .

Why do cows wear bells?

Because their horns don't work.

It's not funny, but you crease in laughter, and as we watch you, so do the rest of us. We can't stop. My sides hurt. I see your hand over your face wiping your tears but still don't see your whole face. But it doesn't matter. I listen to your laughter. I hear your happiness. You are my mum and I'm proud. I'm glad to be your daughter.

Hold that for me, Mrs B. You were there, you'll remember too. Hold that memory for me after I'm gone. Keep it safe. Keep her with you.

Hours pass.

I'm cold. Freezing.

The cell's become darker and the window's now the lightest thing in here. I wonder what the moon looks like tonight. It must be big because there's so much light out there I can see the clouds zooming over the sky.

The wind's blowing in stronger.

My fingers are stiff, my toes numb.

My brain keeps wanting to work out how many hours I've got left, but I won't let it.

I feel cold to my bones.

Maybe I'll freeze to death tonight instead. They'll come in in the morning and I'll be like an ice cube and they'll have to crack my arms and legs to straighten me up. Lift me and drop me back to the ground and I'll shatter into a million pieces. Probably they'd still carry on with this whole charade and put all the frozen, broken pieces of me in the electric chair.

Can't spend the night like this, I think.

I'm shaking.

There's some kind of rhythmic clicking or tapping noise and I look around trying to work out what it is, thinking I'll be able to see in this dark and there'll be some mouse scurrying across me or a spider with clicking pincers.

It's your teeth, I tell myself.

I need to get warm, or at least not get any colder. I try to think of what to do but I can't think.

Hypothermia. Affects your brain function.

I wish I had more than this mangy sheet.

Knock on the door, ask for a blanket, a duvet.

Yeah, right. Can't move. Tired.

My nose is running now. Thought it'd freeze not run. Snot icicles off the end of my nose.

Maybe they've given up on the psychological torture and are going for the physical now.

I'm trembling and jostling and shaking like I'm four years old and need a wee. I can't keep still. I stick my hands under the pillow. Change my mind. Hug it to my chest.

219

Keep your core warm.

Can't feel my feet.

I wish you were with me, Isaac, I think. *Keep me warm. Hold me. Hug me.*

'I am,' he says in my head. 'I'm here next to you. Forget the cold. Look up to the stars with me. We can still share the sky.'

It had to end though, didn't it?

'If my father hadn't . . .'

We were naive.

'No, we were in love.'

Were?

'Are.'

CELL 6

Martha

A crackling sound wakes me from a beautiful dream where you were with me.

The warmth of your arms was around me, your breath on my skin, your heartbeat, your chest moving up and down as you slept. It must've kept my heart pumping blood around my freezing body.

It reminded me of the time in Bracken Woods, lying on a blanket with the orange of the sunset on your face, swearing at myself for falling in love with you. Happier than I'd ever been, but waiting for the crash that would be so loud it would wreck our lives.

The crackling gets louder, thoughts of you retreat and I sit up.

This new cell is tiny. There's just enough space for the mattress, a toilet bowl attached to the wall, and a hand basin next to it. There's no window, only the sliver of a hole, no glass across it and too small to need, or fit, bars.

I inch myself into a square of sunlight coming through it.

The crackling sounds like it's coming from a speaker but I can't see one anywhere.

It stops.

The silence is strange now.

I wait.

'*Death,*' a voice says. '*A permanent end to all functions of life in an organism. Termination. Destruction. Murder or killing.*'

I can't see where it's coming from.

'*Kill: to put to death. Deprive of life. To cause extreme pain or discomfort to. To make something die.*'

It sounds like my old English teacher. Droning and monotone.

'*Die.*'

I think it's getting louder.

'*To cease living. Become dead. Expire.*'

Oh my God.

'*To cease function. Stop. To pass gradually. Fade. Subside. Result of murder.*'

I lie back down and pull the pillow over my head.

'*Murder: the killing of another person without justification or excuse. To put an end to. Destroy. To kill brutally or inhumanely. Particularly with pain.*'

How long is this going to go on for?

'*Pain: an unpleasant feeling . . .*'

You don't say . . .

The Stanton house

'It was just a promise,' Cicero says as he ejects the memory card, turns off the computer and looks to Isaac.

'Doesn't a promise mean anything to you?' Isaac asks.

'Not if someone innocent is going to die if I keep it!' He tosses the card onto the table. 'How could you do that?'

'Because I respect her! Because I'm not some adult who thinks they know best when they don't! She knows what she's doing. We both do.'

'They're going to kill her!' Cicero shouts.

'Do you think I want them to?' Isaac says. 'Don't you think I'd prefer her to tell the truth and fight this?'

'Frankly? No!'

'She has a right to decide! I have to respect that! So do you!' He grabs the memory card from the table and storms towards the door.

'You can't take that!' Cicero shouts after him.

Isaac stops and spins round, staring at the exasperated Cicero.

'Stop thinking you know what's best,' he says, his voice measured and controlled. 'Because you don't always. Neither do I. Or Martha, or Eve or even Max or that scruffy-looking guy, *Gus*, from the High Rises. But together we might, and we have to trust each other to do what's right.

'I can do this. With some help from Max and with some support from you guys and some *belief* that I will do the right thing, then I can do this. Trust me.'

As he walks away and the door silently closes, Cicero paces around the room.

'Jesus Christ,' he says, rubbing his hand through his hair. 'Jesus bloody Christ.' He grabs his suit jacket from the back of the chair and storms out after Isaac.

The house falls into quietness and while Eve slumps down at the table and rests her head in her hands, Max pads into the room. With a glance to his mother, he moves through to the kitchen, pours water into the kettle on turns it on.

Eve doesn't move.

He puts a spoonful of coffee into a mug and takes the milk from the fridge, yet still Eve doesn't move or say a word. After the kettle has boiled he fills the mug, adds the milk, stirs it and places it in front of his mother.

She looks up. 'Thank you,' she breathes.

He sits opposite her, takes a biscuit from the barrel and places it next to the mug.

'What do you think, Max?' she asks.

Max closes his eyes, letting the silence wrap around him.

'Isaac and Martha? I think they love each other,' he says at last.

Martha

Martha sits on a white swivel chair in a small white room. There is nothing else except a computer screen in front of her.

'Hello, Martha,' says a slow, metallic voice from behind the screen.

Martha doesn't reply.

'How are you today?' Each syllable is staccato, the odd word lilting in pitch as it fakes a human tone.

Martha spins the chair left and right, left and right.

'We'd like to talk to you.'

She spins it further, stopping it with her back to the screen.

'You are the lucky first user of our new computerised counselling service – the virtual counsellor.'

Martha scratches her head.

'The viewers at home would like you to turn around. They would like to see your face.'

She doesn't move.

'In order to take full benefit from the virtual counsellor it is imperative that you turn around.'

A whirring begins and the chair moves by itself. Martha fights it, pushing against the ground with her bare feet but still it turns, stopping and locking in place, as she is again facing the screen.

Martha shuffles in the chair, folding her legs up and turning around so the screen focuses only on her back.

'It is imperative that you turn around.'

'Fuck you,' she says.

The lights shut down and the room falls into black. Somewhere a door creaks open.

'Hey!' Martha shouts. Muffled sounds of feet fill the darkness, a jangle of keys, a shuffle of bodies, a couple of thuds and a dull shout.

Silence.

The lights come up again.

Martha is strapped to the chair facing the screen. Her face is red.

'Thank you for your cooperation,' the voice says. 'We would like to know how you are feeling today.'

Martha doesn't reply.

'You have thirty-four hours and fifteen minutes until your possible execution. Correction: thirty-four hours and fourteen minutes. How are you feeling?'

'I want to speak to Eve. She's my designated counsellor,' Martha says.

'The post of designated counsellor no longer exists. Mrs Eve Stanton is no longer your counsellor. We, the VC – virtual counsellor – now provide for all your needs. You may speak to us instead.'

'I don't want to speak to you.'

'With our unlimited database of virtual experiences we can help you deal with your emotions and thus share your problems, feelings and secrets. Would you like to share a secret with us now?'

'Nope,' Martha replies.

'We are sorry to hear that. We sense stress in your voice.'

'*Stress?* Are you surprised? You know what it's like.' She stops abruptly.

'Would you like to share your feelings?'

'No,' she replies again.

'We would like you to share your feelings. Or perhaps you have a problem you would like to discuss.'

'Actually, yes, yes, I do have a problem. Can you fix it for me?'

'We can listen and empathise. We can suggest ways in which you can deal with your problem.'

'OK. My problem is that you're all assholes.'

'We are sorry to hear that. Although we sense your problem derives from a subjective point of view –'

'Subjective point of view and bloody *torture*.'

'. . . and would suggest you look at the problem objectively. This may ease your pain.'

'I hadn't finished.'

'Please continue.'

'I have lots of problems. Shall we discuss them all?'

'Our service is to assist you at your time of need. If discussing all of your problems would be of assistance to you then we shall discuss all of them.'

'Thank you. My first problem, discounting all the . . . *shit* . . . that's going on in the cells, is that I don't have any biscuits and it's making me sad. I miss biscuits.'

'We are sorry to hear you feel sad and are missing biscuits. The death row service on which you are incarcerated provides three meals a day, none of which include biscuits. Searching the database shows us there are no foreseeable plans to include biscuits on the menu, and examining the statistics regarding your impending death it seems unlikely you will be released. We would therefore recommend that in the future you avoid committing crimes which result in your subsequent incarceration. We hope this solves your problem.'

She nods. 'Right. Well, my second problem is that I'd like to see a tree again before I die. It's nice to see something green.'

'We are sorry that the current service does not include the use of trees, yet as it is something green you wish to see, we are pleased to inform you that peas are on tonight's menu.'

'Fantastic,' Martha replies. 'Thank you.'

'Do you have a third problem?'

'I do. Tell me, computer, is this being shown on TV?'

'It is.'

'Is it live? How many people are watching?'

'It is live. Examining the current statistics we estimate that the viewing populace is currently at around . . . twenty-one million.'

'Wow, that's a lot.'

'It is estimated that your execution will attract a figure far in excess of that. Our goal is to exceed 24.15 million, the number of viewers who tuned in to hear news of Kennedy's assassination.'

'I could beat Kennedy.'

'Your current viewing statistic puts you in the all-time top twenty.'

'I bet you'd like that to be even higher, wouldn't you?'

Behind the screen, the mechanism of the computer seems to click and whirr.

'We are here to discuss your needs. We are your virtual counsellor and our aim is to support you.'

'Yeah, yeah, but even more people . . . I could help you with that.'

The computer doesn't reply.

'I do have a secret . . .'

Still the computer is quiet.

'Something I could share with your viewers, that they'd be so shocked at they'd struggle to believe . . . but that I could prove.'

'After examining your personal history, your childhood, your family and friends as well as your school records and lifestyle choices, it seems highly unlikely that you would indeed have a secret that would shock the viewers or that they would struggle to believe, hence our reply is that unfortunately we don't believe you.'

'But you're curious.'

'We don't believe you.'

Martha manages to shrug slightly and her eyebrows lift with a silent question.

'Although we don't believe your secret will shock, you are free to share it with us now if you wish. Unburdening may help you rest.'

'I'll be dead soon, why do I need to rest right now? No, if you want to know, you can do something for me.'

The room is silent. At the side of the screen a red light blinks.

'Tell us your secret.'

'No. You have to do something for me first.'

'Tell us what it concerns and we may negotiate.'

Martha closes her eyes as she thinks, stretching her hands against the clasps they're held in.

'OK. You agree to let me see Eve again, straight away, now, I want to see her now, and I'll tell you who it's about.'

'We don't believe we can trust you.'

'Snap,' Martha replies.

'We believe finding Mrs Stanton may be difficult.'

'I don't think so. I should think she's already here.'

Again there's silence.

'We agree to you seeing Mrs Eve Stanton one more time.'

Martha stifles a smile. 'Good. My secret concerns Paige, and my *relationship* with him, shall we say?'

The clasps around her wrists loosen.

'You will tell us your secret after you have spoken with Mrs Eve Stanton.'

The door opens and a guard enters.

Martha shakes her head. 'No. I'll tell you my secret, everything I know, at my final words tomorrow. Just before I die.'

Isaac

'What are you doing?' Isaac hisses.

On the massive television screen hung on the wall in front of him, he watches Martha be led away by the guard. The white counselling room is replaced with the blue of the studio, Kristina's red lips hanging open in mock horror and her thickly mascared eyes glancing skyward. Next to her, the eye logo with the words slowly turning.

'Turn that rubbish off.' Isaac's mother wanders into the room, pink velour trousers and a white sweatshirt. Her face is glowing as she dabs at it with a towel, her hair slightly damp. 'As if it wasn't enough to have lost my husband, I have to contend with that girl's face everywhere I go.'

'He was my father too.'

'Kind of. But you don't seem exactly cut up about it now, do you?'

'Come on, Patty. You know what he was like. You know what he was doing at the High Rises.'

'If you're going to call him your father, you can call me your mother.'

'I remember my mother; she was a better woman than you could ever be.'

'If you could remember her, you'd remember she was a whore!'

233

'She slept with men for money so she could eat and so she could feed me – it was the only way we could survive. What's your excuse?'

Her slap stings his face and he gasps in shock.

'Whatever he was doing,' she hisses, 'it doesn't mean he deserved to die.'

'An eye for an eye?' he says staring up to Patty in indignation, a red print of her hand across his cheek.

'Yeah, an eye for an eye. She killed him, so she deserves to die herself.'

'One rule for them, one rule for us, is it? Anyway, did she really kill him?'

'Christ in heaven above, Isaac, are you as naive as you sound? You know who she is, she had every reason to want to hurt your father. Never thought she'd actually go through with it.'

'What are you talking about?'

'I've got to go.'

'No, Mother.' He grabs her round the wrist and she stops dead.

'Call me Mother now you want something.' She looks down to where he holds her. 'Isaac, sweetie, don't get hung up on this. I know it's upsetting. I mean, I'm shocked, but your father, he was stupid. Some might say he had it coming. I just thought it'd be the mother not the daughter . . .'

Holding her wrist up, he moves his face close to hers. 'He ran her mother down,' he whispers, 'but that's not what you're talking about, is it? What do you know?'

'Plenty of things, but none that are any of your business.'

'Things to do with Martha?' He lets go of her wrist. 'I think we should talk.'

'I don't,' she says, straightening her clothes and her hair. 'I've got to go.'

'Mother, this is important.'

'So is lunch with my friends.'

'More important than a talk with your son?'

'I don't have a son,' she says. 'And if you know what's good for you, you better work out what side you're on.'

Martha

'Thou shalt not kill,' a voice says. *'One of the ten commandments, also known as the Decalogue, which are . . .'*

The door to Martha's cell opens and Eve steps inside.

'. . . found twice in the Hebrew bible . . .'

'Remember the camera,' Martha whispers as she stands from the mattress on the floor, no bed frame, no chair.

'. . . first in Exodus . . .'

Eve nods. 'What's that voice?' she says.

'. . . then in Deuteronomy . . .'

'Some kind of moralistic running commentary for the day,' Martha says, her voice low and monotone. 'There were word definitions at full blast all morning.'

'. . . some state that God inscribed . . .'

Eve frowns at her.

'Like, the definitions of *kill* and *murder*,' Martha adds. *'Death,* stuff like that.'

'. . . his ten commandments onto stone tablets . . .'

'Seems it's moved to religious morals now,' she continues. 'You wouldn't believe the shit I've learnt.'

'. . . and given them to Moses . . .'

Martha slumps to the floor. Her face is haggard, bags under her eyes, her mouth lolls open as if it's effort to control it. She nods. 'You wouldn't . . . No, it doesn't matter.'

'. . . *on Mount Sinai . . .*'

'It'll move on to Islam next,' she mutters. 'Seems to be a cycle. Least it's quieter than the word definition things'

'. . . *the Qu'ran includes similar verses to these, which some scholars call . . .*'

'See?'

Eve nods and sits next to her. 'Look at me instead,' she says. 'Try to block it out for a while. Listen to my voice.'

Martha shuffles and turns to her. 'Yeah,' she says.

'. . . *instructions, as . . .*'

'This cell's tiny,' Eve breathes. 'I've never been in one before.'

Martha shrugs. 'Don't need much,' she says.

'It looks smaller than on the TV,' Eve continues, 'and the ceiling seems lower.'

'It feels like a coffin,' Martha says. 'But it's warmer than the last one so . . .'

They sit on the mattress, their backs to the camera. Eve rests her bag next to her feet and unzips it.

'. . . *found twice in the Qur'an . . .*'

'It was the closest thing I could get to a tree,' she whispers, and she takes out a small twig, barely the length of her hand, with leaves still attached that are golden yellow and ready to fall. 'But it's not very green.'

Martha smiles. 'I said that for you,' she says. 'It did make a difference.'

'Thank you,' Eve replies. 'I should think they'll take this off you, but . . .' She shrugs.

The voice continues but Martha rubs her fingers across the

rough of the bark and the dry of the dying leaves, trying to distract herself.

'I went to Gus's house,' Eve whispers.

Martha glances to her. 'You got the . . . ?'

Carefully Eve puts a finger to her lips and barely noticeably, she nods. 'I read everything,' she breathes.

'Even . . . ?'

'Your mum's letter? Yes.'

Eve takes a packet of biscuits from her bag, peels it open and places it in front of Martha, hidden from view of the camera.

'Were you shocked?'

'No,' Eve whispers. 'It all makes sense now. Were *you* shocked when you read it?'

Martha takes a bite and chews, taking her time as she swallows and glances sideways to Eve. 'I feel sorry for my mum.'

Eve nods. 'I understand that,' she says. 'Who else knows?'

'Can't be many or he wouldn't have tried to keep it quiet.'

'You think it'll change things?'

'Not by itself, no, but it's more ammunition to make them listen. Well, listen to Isaac, anyway.'

'You know the CCTV at the underpass was working the night your mother was run over?' Eve asks.

Martha turns to her. 'No, I didn't.'

'You could prove he killed your mum.'

'By itself that's not enough to do anything either, though, is it?'

'Why?'

'All it does is show I had the perfect motivation!'

'Anger and revenge?'

Martha nods.

238

'Why didn't you and Isaac think all this out properly beforehand?'

'Huh. Y'see, you're forgetting something fundamental.'

'What?'

'That until Jackson turned up that night we had no way to do anything. We had the papers Isaac had stolen, and Mum's letter, but there wasn't anything we could do with them. Anybody of any influence wasn't going to listen. No policeman would've touched it. No politician, no journalist. And even if they had listened, were interested or whatever, they couldn't have done anything. His influence was too wide.

'All I ever wanted was for truth and justice for Mum and Ollie, but together, me and Isaac, we realised we could do more, if only we could find a way.

'I suppose it's stupid – who are we to do anything? – it should be someone like you or Cicero. Not teenagers, but . . .' She shrugs, wipes the biscuit crumbs from her lap and looks back to Eve. 'Until Jackson fell to the ground with a hole in his head and the police cars came with their sirens and blue lights, and all that, we had no way to carry it out.

'Suddenly there's the body of one of the most famous men in the country at my feet, police on their way, likely media too and I know what to do. The plan, if you could call it a plan, was a couple words spoken between us in the few minutes it took for the police to arrive. Everything before that was just hope.'

'Then why do it?'

She leans in towards Eve and lowers her voice. 'Because there comes a time when you have to choose apathy or action. I could've stepped away and gone back to the shadows and carried on living hand to mouth, watching the injustices mount up around me, thinking 'what if I'd done this, or done that, there's another like Mum, another like Ollie' or I could've stood up tall and told the world I'd had enough, as had so many, *many* others, and take the consequences and pray those consequences could change the future.'

'But, Martha, by the time this comes out, whether at your final words, or if Isaac says something at the victim speech, people won't suddenly feel sorry for you and vote for your innocence, and even if they did, it'd be far too late.'

Martha huffs at her. 'This isn't about saving my life. If it was, I wouldn't have pleaded guilty. It's about something bigger. I will die tomorrow, but people will know the truth about Mum and Ollie, and about Jackson and all the stuff he was caught up in. And with it, I hope, will be a chance for a new justice to be born. A fairer one where people have their eyes open and aren't led by publicity and media.'

'You are certain that you want to die for such an *un*certain hope?'

'If I didn't think it could at least start things, then what would the point of this be?'

'In all my time here, Martha, not one person has pleaded guilty so freely and been so open to their own death. I don't know what to make of you. I feel like I've failed you.'

Martha stares at Eve for a moment. 'Really?' she whispers. 'Not *one* person has pleaded guilty so freely?'

Eve shakes her head and frowns.

Martha leans in. 'What about your husband?' she whispers in Eve's ear.

Eve's breathing stalls.

'We all know in the Rises,' Martha continues. 'He didn't kill that man, you did. It *was* self-defence, but I'm betting he took the blame so you could live, so you could be there for Max.'

'Martha, nobody . . . Max doesn't . . . I told Jim not to . . . I didn't . . .'

'Doesn't even Cicero know?'

She shakes her head again.

'I know that's why you understand me and I know you understand why I'm doing this.'

The door behind them opens again. Eve pushes the biscuits under the mattress and grabs her bag.

'Time to go, Mrs Stanton,' the guard says.

The two women stand up.

'I won't be able to see you again,' Eve whispers.

'What happens tomorrow?'

'Tomorrow?' Eve takes her hand. 'You'll spend the day in Cell 7. It's bigger than this. Have you seen it on the television? On the programme?'

'I saw it when Ollie was executed . . . but I don't remember.'

'I said it's time to go,' the guard says.

'The chair is in there too.'

'The chair? The chair that . . . where I'll . . .' Martha's voice cracks.

Eve nods.

Martha takes a tentative step towards her. For a second she pauses, then she closes her eyes and drops her head into her hands.

'I'm scared,' she whispers.

Gently Eve takes Martha's hands away from her face. 'I'll never forget you,' she says, her eyes filling.

Martha's breath judders in, her body trembling as panic threatens her and she gulps and gulps at the air to steady herself.

'Tomorrow,' Eve whispers, 'close your eyes and imagine the tree in the breeze. Be the bird that sits in it, then let yourself fly away.'

Martha leans towards her. 'Tell Isaac . . . tell him I'm sorry . . . tell him . . . I love him.'

The guard pulls Eve away and tears flood down her cheeks.

'I'll tell him,' she shouts as she's dragged away. 'I promise. I'll tell him.'

The door slams and inside Martha collapses onto the mattress. She turns away from the camera and pulls the blanket around her.

'Be with me, Isaac,' she breathes, and she closes her eyes. 'Hold me, stop me from feeling so alone.'

In her imagination he's behind her and his arms are around her. He's whispering in her ear that he loves her and they will always be together.

Death is Justice

Already on air for some hours. The lights are low. In shadow, Kristina sits in her usual seat at the end of the long desk, Joshua to her side. To the right the screen shows Martha lying on the mattress with her back to the camera.

The cell seems bigger, cleaner, brighter, whiter. The mattress looks thicker, the blankets softer and the untouched food on the tray more appetising.

KRISTINA: This is precisely why it was necessary to take away the post of designated counsellor. The problem, you see, with human interaction is feelings and emotions can sway judgements.

JOSHUA: It does seem that Counsellor Stanton has developed something of an attachment for our accused.

KRISTINA: Indeed, and it's simply not right. One needs to keep a professional distance. This woman has had sympathy with the girl since Cell 1.

JOSHUA: I wonder though, Kristina, viewers, audience, if this is a direct influence from her own tragic experiences.

KRISTINA: Hardly tragic!

Joshua glances briefly at Kristina.

JOSHUA (laughing): Well . . . I imagine your husband being executed is pretty high up on the stress-o-meter, Kristina!

He turns to the audience and they laugh with him.

JOSHUA: It was an infamous case. Jim Stanton, her husband, was executed for killing a man he claimed was attacking him. He said he acted in self-defence and the killing was accidental. It was a change in public opinion we've not seen the like of before or since: 92% voting not guilty until the evening of Cell 6, when a police document leaked to the newspapers showed that the man died from a blow to the *back* of the head – so not self-defence but a cowardly attack.

KRISTINA: You certainly remember your facts, Josh!

JOSHUA (smiling): Well, come now, Kristina, it's all in my new book, don't you know?

He holds up a hardback book with the title – *What They Deserve?* – emblazoned across it, and opens the cover to his photograph on the inside.

JOSHUA: With a lovely photo of myself.

He winks and a murmur breezes over the audience.

JOSHUA: But on a serious note, it examines what we as
a public think a criminal should suffer for their
crimes.

KRISTINA: Death, it seems.

JOSHUA: In many cases, it does, but not in all. It's interesting
to see that the old adage of 'an eye for an eye' still
resonates deeply with many moralistic people. The
saying that inspired the law, this company and our
logo. A saying that is found in the Bible, but often
misinterpreted as literally meaning –

KRISTINA: Thank you, Joshua, but if I can just stop you there
before we launch too deeply into opinion.

The camera zooms in on her.

KRISTINA: As always for our Cell 6 prisoners we're taking
calls from you, the voting public, hearing your
opinions on this case. But before we do, let's
take another look at what makes this case so
important and fascinating for so many, graciously
worded by our wonderful PM.

She smiles to the camera, which turns towards the screen on the right, filled by an image of Lady Justice on top of the Old Bailey, looking over the City with her arms outstretched, her double-edged sword high in one, her scales balancing in the other.

A caption slides in from the right: 'Culpae poenae par esto'.

Underneath the translation appears: 'let the punishment fit the crime'.

Another appears – 'Bonis nocet quisquis malis perpercit' – with its translation: 'whoever spares the bad injures the good'.

PM VOICEOVER: Our laws and morals have been our compass for many years and have guided us through wars, uprisings, civil unrest, recessions and religious turmoil, ensuring that even when we are put to the test, we do what is right for the people of our nation.

The screen changes, focusing down a long, gloomy corridor with closed metal doors along it and a dim light above. Bars slam across in front of the camera; a deep clanging resonates.

PM VOICEOVER: Those who fall foul of this moral standing will feel the full weight of the law.

The camera pulls back along the corridor, light seeping through until the screen is nothing but bright white.

PM VOICEOVER: Six days ago a crime was committed that
has shocked our nation to the core.

Photographs of Jackson flick over the screen: a skinny boy
of six or seven, sitting in the gutter near the High Rises, dirt
on his face, a piece of bread clasped in his hands. Another of
him as a young teenager, skinny jeans and a sneer; a cigarette
between his fingers as a police officer stands in front of him.
Another and he's around eighteen, his arm hanging around
a slim woman with long hair, both with a bottle of wine in
their hands.

PM VOICEOVER: Jackson Paige could have stayed like this,
but he chose not to. He grew up in the
most terrible circumstances imaginable,
but worked to take himself out of squalor
and live the life he truly deserved.

The picture changes again. A shot of him as a twenty-something
man, a battered suitcase in his hand and a nervous grin as he
waves to a camera.

PM VOICEOVER: First coming to the public's attention as he
entered into television's ground-breaking
reality TV show – *Them Versus Us* – pitching
some of the country's richest against the
poorest, his charm put him in our hearts
and he not only walked away with well
over a million pounds in prize money . . .

On the screen an ebullient Jackson stands with flowers around his neck, a spewing Champagne bottle and a smiling young woman.

PM VOICEOVER: . . . but also his soon to be wife, young socialite Patty West.

A wedding photograph on the front cover of *Celebrity Goss!* magazine appears.

PM VOICEOVER: Together they dominated the pages of celebrity magazines, parties of the rich and famous, were frequent chat show guests, made countless public appearances, and he became a major figure for many leading charities as she supported his growing career and importance. They typified the perfect couple.

A series of images follow, each with Patty and Jackson looking glamorous and generous as they hand out oversized cheques, or sit at bedsides of the ill and suffering.

PM VOICEOVER: The epitome of their care for the community came when tragedy struck as Jackson was returning from supporting a food bank close to his old home in the High Rises. A struggling young mother threw herself from her balcony. The first on the scene, Jackson was heartbroken over the impending plight of the son left behind, and together he and Patty took him into their care and adopted him as their own. No expense was spared in the young orphan's upbringing and further charity work within the Rises was instigated.

A grainy black and white photo fills the screen: Jackson on his knees next to a young boy with tears down his cheeks.

PM VOICEOVER: He was a figure of hope for many, a charity worker, a public idol. He was a true prince, although born into pauper clothing, yet he was taken from us in a meaningless and shocking act of violence.

A still from the police head-cam fades in – Jackson's blood-stained body lying in a wet road, half hidden by the shadow of the underpass.

Music begins: the slow, emotive sound of violin strings.

Images of people wrapped in sadness appear on the screen, faces streaked with tears or paused in anguish. Young children leaving pictures they've drawn at the site where he fell. Teenage girls holding single roses, grown men patting each other on the back, women with hands clasped across mouths and boys with heads angled down and faces hidden in hoods.

PM VOICEOVER: All because of this girl.

A smiling school photograph of Martha glares bright on the screen. Her hair is curled, her shirt is ironed, her jumper is clean.

PM VOICEOVER: At 8.30 last Monday evening, Martha Elizabeth Honeydew took this weapon . . .

A police photograph of the gun is shown.

PM VOICEOVER: . . . and offloaded bullets into Jackson Paige until his body fell to the floor in front of her and his blood seeped into the ground.

A grainy video clip begins: the feed from the police head-cam again, streets zooming, blue lights flashing, headlights falling onto Martha holding the gun, running forward, police gun pointed towards her.

POLICE OFFICER: Drop your weapon! Drop your weapon!

Martha drops the gun and puts her hands on her head.

MARTHA: I did it. I shot him. I killed Jackson Paige.

Again the screen changes: a large room, one wall made of glass, a solid door and bare floor. The light is dim, illuminating pools of the room but leaving corners and edges in shadow. In the middle is a solid wooden chair, a high, straight back, with five leather straps – two at ankle height, two across the arm rests, and one on the back of the chair at chest height. At the top a metal crown is attached to an adjustable arm.

PM VOICEOVER: What is there to debate?

The music fades and the eye logo fills the screen as the camera pans back to Kristina and Joshua. The studio is silent, the mood sombre.

KRISTINA: Indeed. And we extend our thanks to the PM for taking time from his holiday to record those words for us. It most certainly means a great deal.

She pauses, takes a tissue from a pocket, dabs her eyes and looks back to camera.

KRISTINA (a half-smile): But on our show, and in our country, we pride ourselves on our democratic system and a voice for all. Join the debate on social media now, share your opinions, phone us and leave your messages. We'll be back after these words from our sponsor, Cyber Secure, to hear your thoughts, but first let's see those all-important voting numbers . . .

Martha

My head's back and forth today. Confused. Thoughts and ideas drift in, mix up, drift out, then back. I can't settle. Can't sit still. My brain can't rest.

Y'know, what's surprised me is the amount of time I used to spend thinking about the future. Not big stuff, but like what I'd have for tea tomorrow, what'd be on TV next week. If it'd snow this winter. Things like that.

I'll find out what I'll have for tea tomorrow but that's about it.

It's hard to think about the impending *nothing*. What it'll be like to not . . . *be* . . . any more.

No thoughts. No memory. No TV next week, or snow this winter, or bird song in spring or . . . or . . . daffodils or conkers or rainbows . . . or . . . lightning . . . or . . .

Shit, girl, just shut up.

Just. Shut. Up.

I close my eyes, trying to ignore my own worries, but then all I see in my head is a vision of this silly cow reaching out for a gun and I'm shouting at myself – 'Put it down! Don't do it!'

The bang was so loud, and the flash from the gun so bright, and all it took was a fraction of a second and the tiniest movement of one finger to end a life. What was it that scientist said? Newton, was it? *For every action there is an equal and opposite reaction?*

Doesn't seem quite right. Move your index finger and someone dies.

It'll be the same tomorrow, won't it? Dial a few digits on your phone and I'm a goner.

They have the power over my life, the responsibility to do the right thing.

We had the responsibility that night, yet it was the first time the power had been in our favour.

With hindsight, I see now, from here in my cell, that everything had been tumbling forward to some point in time I couldn't quite see and it all had to come to an end at some point, and the longer it went on, the more speed it was gathering and the more mess it was going to make when it was forced to stop.

My God, will this make one hell of a mess.

People will talk about it. They'll remember. I hope they will act.

It's a month before *that night*. We've had dinner with Mrs B, you bought the food, she cooked it. We hadn't seen meat in a long time and when the smells of cooking started through the corridor along our floor, we thought we'd start a riot.

You never rubbed it in our faces that you had money and we didn't; you were the most down-to-earth snob we'd ever met!

But you weren't a snob, were you? Because you were from the Rises really.

'The praise Jackson got for your rescue,' Mrs B said as you carved the chicken. 'Newspapers, they adored him for it.'

'I don't remember,' I said.

'You were six years old, just like him. What about you, Isaac? You remember?'

You shook your head. 'Not at all, Mrs B. Although I think if I had lived near you as a child, I wouldn't have wanted to leave.'

She smiles at you – you know how to charm.

'Story of your mother was tragic,' she said. 'Good lady, would do anything for you. Never understood why she did it.' She passed a plate up to you.

'Did you know her?' I asked Mrs B.

'Saw her about. Lived near friend of mine in Bluebell House. Friend told me after that she always had a smile, couldn't have thought she was so depressed.'

Isaac rested his knife on the plate.

'Oh the commotion . . . the *mess*. 'Course then they put bars across windows, stop others jumping.'

Your eyes closed. I rested a hand on your leg.

With a shake of her head Mrs B continues. 'Amazed how quick Jackson got to flat. Said it was to check you were OK, thought you could lean over and see her dead, maybe fall over too. Came out with you in his arms, tears down your dirty face. Press were there with that Patty woman already.'

'Did he see it happen?' I asked. 'What was he doing around here?'

'Said he remembered where he came from, his . . . what is word . . . *seeds*?'

'Roots,' I corrected.

'Yeah, that. Said he came back to give food and things, go see young families, keep people going. Me? Don't think it was simple like that.' She shrugs, her mouth turning down. 'Who am I to say, maybe he was walking near when it happened.'

I watched her fingers tapping against her lips and waited for her to carry on, but she didn't. Jackson Paige coming up in conversation usually meant the air would be blue with every expletive she knew and she never cared who overheard her and if they agreed or not.

What was different?

Because Isaac was there and she didn't want to bad-mouth his father?

I was touched she thought that much of him.

'But how did he know which flat it was?' I asked.

She looked at me with her eyebrows raised as if telling me I was out of order. 'Lots of questions, Miss Martha, you should be police! I don't know answers.'

I let it go. Whatever I thought, or she thought, or even Isaac thought I suppose, fact was he still brought him up. Still adopted him and he didn't have to. Could've left him to go in an orphanage or institution. Why? The good in that didn't balance with everything else I knew of the stinking shit of a man.

But your head was ticking.

'What about Patty?' you asked, cutting into a Yorkshire pudding. 'Your stepmother?'

You nodded. You put the slice into your mouth and didn't take your eyes from Mrs B as you chewed.

She lifted the gravy boat and shrugged. 'Only saw her in real life that day. She was pretty. *Beautiful.*'

'Clever?' you asked.

'Couldn't say.'

'Manipulative?'

'Couldn't say,' she repeated. Then, as if she couldn't contain it any longer she put the gravy boat back on the table and sighed. 'What's that saying you have here . . . under great man . . . no . . . behind great women . . .'

'Behind every great man stands a woman?' you asked.

Mrs B nodded and smiled. 'That's it!'

You stared at each other and slowly her smile faded.

'That's it,' she repeated with a whisper and a nod, and something passed between the two of you that I was not party to and for the first time I questioned whether Patty was really the dumb blonde she played.

When we'd finished eating we went back to my flat. We sat on the floor of the tiny living room, the curtains closed and the lights off. The fire was one of those with glass lumps on to look like coal, a light underneath and a fan. I took the glass off, turned the light and the fan on and we lay down watching the orange and yellow shapes dancing on the ceiling.

In the background was the low chat of voices from flats nearby, a rumble of a car outside, a police siren, but all of it was a world away. We were alone and we knew our time was coming to an end.

I rolled over to my side and watched the lights on your face. The edges of your mouth tilted in a smile as you caught me and I traced them with a finger.

'That tickles,' you said, so I moved down your cheek and your jaw instead. Then your neck, over your Adam's apple. Then to the first button of your shirt.

Your breath quickened.

'Martha,' you whispered.

'Shhh,' I replied and I leant over and kissed you on the mouth. My fingers undid the second button, touched your chest.

Gently you pulled away, brushed the hair from my face and looked at me.

'Martha,' you whispered, 'I've never . . .'

You let the rest of the words hang in the air.

'Me neither,' I replied.

'Are you sure you want to?'

I nodded.

You'll remember what happened next. How could you forget?

You kissed me back. We kissed each other. We melted into each other, nervous and awkward, with hormones and desire and lust that I didn't know I had inside me.

Clothes came off and your skin was hot and soft, your chest fluffy, your arms strong, your fingers delicate but clumsy.

I wanted to touch everywhere but was scared to. I wanted you, loved you, couldn't imagine anyone more right for my first time than you.

My nakedness embarrassed me, but so did yours. We watched each other's eyes for reassurance, sniggered at our ineptitude, smiled for comfort, listened to our ragged breaths when things came together. As we moved, our hearts beat faster and our bodies clung to each other with sweat and nerves and carpet burns to our knees and elbows.

We shared the sky, we shared the stars, now we shared our first time.

I dragged the throw from the sofa and we lay naked under it.

'You seduced me,' you said with a smile.

I laughed at you. 'I don't think so!'

'I'm not complaining.'

In a neighbour's flat a clock struck twelve.

'Midnight,' I said. 'Your parents are going to be suspicious.'

You propped yourself up on an elbow. 'I wish I could stay.'

I was thinking the same but shook my head. 'Don't give him reasons to follow you here,' I said.

'You know what Mrs B was saying earlier . . . she was wrong, he wasn't there to give out food parcels,' you said.

'I know,' I replied.

'You know my mother, my *real* mother, not Patty, well, after my father died her and Jackson were . . .'

I rolled over, watching your eyes glisten in the light.

'He was in her flat before . . .'

'It doesn't matter any more,' I whispered.

'It does,' you replied. 'I know she didn't jump.'

I watched the colours reflecting on your skin and sensed your pain.

'She had her problems but she never broke a promise – not even on her blackest days. It was my birthday the next day, the *very next day*, and she'd promised to take me to the zoo, she had the tickets, had even made a picnic to take. She was in good spirits. It made no sense.'

'Are you saying he pushed her? Why would he have done that?' I whispered.

'I don't know,' you replied. 'Maybe she threatened his cosy life. Maybe he was on some power trip to prove something; maybe he just enjoyed it.'

I watched the memories and the years of trying to make sense of it tear through you, all the while with a question in my head that I knew I shouldn't ask.

'Isaac,' I whispered, resting a hand on yours. 'Why did he adopt you?'

Slowly his face turned to mine.

'It made him look good, didn't it? Adopting me, a poor orphan boy from the Rises. Makes him look kind and sympathetic. People admire him for it, you know. They like him. Respect him. What a good guy, they think.' You shook your head. 'I don't think it was his idea. The more I think about it, the more I think someone else was pulling his strings all along. And the more I think about it, the more angry I am.'

'It's pointless being angry,' I whispered. 'It won't change anything.'

'Nothing will ever change,' you said. 'The longer this goes on the more I'm sure of it. It's all pointless; you know it as much as I do.'

But with those words something happened, a feeling washing over me like waves of a cold sea. Like I'd been slapped awake or missed a step going downstairs.

'Yes it will,' I said with total conviction. 'Something will happen and things will change. They have to.'

And something did, didn't it?

Something fucking did.

CELL 7

Martha

The door to Cell 7 opens and I step inside.

The chair stands in the middle of the floor, straps around it, waiting for me.

I stop, can't move.

There's a whirring sound and I look up to the top of the wall; a camera's pointing at me. I want to smile at it, wave, give it the finger or shout at it but I can't do a thing

The door slams behind me and I jump, give a scream of shock, that I wish I hadn't. Don't want to show weakness but my heart's pounding so much I'm sure everyone watching will see my whole body shaking with it.

I stand in the gloom not moving, staring at the chair and the straps.

On the wall, the clock ticks.

'The time,' a stunted electronic voice announces, 'is 8 a.m. You have: thirteen hours until your possible execution. The current stats are: 97% in favour, 3% against. We will update you in: one hour.'

Shit.

Isaac

In his room, Isaac turns off the television.

He takes a deep breath and looks down at the array of things over his desk: photographs, documents, a memory card . . . He picks up an envelope – 'Last Will and Testament' it says across it – and puts the other things inside.

He looks at his watch.

'Twelve hours and fifty eight minutes until your possible execution,' he says.

Eve

Eve stares into the mirror of her dressing table. Her hair is done, but her face is bare of make up.

'You know they'll bring up Dad,' Max says from the doorway.

Eve nods. 'I know,' she whispers, 'but I have to do this.'

'Do you want me to come with you?'

She turns to look at him.

'I don't mind,' he says.

She nods. 'That'd be good.'

Cicero

'You're not a judge any more,' Cicero tells himself as he smears his face in shaving foam. 'What you think doesn't matter. Nobody cares.'

He wipes the steam off the mirror so only his eyes show, and he stares into them. 'But I know innocence when I see it,' he whispers, 'and I know corruption.'

He draws the razor down his skin.

'Your time of influence has gone, old man,' he tells himself. 'All you can be now is a shoulder for others to stand on.'

His stubble crackles against the blade. 'Weak, useless shoulders,' he mutters.

Death is Justice

Flecks of white buzz and crackle on a dark blue screen. The eye logo blinks and the words 'An Eye For An Eye For' spin in a circle around the black pupil.

MALE VOICEOVER: An Eye For An Eye Productions brings you . . .

The words stop spinning. The sound of electricity fizzes again and the font of the words goes from smooth to jagged. The eye reddens and closes.

MALE VOICEOVER: . . . today's show *Death is Justice* with our host . . .

The blue fades and lights come up on Kristina seated at her usual place, perfect hair, perfect make up.

MALE VOICEOVER: . . . Kristina Albright!

KRISTINA: Good morning, viewers. What an exciting week we've had here on *Death is Justice*, and, boy, have we been serving up some justice for you!

267

The studio audience applaud.

KRISTINA: Three executions in three days are sure to make our streets safer. You can walk home from school or work, knowing that there are three fewer criminals out there. Together, with our police and your votes, we're making a difference and making our country a better place to live in.

The applause increases.

KRISTINA: And it seems tonight we'll be bringing you more of the same, but we do still have some hours to go. Let's have a quick look and see what our accused is doing right this very second.

She stands and moves over to the screen on the right.

KRISTINA: Viewers, this is our live feed from Cell 7. For those of you who aren't familiar with this, Cell 7 also doubles as the execution room. The accused spends the day in there, able to walk around, examine the death chair, have their last supper, until voting closes at 8.30 this evening.

She pauses and looks at the screen – Martha standing in front of the door, white prison overalls and bare feet on the concrete floor. Kristina smiles.

KRISTINA: She looks a trifle worried, doesn't she?

The audience laugh.

KRISTINA: We've been busy taking your calls about our killer, Martha, and reading your texts and emails, and here to go through them with us now is the one and only Joshua Decker.

Dressed in a tight-fitting grey suit and tie, Joshua strides onto the set, a hand raised to wave to the audience, who whoop and cheer.

KRISTINA: Delightful to see you again, Joshua, and we do seem to be seeing a lot of you lately.

JOSHUA: Thank you, Kristina. It's always a pleasure to be here.

He turns to the audience and smiles; a murmur travels around.

JOSHUA: And I'm hoping I'll be able to see a lot more of all of you in the future.

Kristina's smile creases, she turns away, focuses on the screen.

KRISTINA: Let's have a look now at some of those opinions coming in.

JOSHUA: Of course.

Joshua taps the interactive screen, dragging boxes of text across, tapping and enlarging some.

JOSHUA: As you can see, Kristina, emotions are really running high. It seems our viewers have little sympathy for 'Martha the Merciless' as the press are cruelly calling her.

KRISTINA (laughing): I hadn't heard that one!

Joshua points to the screen.

JOSHUA: Take a look at some of these – 'She should rot in hell,' says Tony. 'How can a teenager be so evil?' asks Chandra. 'Society should be ashamed of itself for letting immorality breed,' a really tough one there from Caswell. But this one especially caught my eye: 'What can society expect but wanton death and destruction when our morals have been in decline for so many years? It isn't surprising that a teen should commit such a crime when they are brought up within inadequate families. The blame should lie with the mother.' And that's from Geri. No surname there for Geri. But can we really put the blame at the feet of the mother who, by all accounts, suffered her own –

KRISTINA (interrupting): Well, viewers, it's *your* opinions we'd like to hear on this. What do *you* think? We've certainly heard that argument before. How much of the responsibility should the mother take?

JOSHUA: We have a call coming in about that right now. Hello, caller, what's your name?

CALLER 1 (STEVIE): My name's Stevie and I wanted to ask about the video camera.

Kristina and Joshua frown at each other.

JOSHUA: Sorry, Stevie, we were asking whether the lack of a family unit can affect the behaviour of a child.

STEVIE: Yeah, right, I get that, but right, I was caught sleeping rough at the underpass last night, right, and the police told me that they saw me on the video thing. The CCTV, yeah? So, if that's still working, how come they haven't got it from when Jackson was killed?

KRISTINA: Stevie . . .

STEVIE: Cos, I think maybe they have, but then why aren't they showing it? Ask yourself that, hey – why aren't they showing it? Well, I reckon it's cos . . .

The line goes dead.

JOSHUA: Stevie? Stevie . . . ?

KRISTINA (smiling): I'm sorry, viewers, seems we've lost
　　　　　Stevie. I wonder how he could afford the phone
　　　　　call anyway . . .

JOSHUA: Do we have another caller? Yes, we do. Hello,
　　　　　what's your name, and what do you wish to share
　　　　　with us today?

CALLER 2 (LUKA): Hello. My name's Luka, and I wanted
　　　　　to ask a question about Martha and
　　　　　your show the other day.

JOSHUA: Go ahead.

LUKA: Your guest said that you didn't need evidence because
　　　　　you had motivation, but then he failed to say what the
　　　　　motivation was. Could you tell me what motivation she's
　　　　　supposed to have, to have wanted to kill Jackson Paige?

Kristina glances sideways.

KRISTINA: Er . . . well, Luka, this was discussed in depth
　　　　　the other evening, and I would suggest you log
　　　　　on to our website and watch it in full, where I'm
　　　　　sure you will find your answers.

LUKA: I did log on. There are no answers. I told you, he didn't say what her motivation was, and I don't get why she did it. And why would she admit to it if she knew she was going to die?

JOSHUA (quietly): Maybe she felt she had nothing to live for . . .

LUKA: And what's this secret she says she has? What if that changes things? Then it'll be too late, won't it?

KRISTINA: Thank you for ringing. Do we have another caller?

She holds a finger to her ear. Sweat's gathering on her top lip.

KRISTINA: Yes, we do. Hello, caller, and welcome.

CALLER 3: Hello, Kristina. I do hope you're not going to cut me off too?

She laughs nervously.

CALLER 3: In the years since the introduction of the voting system over 2,500 people have been executed. Since their deaths, evidence has been found that more than fifty of those were innocent, yet not all cases were analysed.

KRISTINA: Meaning 2,450 were guilty.

273

CALLER 3: Potentially. Yet also that more than fifty killers haven't been prosecuted for their crimes. Also in those years, increasing living costs have priced phones and the internet out of reach for around 45% of the population . . .

KRISTINA: They could use public systems . . . libraries . . .

CALLER 3: Which still have to be paid for, again are far too expensive for many and are increasingly inaccessible. Looking at the voting records, which I have here in my hand, I can tell you that in the current case of Martha Elizabeth Honeydew, 98.3% of the votes come from areas with the same revenues as the City and the Avenues. In fact, 56.2% of the total vote, the *total* vote, comes from one phone number. *One* phone number. Would you like to know whose?

KRISTINA: I'm sorry, caller, what did you say your name is?

CALLER 3: I didn't. That phone number . . .

KRISTINA: And how did you get those telephone records?

CALLER 3: How I got them isn't important. Kristina, are you interrupting me to stop information reaching your audience and your loyal viewers? Surely you respect them enough to allow them access to the truth so their choice in vote can be an informed one?

KRISTINA: I –

CALLER 3: It's the phone number of William Crawford. Do you know who he is? He was Jackson Paige's lawyer and is still acting on his behalf. Tell me, Kristina, why do you think he would be doing that? Why does he want this girl dead?

KRISTINA: Audience, viewers, I have to ask you to discount this information. This is slander against one of our most prolific and successful lawyers in the country. There is no evidence –

CALLER 3: Sorry, Kristina, did you say evidence? You *want* evidence now do you? Not just motivation? Well . . .

The screen flickers and the statement of telephone records for the lawyer comes into view, the amount of calls to the 'guilty' line clearly visible.

The audience gasp.

KRISTINA: Caller? Where did you get this? This is illegal. This cannot be shown on television.

The phone line goes dead but the phone records stay on the screen. Joshua does nothing but watch over the audience, a hint of a smile flicking the corner of his lips.

KRISTINA: Viewers, I must apologise for the hacking of our system with inappropriate and potentially forged documentation. We'll be back with you after this short message from our sponsor, Cyber Secure.

She smiles a plastic smile.

Cicero

Cicero wipes a towel across his sweating face and exhales loudly.

'Did I do all right?' he asks.

'You did great,' Max says. He takes the phone from him and slips a cover from the mouthpiece. 'They'll never know it was you.'

'They better not. How did you get those records anyway? Does your mother know?'

'Oh, I did them on the computer . . .'

'But?'

'It's only what's happening anyway, isn't it? You know the votes are fixed.'

'Not *fixed* exactly, but . . .'

'The people with money rig the phone so it votes again and again for what they want the outcome to be – that's fixing, isn't it? Everyone knows that's what happens. We just got them thinking about it a bit more.' He unplugs his computer. 'I've got to go, Mum's waiting for me at the TV studio.'

'She's going on *Death is Justice*?'

Max nods.

Martha

This cell's the worst. I thought it would be small, clean and white, bright lights . . . clinical. But it's dark and miserable. The air's cold. There's goosebumps on my arms, the concrete on my bare feet is freezing but there's nowhere to sit. Only that awful-looking chair with the straps.

It reminds me of an old-fashioned dentist chair.

'Sit here, little girl,' the dentist would say, a dirty apron tied around him, splattered with blood, his face covered with a mask. 'Let me put the straps around you, you'll be more comfortable that way.'

Oh, shut up, just shut up, Martha.

It's hard to think that in a few hours all this going on in my head will have stopped and I'll just cease to be.

Does anyone have a soul? Do I?

I remember watching this thing on TV, it said that in the moments after you die, you lose twenty-one grams in weight. Some people thought that was the weight of your soul. You lost it because it'd left your body.

Funny, that.

Does that mean a ghost weighs twenty-one grams?

I don't know. I don't know anything any more.

I move to the other side of the room and rest my palms on the glass screen that separates the cell from a viewing area.

When I take them off again I can see my smeared fingerprints and I look for other people's; maybe the guy who was executed yesterday, the one I chatted to, or the one before that.

The guard told me it's been the busiest week they've had in ages.

I can't see any though. I suppose they must clean the glass. I wonder if they wash the chair down too.

It's weird to think that I've been here before, but on the other side of the glass, watching Ollie. As I was the closest and only family to the victim – my mother – I was given the opportunity to make a speech.

I chose not to. I had stuff to say but it was private stuff, not for the media to turn into something to be quoted out of context and splattered over newspapers to make them money.

They asked if I wanted the glass down too – so I could 'see the execution better', they said. I told them that if it was up to me the execution wouldn't be going ahead anyway, and if it absolutely had to, it would be somewhere private where Ollie could die in peace, not with a million anonymous faces staring at him.

I don't know what other people chose. I've never watched it on TV. It felt disrespectful not to, but like I was spying if I did.

Mrs B was happy with my choices anyway. Well, as happy as you can be when they're killing your only son.

There are chairs in the viewing area on the other side of this glass. Rows of them going back – I can't tell how many, it's too dark, and I can't remember from before. Ten rows? Maybe more.

It's like a cinema and I'm the film.

Live action, hey?

Who'll come to watch me die?

Mrs B? No, I don't think she could stand it.

Friends from school who I've not seen since Mum died and I had to drop out? Maybe.

People from the Rises like Gus? The homeless guys who were there that night? No, I don't think so.

Eve?

The press?

Isaac?

Isaac, I know you will be.

I've left everything I own to Mrs B, but I've asked for my ashes to go to you. You'll know where I want to be sprinkled. I can see you now as I close my eyes and rest my head on the glass; you're walking down the path towards the woods. It's cold, winter, the wind is howling around you, blowing your hair around your head, your collar's up, your shoulders hunched, you're staring off to the tree line in the distance.

My twenty-one grams is walking with you but you can't see me. I want to hook my arm in yours, slip my hand into your pocket and feel your fingers grab onto mine.

I hope you sense me with you, but I fear you won't.

At the clearing in the middle of the trees, the place where we sat together around the fire we made, the place we first kissed, where we lay with sunrays on our skin, will be where you leave my ashes, and when you want to remember me and the times we had, it'll be the place you return to.

And when everything is shit, when fighting is so hard, it'll be the place you come to feel stronger again.

I will miss you.

You lit my life when everything was in blackness.

You woke me and gave me strength to be myself again.

You gave me reason to wake in the mornings, to eat in the days and to smile again.

And although tomorrow I won't be here, the reason I will die, is reason *to* die.

You will see to that.

'The time,' oh, that voice again, 'is 9 a.m. You have: twelve hours until your possible execution. The current stats are: 96.5% in favour, 3.5% against. We will update you in: one hour.'

This is the worst; let it happen now.

Are you waiting for me, Mum? Ollie, are you there too?

I slam my fists against the glass.

'Do it now!' I shout, banging my fists again and again. 'Kill me now!'

As I stop I hear the whirr of the camera but nothing else.

I slump down and rest my head on the floor.

Remember what we said, Isaac – I can be the martyr but you have to be the fighter. I close my eyes.

We'd been seeing each other for eight months when he found out. Lord knows how we'd managed to make it that far. 'Because he's always busy,' you told me. 'He doesn't care what I get up to.'

But you'd been suspicious for a while. Thought he was tracking your phone, so you'd started leaving it with a friend. Comments too, you told me, about how important it was to go out with the *right* people, or that you never brought any girlfriends home.

The night he found us, actually *saw* us, I was there at the station to meet you, waiting on the platform. It was a warm summer evening, the sun just dipping behind the tall buildings, a beautiful orange hue cast on concrete. The sun could make even the High Rises look attractive.

You smiled at me as you stepped off the train, took my hand and together we strolled away.

'You want to go to my place?' I asked.

You shook your head. 'Let's sit in the sunshine somewhere,' you said.

We grabbed some drinks and crisps from the corner shop and strolled through the streets towards the park.

People around us were in good spirits. Some I knew stopped to say hello and asked about you. You didn't tell them you were Jackson's son, but most recognised you.

'See your old man round here a lot,' one said.

You weren't surprised.

Some guy asked if you'd got any supplies from your dad. We walked away.

As we walked, you put your arm around me and drew me towards you, taking my face in your hands as you bent to kiss me. 'Thank God I'm not actually related to him,' you said. 'You don't have to worry about me turning into some psycho, unfaithful, womanising, drug dealer.' You smiled at that, but I knew it was no joke.

We could've only walked a few more steps before we heard the roar of the car. We both froze, do you remember that?

The car screeched to a halt in front of us, and Jackson launched himself out.

I don't remember all of the conversation, if you could call it that, all the ranting, the shouting and swearing, but I remember how much he scared me, and I remember that one thing he said.

'The women here are the ones you have sex with,' he said. 'The ones over there are the ones you marry. You can come here to get your kicks but you don't take these home and you don't get caught.'

At that you hit him.

When he'd got over the shock he hit you back. Knocked you to the floor.

As I bent over you, helping you to your feet, I looked back at Jackson. I remember shaking, but I wouldn't let him see.

'You killed my mother,' I hissed at him.

'Huh,' he replied. 'Who's your mother?'

'Beth Honeydew.'

People were starting to gather, standing near me and you, staring out at Jackson with sneers. He seemed off-balance, like my words shocked him.

'You know who I am?' I asked him.

He spat on the ground. 'A slag like your mother,' he said.

I remember the fear I felt as you launched yourself back up off the ground and towards Jackson. I tried to pull you back but you squirmed from my grip and were at him and I thought you were going to kill him. People around us shouted and jeered, others came from across the park and the underpass.

But before you even touched him, everything stopped.

Fear rolled over me. I stepped back with everyone else, and silence blanketed everything.

He'd put a gun to your head.

'Don't,' he said. 'Don't throw your life away on shit like her.'

Your face writhed with anger. 'You wouldn't shoot your own son.'

'No,' Jackson said, 'if I had a son, I wouldn't shoot him. But you're not my son, are you?'

The rage was bubbling from you, but you were helpless. He shoved you in the car and all I could do as he drove you away was watch.

It was Gus who came up to me, put an arm around me and walked me home.

'I've never seen a gun before,' I muttered to Gus.

'And you don't wanna see no more,' he said. 'Weak men use 'em.'

'What do you mean?' I asked, the low sun reaching out shadows of buildings like fingers stretching to get me.

He lifted a hand, all his fingers folded but for his index one. He curled it, mimicking shooting a gun. 'Takes more effort to think than to pull a trigger.'

I never told you that. Profound? True? What do you think?

Maybe, hey? But when your only other option is dying, you don't stop to think.

Huh, look at me saying that.

Thinking back, all the times we'd wandered through the Rises together, and all the times people told us Jackson had been around, it wasn't surprising, I suppose. We'd been found out. The gun to your head was the first warning, the trashing of my flat was the next.

We ignored them both.

Eve

Outside the studio a crowd has gathered. People wrapped in coats and scarves, waving placards and chanting slogans.

A Life For A Life.

We Demand Safe Streets.

Across the other side of the road, in relative safety from the crowds, stands Gus from the High Rises. He holds a soggy piece of cardboard, stained with food and dirt. Across it, in smeared black ink are the words – One Person, One Vote.

He holds it to his chest and moves from foot to foot to keep warm. His thin sweater and trousers blow and flap in the wind. He has no jacket, hat, gloves or scarf. He shivers.

A taxi pulls around the corner, slowing down as it approaches the crowd of people. A few of them turn to the car, peering through the glass to see who's inside.

'Counsellor!' one of them shouts, and a few more turn around.

'Eve Stanton!' another says, and as word goes through the crowd they swarm on the car, banging on the windows, the bonnet, the roof, their noise increasing, and in seconds it can't move forwards or backwards and it rocks violently back and forth as they push and pull on it.

Gus drops his cardboard and runs across, shoving his way through the people. Some force him back but he slams into them, grabbing and pushing until he reaches the door.

Yanking it open he grabs Eve and pulls her out, Max following close behind, just as the car lurches too far one way and goes over.

A roar lifts up from the crowd, so many thinking she's still inside. Gus wraps an arm around Eve and forces through them with Max right behind.

Demonstrators jump on the up-turned car, their chants louder and louder and their banners waving high.

Make Our Streets Safe!

Kill The Killers!

Death Is Justice!

'Quickly,' Gus says to Eve and Max. 'If they realise you've escaped, we're done for.'

Death is Justice

Seated at the desk, the studio lights glisten on Joshua's skin as he turns to camera. Next to him, Kristina, in a lemon pinstripe dress, is smiling at the scene of destruction showing on the screen.

JOSHUA: Kristina, it seems that banner is advertising our programme!

Kristina laughs at him.

KRISTINA: So it does. But of course, we *are* the place to be for all the latest news and gossip about our accused and their crimes. Speaking of which, haven't we got a scoop today?

The studio audience suck in a breath.

JOSHUA: I'm sure you eagle-eyed viewers out there saw our guest fighting her way to the studio just then. Yes, coming to talk to us today, and give us her opinion on the killing of Jackson Paige, is none other than designated counsellor . . .

KRISTINA (smiling): *Ex*-designated counsellor!

JOSHUA: Ex-designated counsellor, Eve Stanton. Eve's managed to cause a storm of controversy, but before we invite her in, let's give you those all-important numbers once more. Dial 0909 87 97 77 and to vote GUILTY add 7 to the end or to vote NOT GUILTY add a 0. You can also vote by texting DIE or LIVE to 7997. To vote online visit our website www.aneyeforaneyeproductions.com, click on the 'Martha Honeydew Teen Killer' tab at the top and log your vote. Calls are charged at premium rate, please seek bill payer's permission, texts cost £5 plus your network provider's standard fee, voting online is also £5 after an initial registration fee of £20. For full Ts and Cs visit our website.

A blue band with the numbers and details written in silver glides across the bottom of the screen. Joshua looks into the camera but he doesn't smile.

Isaac

'I don't know why you keep dialling, sweetie, it's a waste of money. Your father's lawyer's got it sorted – that girl's going to die.' Isaac's mother stretches a brush of pink down her thumb nail as she sits at the kitchen table, her long legs extended from her dressing gown, her blond hair falling over her shoulders.

Isaac looks up from his phone. 'You're all heart,' he says.

'Well, she'll get what she deserves.'

He sits down opposite her. 'Really? You think she deserves to die?'

'She killed Jackson!'

'Did she?'

'Said she did.'

'Do you never think that there should be more certainty before we take a decision to execute somebody? Proper evidence.'

'As my hairdresser said to me yesterday, it's our responsibility as voters to tune in and watch *Death is Justice*. You can get all the information you want by hearing what the experts say.'

'Mother, that programme is biased.'

'They are doing us an important service. Look how much safer the streets are since we did away with courts. And we, with the money we have available, have a *responsibility* to society to vote as much as we can.'

'What about the people who can't afford it?'

'Well that's exactly why we should vote more.'

'But what if they want to vote differently to us?' Isaac shouts.

'Why would they? She's guilty. She said she is.'

He stands up, his hands out in exasperation. 'Can you possibly be as dumb as you sound?'

She looks at him sideways and says nothing.

'Just because she says she did it, doesn't mean she actually did.'

'If that's right,' she says, 'then she deserves to die for being so goddamned stupid!'

He stares at her.

'You should just be glad that your father took you out of that place and gave you a good education and a future.'

'Yeah, let's talk about that, shall we? Why *did* he do that? Was it really *his* idea?'

She finishes painting her nails and replaces the brush into the bottle. 'You never asked that when Jackson was alive. Why now when he's dead? What does it matter why? He did it because he was a kind, caring man, that's why.'

'Who killed people and manipulated others, and sold drugs and had affairs . . .'

She stands in front of him, puts a finger over his lips and smiles.

'Well, aren't you growing up fast? You know what I learnt when I was younger? I learnt when to shut up and when to look the other way.' She moves her finger and points at him instead. 'Think what you could've ended up like if he hadn't taken you out of there, before you take that high moral tone. You'd be just like that useless, hot-headed orphan girl.'

'As Jackson killed both of our mothers, seems I am already like her.'

She smiles coldly. 'Adopting you *did* make him look good. Both of us, really.'

'The adoption was your idea?'

'Should've dealt with the girl a long time ago though. She was always a nagging loose end. Thanks to you, we finally are.'

'What do you mean by that?'

'It doesn't matter who pulled the trigger that night,' she whispers, and she raises her right hand, makes a gun shape with her fingers, and as she points it at him, she winks.

His face drops, his mouth opens to speak but the words are gone.

'And we still look good. Oh, the sympathy I've been given.'

'I . . . you . . .' he says.

'Speechless?' she says. 'That's not like you.'

'Martha . . . she . . .'

'It is *so* funny how much you care about the little people!'

She laughs and as he watches her face contort, he breathes deep and steadies himself.

'I wonder if you'll still be laughing,' he says, 'when Jackson's will is read.'

Her smile fades. 'What did you say?' she asks.

'Oh, didn't you know he changed it?' His voice judders but he carries on. 'Perhaps rather than assuming he was disappearing off to sleep with other women, you should've considered the possibility that he was visiting his lawyer instead.'

'He wouldn't dare!'

'Yet . . .' He lets the idea hang in the air for a moment. 'Seems he was a little fed up of your controlling ways,' he says, and with a smile he walks out of the room.

Martha

'The time: is 11 a.m. You have: ten hours until your possible execution. The current stats are: 95.5% in favour, 4.5% against. We will update you in: one hour.'

I don't remember hearing the one at ten o'clock. Was I asleep? Did they actually do it? Maybe they're taking extra hours off me for fun. The next one will be one o'clock, or two, even.

It said 95.5% in favour. It's going down, isn't it? Maybe it'll keep going down. People won't believe I'm guilty. I won't die.

But I wanted to die. I said it was the only way.

It is.

But I'm just a girl from the Rises.

You're a girl whose name people will remember for the change that began with you.

No, it won't work, and I'll be dead anyway.

That's because you're a killer and you deserve to die.

No, I'm not! No, I don't!

Shit, stop talking to yourself. You're going mad. Stop it.

Look, there he is through the glass. See him? He's sitting in the front row. He's waving to you. See how happy he looks?

He does look happy, he's smiling.

See what he's got in his hands?

No.

293

That envelope. It says 'Last Will and Testament'. It's his father's. He leaves everything to him. That's why he's happy.

Why? Because he's got his father's money?

Yes, he's going to watch you die and he's not going to do anything. You killed his father for him, you see? Now he's free to do what he likes with all that money.

That's not true!

Look he's leaving now, can't be bothered to wait for you to die. He's waving again. He's not doing anything but leaving. See?

No! No, Isaac, no! Shut up! Shut up! Stop arguing with me. You're not real. You're me. You're just me, worried and scared. Shut up, shut up!

I bang my hands again and again on the glass.

'Isaac!' I yell. 'Isaac!'

Death is Justice

Kristina shakes her head at the audience, the live feed of Martha on the screen to the right, Joshua next to her.

KRISTINA: We've not seen someone lose it quite so early in the day for a while now have we, Joshua?

JOSHUA: No, Kristina, you're right. And how strange it is that she's shouting the name of the deceased's son.

KRISTINA: Indeed. One for our viewers to ponder there, I believe. But right now, let's turn our attention to our studio guest today.

The live feed on the screen is replaced by a photograph of Eve walking into the prison building.

KRISTINA: In the time since she's held the position of designated counsellor, she has adamantly refused to appear on our show, yet as an exclusive for you, viewers, we have her here tonight!

JOSHUA: Please welcome . . . Eve Stanton!

The eye logo takes its place on the screen as Eve strolls out from backstage. Her head is angled upward as she walks forward, and she extends a hand toward Kristina and Joshua.

Joshua stands up and takes it with a smile. Kristina ignores her. The audience are silent.

JOSHUA: Eve, please take a seat.

At the high desk, Joshua moves to the side and Eve takes her place in the middle. Her stool is slightly lower than the others.

JOSHUA: What an honour it is to have you here with us today.

EVE: Thank you.

To the studio audience and viewers at home, Eve's voice is quiet, yet in reality, her microphone has been turned down.

JOSHUA: Could I ask you why, after so many years of avoiding the public eye, you've chosen now, with this landmark case, to talk to us?

Eve gives a brief smile.

EVE: Well, to be honest with you . . . a few reasons really. Firstly that I didn't want to accidentally pervert the course of justice.

KRISTINA: That's a somewhat outdated phrase! I haven't heard that since before the introduction of Votes For All. It's hardly relevant nowadays – the voting system eradicated the potential for that, surely?

EVE: Yes, in the conventional sense, I agree. My concern was more that I would inadvertently bring in any feelings or emotions I'd garnered from the accused, perhaps via stories they often share with me about their childhoods or loved ones, and that any sympathy I may accidently feel for the person the accused was *before* they became killers, may come with me and I may demonstrate that in something I said.

KRISTINA: You're saying you feel sympathy for these killers?

EVE: I'm saying, in a session with me, the accused will often share stories that remind me of the person they were before they killed someone.

JOSHUA: That they were once human?

EVE: That they were, yes, and still are. But my concern was that any question I answer may be coloured by that, which may then influence the voting of your viewers – and that is a lot of people.

KRISTINA: It sure is!

EVE: And influencing the voting of those thousands . . . hundreds of thousands . . .

KRISTINA: Millions. Our viewing figures regularly top the chart with figures such as 13.1 million. We estimate that tonight's execution will bring the highest TV viewing figure since the funeral of Princess Diana.

EVE: So imagine if I should inadvertently say something that would affect the votes of that many people.

JOSHUA: Sure. I see your point.

Eve looks to the studio audience with a smile.

EVE: I've always wanted to come on. It's truly my favourite programme. My son and I tune in all the time.

Kristina sits up taller.

KRISTINA: Even though your husband was executed on our show?

Eve's smile fades. She fiddles with her chewed fingernails.

EVE: I must admit sometimes it's been hard. There have been times where everybody on death row has looked like my husband, and I could see him sitting in that chair again. But I have to remind myself that Jim was not the person I thought he was when I married him.

JOSHUA: What do you mean, Eve? Can you share that with us?

Her eyes fill with tears.

EVE: I married an honest, hardworking, gentle and kind man.

JOSHUA: Yet he turned into a cold-blooded killer.

Joshua rests a hand on hers.

JOSHUA: I'm so sorry, but, Eve, we've all been there, haven't we viewers?

He looks to the audience then into the camera.

JOSHUA: Not to the same degree, but we've all been taken in by someone, gone on a date with someone, had a relationship with someone, who turned out to be a *liar*, or a *cheat*. Haven't we, ladies and gentlemen?

Applause ripples through the audience.

JOSHUA: Eve, we feel your pain.

He lifts a box of tissues from under the desk and passes her one. She dabs at her face, sniffs and looks up to the audience.

EVE: Thank you. It's been so many years now, and I feel like I should be over it, but it still comes back to me. It haunts me.

The audience applaud again.

JOSHUA: And I suppose that was another reason you felt it difficult to come on here?

She nods.

JOSHUA: We're all your friends here, Eve. We all support you.

He looks into camera, then to the studio audience.

JOSHUA: Don't we, viewers?

He smiles at them and they cheer and clap.

JOSHUA: But, Kristina, you're awfully quiet. Do you have something to add?

KRISTINA: Well . . . I'm curious.

JOSHUA: Do share.

KRISTINA: I'm curious, Eve, as to why you've chosen now to come on our show.

Eve takes a deep breath, dabs her eyes, brushes her hair from her face and sits up straighter.

EVE: I'm sure you're aware that the counselling system on death row has been updated . . .

JOSHUA: Oh yes, quite the scandal.

Eve flicks him a smile. Kristina glares.

EVE: It's a fabulous new system really, that allows viewers unprecedented access to the accused . . .

KRISTINA: I'm surprised you feel that way.

EVE: Progress should be welcomed, don't you think?

KRISTINA: Yes, but it makes you unemployed, and you were such a staunch advocate of the counselling system that is being replaced.

Eve takes a breath, looks to Joshua, the audience, into camera and back to Kristina. A glimpse of a smile.

EVE: There comes a time in your life, I believe, Kristina, where you have to accept that your time with something is done. For whatever reason – superior technology, new innovation, a more efficient system, a . . .

She glances to Joshua and back to Kristina.

EVE: . . . a younger co-host – you are surplus to requirement.

Kristina's face stiffens.

A few audience members snigger.

EVE: You can either accept that with grace and dignity or fight it and look a fool. I can't say I've enjoyed every minute of being a designated counsellor – it's been tough, but it's been hugely rewarding. However, I'm done now, and as I'm done, this is my last chance to come on this icon of a television programme.

JOSHUA: Well, it's delightful to have you, and we'd welcome you back any time, wouldn't we, viewers?

They applaud again.

JOSHUA: But tell me, the accused, do they talk of their crimes? Do they share all the juicy details?

The audience sucks in a breath. Eve bites her lip and glances around.

EVE: I shouldn't tell you really, should I? That would be betraying a confidence.

She glances around again. Kristina opens her mouth to speak, but Eve breaks in.

EVE: Yes, Joshua, they do. Often. Sometimes it gives me nightmares. Sometimes it makes me feel physically sick.

JOSHUA: Even those who say they're innocent?

EVE: Of course! Didn't you know – everyone on death row is innocent!

She laughs at her own joke and the whole studio joins in.

EVE: But on a serious note, it reminds me why they are where they are, and why we're doing what we're doing. It reminds me also of how, and why, the death penalty has evolved over the years: from firing squad, to hanging, to electrocution; from years, months and weeks spent in cells to a slim-line seven days; from battles in courts between lawyers, difficulties with juries and judges, claims over malpractice, inadequate evidence, *faked* or *tampered* evidence, to a sleek, efficient system. The system is a life force and it evolves as every life force does.

She pauses, looks over enrapt audience faces.

EVE: And now, even though for these crimes the court system has finally been done away with, the whole system will still keep evolving. Why? So our streets and our homes are safer places to live. So our children can walk home from school, our grandparents can go to the shop, our daughters can be out alone and our sons don't fear gangs.

The audience applaud wildly, a few stand up. Joshua nods his head and claps. Kristina does nothing.

Slowly the audience noise dies down.

KRISTINA: Eve, let me ask your opinion on this landmark case here. Martha Honeydew. She's the same age as your son, Max, I believe. How would you feel if it was your son facing execution tonight?

EVE: I wouldn't be happy. Not because he'd be facing execution, but because he'd committed a crime that warranted it. I'd feel I'd failed as a mother.

JOSHUA: Something we were talking about only the other day. This girl, this *child*, her upbringing has been –

EVE: She's not a child, she's a young woman.

KRISTINA: So you believe she should be executed?

Eve looks down, holding the tissue over her mouth.

KRISTINA: Sorry, Mrs Stanton, I didn't hear your reply.

Eve looks up to the audience.

EVE: I've been a designated counsellor for six years and in that time I've been counsellor for more than 250 accused who've gone on to be executed and fewer than twenty who've gone on to be released. Before I was designated counsellor I was prosecutor for the Crown. Over all those years I've seen, met, spoken to, dealt with, some truly horrible people, but I've watched them cry like babies at the prospect of death. I've seen them beg for mercy, look to God for forgiveness. I've also been unfortunate enough to meet some genuinely nice people in my time. And I say unfortunate because for whatever reason, these people have fallen foul of the law. Some have been guilty, circumstance pushing them somehow into terrible situations – defending their child, for example. Wouldn't we all do whatever it took to defend our child?

A murmur of agreement sounds around the audience.

EVE: Others, *few*, have been wrongly accused.

JOSHUA: Terrible.

KRISTINA: How can you *know* that?

Eve ignores her, still looking out to the audience, then to the camera.

305

EVE: With all the experience I've had prosecuting and as a counsellor, and the experience of being fooled by someone close to me, I can say with all certainty, that I am now a good judge of people. I can see it in them.

The audience hang on her every word.

EVE: I can see the madness of some who don't truly understand what they've done. I can see the anger in others that has driven them to it. I can see the hate, the downright nastiness, the ugliness of a personality that just wants to hurt, or the greed of someone killing for their own gain. But . . .

She raises a hand, sits up, looks over every single face and right down the lens of the camera.

EVE: I can see remorse in those who didn't mean to do it, I can see the guilt in those who thought it was their only choice and I can see the frustration in someone who is innocent.

JOSHUA: Tell us what you saw in Martha's eyes.

Kristina tuts and folds her arms across her chest.

EVE: I saw none of those things.

She lets the words hang. The audience, Joshua and Kristina are enrapt.

EVE: I saw desperation.

JOSHUA: Desperation?

EVE: I saw a young woman who'd been pushed to despair. Not anger or frustration, madness or ugliness or greed or any of those things. I saw someone in a corner. Who's fought through everything life's thrown at her until she could take no more and has stood up, in desperation, and said 'Fuck it'.

The audience gasp at her language. Joshua titters awkwardly.

JOSHUA: Eve, I have to remind you that we're before the watershed, please . . .

EVE: I apologise, I would hate to offend any of your viewers, but sometimes –

JOSHUA: I understand, please continue. Without the profanity.

EVE: I, and this will sound controversial . . .

JOSHUA: Go ahead.

The camera zooms in on Eve. Her eyes are closed, her head lowered. Anticipation drapes over the studio, the audience and the viewers at home.

Eve lifts her head and opens her eyes, the watery blueness of them reaching out to people's souls.

EVE: I believe she is innocent.

The audience gasp.

EVE: I believe she is covering for whoever did kill Jackson Paige. Something about it doesn't add up.

JOSHUA: Yet . . .

He stops, gasps, looks at the audience, then Kristina. He touches his ear.

JOSHUA: Control? Yes, can you search through yesterday's clips, please?

KRISTINA (hissing): What are you doing?

JOSHUA: Viewers, I'm not sure if you remember, but . . .

He focuses back on the voice in his ear.

JOSHUA: Yes, the section with Martha Honeydew in the new VC room, please, yes, search it for the word 'secret'.

The audience gasps, a murmur rolls over them. Joshua looks to the audience.

JOSHUA: Yes, I'm not sure if you will remember but, yesterday in the new virtual counselling room, Martha had something very interesting to say. And this could quite easily tie in with the claims of our esteemed guest here.

He puts a finger to his ear.

JOSHUA: Yes, we have it, thank you, control.

Yesterday's footage of the virtual counselling room appears on the screen – Martha shaking her head at the computer screen.

MARTHA: No. I'll tell you my secret, everything I know, before I die tomorrow.

It replays again. And one more time. The third pausing on her face looking into the camera. The studio falls silent.

JOSHUA: Suppose that secret is who the killer really is. Suppose she *is* innocent?

In a million homes across the country, in bars and restaurants and shop displays, viewers pause and stare at the face of Martha Honeydew.

JOSHUA: We can but wait.

Martha

'The time is: 4 p.m. You have: five hours until your possible execution. The current stats are: 76.4% in favour, 23.6% against. We will update you in: one hour.'

Shit, I must've fallen asleep.

God, it's dark outside. I've slept on my last day. Four o'clock, did that say? Hell.

Oh, my head's spinning. I feel sick.

Five hours left. That's 300 minutes. That's ... 18,000 seconds? Is that right? Less now. I'm glad there's no clock in here.

Jesus, it's cold on the floor. I should stand up. I'll get ill. Huh, what's that matter any more? I could do all those things you're not supposed to now. I could walk around outside without socks on, or a hat – that's where you lose most heat, of course, weren't we all told that as kids? I could stand in the rain – *you'll catch your death*, Mum used to say. Well, guess what, Mum? Yeah, I caught it, but not like that!

I could smoke, take drugs, cross the road without looking, ignore the train barriers, do whatever!

Hang on, what did it say? Seventy-six percent in favour? That's not what it was before. It was higher. It was ninety something when I came in here. What's going on? Why's it gone down?

Because you're innocent.

Shut up.

You didn't do it. You know who did.

Shut the fuck up.

I rub my eyes and the door behind me slams. I spin around.

'Thought you might like an early dinner, miss,' a guard says. 'Seeing as . . . well, y'know . . .'

I stand and walk over to him. I feel unsteady. Dizzy.

'Thank you,' I mutter. I've not seen this guard before. They don't normally come into the cells, but I suppose this is different. 'It smells wonderful,' I tell him.

'Chicken tikka masala, pilau rice, peshwari naan. Followed by sticky toffee pudding an' custard.'

'They're all my favourites,' I say.

He grins. 'Good that, in't it? Like yer mum used to treat you to when she were alive.'

I feel a smile coming over me. I look down to the food, steaming hot, and back to the guard, but he's not there. Mum is instead.

Sickness pours through me. 'Mum?' I say. 'God, Mum, I've missed you so much.' She smiles at me, my eyes fill with tears. I wipe them roughly with my hand and everything blurs. I blink, wipe them again and again, and as my vision clears I realise that nobody is standing there. There is no Mum, no food, no nothing.

My head clears. I stumble across the room and sit on the death chair.

As I pull my knees to my chest, I look out across the empty room.

'I'm scared,' I say. 'But that's OK.'

311

Eve

Eve stumbles backstage. Max takes hold of her and hugs her tight as she cries in his arms.

'I didn't mean it,' she whispers in his ear. 'About your father. I didn't mean a word.'

'I know, Mum,' he replies, gently rocking her. 'And so does he.'

She pulls away from him, tears pouring down her face, but he takes her hand and leads her away from the hubbub of people and into the shadows.

'You got the audience on your side. They were eating out of your hand.'

'I hated saying those terrible things, but I had to make them believe me,' she replies. 'What is the vote doing?'

'It's going down,' he says, nodding.

'I hope it's enough. And all the time we're doing this, she's still got something up her sleeve and she's still saying she's guilty. I don't understand it. She and Isaac, they're up to something.'

Isaac

A long white limousine pulls up at the manicured lawns of the Paige house. Isaac adjusts his tie, brushes down his suit and strides to the front of the house.

'They're here!' he shouts.

As he opens the door to a uniformed man and woman, his mother drifts down the elaborate staircase behind him.

'Please,' he says, 'come in.'

They nod, step into the house and go to shake his mother's hand. As Isaac turns and sees her he stops abruptly, staring at her. 'You can't go in *that*,' he says.

'Isaac,' she replies, 'please, we have guests.'

'It's inappropriate,' he splutters.

The guests look away. 'The skirt is too short,' he says, 'and it's *pink*, and the blouse thing is . . .' he gestures towards a frilly white top, see-through and low, 'is . . . Mother, you can see your bra!'

'So?' she says.

'We're going to an execution,' he hisses. 'You should show some respect.'

'To her? The girl who killed my husband? Took away my happiness?' Her voice becomes louder and higher as she speaks.

'Mrs Paige,' the man says. 'There are a few things we need to go through. We're the security officers who are going to accompany you both during your difficult time today. If we could sit down somewhere, and perhaps you and your son could discuss this later.'

'Yes, sir, I'll sit down with you because I don't need to discuss anything with my son.' She turns to Isaac. 'Honestly, you need to lighten up.'

'Mother . . .'

Patty's high heels click on the marble floor as she strides away, leading the guests into the living room. Isaac follows, shaking his head.

'Mrs Paige,' the woman says, 'we work for the company that runs *Death is Justice*, the programme which, as I'm sure you're aware, has exclusive rights regarding the cases on death row including, but not limited to, the running of the voting system, dealing with prisoners and all relevant interviews, and the management of both the accused leading up to execution day and the execution itself, and by natural inclusion of that, all aspects relating to the relatives of the deceased and management of the rights regarding the attendance of the execution.'

'OK,' Patty replies.

'We've come here to run through with you precisely what will happen and answer any of your questions. It is our utmost priority that the procedure this evening runs as smoothly as possible, and you and your son are not put under any undue stress or hardship. Having worked with many grieving families in the past we understand what a difficult time this can be for you.'

'Seeing that girl die will be one of the happiest moments of my life.'

The security officer takes a breath and shuffles in her seat. 'I do have a responsibility to you, Mrs Paige, to remind you that it isn't a certainty that she will be executed. You do need to bear that in mind. We have, in the past, seen some quite surprising changes in the last few hours, or even minutes.'

'She's dead. You mark my words.'

'Mother, the stats have changed a lot today.'

'They have?'

'They have, Mrs Paige.' The woman taps away at a hand-held device. 'The "guilty" votes have fallen by 23% in the last eight hours. The current stats are 74% for execution.

Patty's painted eyebrows lift. 'Well, that's a surprise.' She gives a nervous laugh. 'If you good people could excuse me just one moment.' As she stands up and strides from the room, she takes her phone out of her pocket, pressing in a number, and before she is out of the room, she's speaking into it.

'Yes, this is Patty Paige, I need to speak to my husband's lawyer, William Crawford, right now. No, it won't wait.'

Isaac watches the security officers. He knows what's going on, he knows what his mother is doing; he's sure they do too, yet they say nothing.

Their heads are low, as if their bodies are there but their minds aren't.

'William? Yes . . . Now, you listen to me, I pay your wage . . .' For a moment his mother's voice quietens and he has to strain to hear, and even then all he can make out is mumbles.

'YOU WILL!' Patty shouts those two words. The guests jump and look up, first to Isaac then to each other.

315

'I don't care what it takes!' his mother yells. 'Or what you have to do. My husband and I have been loyal to you, we set you up in business, and you owe us. This is how you repay us? . . . and do I need to remind you of the information I hold?'

'You know what she's doing, don't you?' Isaac asks the officers.

'As neither myself nor my partner here are officers of the *law*, whatever it is your mother is doing is not our concern,' the woman says.

'She's rigging the votes.'

'It's not our concern.'

'You're not interested in justice, then?'

'Justice is served by the people. A million voices giving a truly democratic decision.'

'This is a joke.'

'What's a joke?' Patty comes back into the room, a lighter step, a smile creeping to her face.

'Nothing,' he mutters.

She sits down next to Isaac. 'Now, where were we?'

'Mrs Paige, I just have a few questions to ask you to ensure the smooth running of this evening's procedures. We have a number of viewing options available to you and your son and it's simpler if we talk through these now.'

'I want to see her face,' she says.

The man stares at her. 'OK. That would be the answer to one question, but if I can run through the actual event with you . . .'

'No need,' she replies. 'I've watched the programme. There's a screen, is there not? A glass wall or something? I noticed sometimes it's there and sometimes it isn't.'

'That's changed now,' he says. 'There is a window of safety glass between the audience and the accused but we found removing it caused issues.'

'I don't mind issues!'

'There were problems with associated smells . . .'

'I don't care.'

'And the accused has been known to spit into the audience.'

'Let her try it and I'll spit back in her face.'

'Either way,' the officer continues, 'the screen is now locked in place from the central computer system.'

Isaac looks away. On the sofa next to him is a folder; he rests a hand on it.

'One question though, Mrs Paige, if you don't mind?' the man says. 'Would either of you like to say a few words to the guests and the press at the execution?'

'Will the press be in the room?' Isaac asks.

He nods. 'Always. It's vital to us as a record of procedure and to follow the responsibility we have to the voting public to ensure their wishes are carried out to the full.'

'I'd like to,' Isaac says, jumping in quickly.

'Then we're done here,' the woman says, looking at her watch. 'Time to go.'

'Already?' Patty replies.

'I'm afraid so, Mrs Paige.'

With a nervous sickness rushing through him, Isaac picks up the file from his side and follows them from the house.

Martha

'The time is: 7 p.m. You have: two hours until your possible execution. The current stats are: 77.6% in favour, 22.4% against. We will update you in: thirty minutes.'

Every thirty minutes now, hey?

Two hours of my life left and all of it available to watch on live TV.

At a premium now too.

Who'd have thought I'd be so interesting that people would want to pay to watch me die. There's voyeurism for you.

How many people will watch my last breath?

More than watched Jesus's! Ha ha!

God, I hope I don't wet myself or anything, you know, when I die – or fart, because they say you do, don't they? Oh, that'd be awful. But hey, I'll be dead, so I won't care.

Unless I'm a ghost, then I'll cringe and bury my head.

I don't mind other people seeing me like that, but not you, Isaac, I don't want you to remember me like that.

I want you to remember me smiling, close to you, holding your hand or kissing you, lying in your arms.

Before all this.

The homeless had started drifting back to their old place at the underpass. It was protected from the wind and the weather and it kept more of the warmth from the fires they made in those metal bin things. Jackson had given them money to keep quiet after my mum was killed, and for a while they cleared off into hotels or B&Bs and the like, but a few at a time they came back to what I suppose they thought of as their home.

A couple of them raised a hand to me as I passed through that night, a few put their heads down, I suppose not wanting to be reminded of what had happened. They all knew who I was, see. *That orphan girl*, they'd say, or *her daughter*, or *that poor girl*.

Only one or two actually knew me by name, those who'd come to her funeral and stood with heads hung in shame for not being allowed to tell the truth.

It's OK, I told them, *I get it, I know, I understand*.

I was raging, steaming angry, but with society, not them.

The train lit its way through a gloomy station. Warm, welcoming carriages but for the smell of piss, sweat and alcohol. Y'see, the Rises might have a lot of nice, genuine folk in it, but it's also got its fair share of drunks, druggies and idiots just like anywhere and they were the kind who'd use the train as somewhere to hang around in.

You, though, kept to yourself on the train, propped in a corner with your hood up, a bottle in your pocket because it made getting out of trouble easier, you said, but I saw you stand and move towards the door, and as the train stopped and you stepped out, your smile warmed me more than any hot drink or fire could've done that night.

We strolled through the frost with our arms linked, talking about what we could do, and we paused under a streetlight

319

and kissed, and you looked down at me and I could see it already in your eyes.

'We have to do something,' you whispered. 'We can't carry on like this. He knows we're still seeing each other. He'll hurt you, you know he will.'

'Then let him.'

'No . . .'

'I'm sick of being intimidated by him, Isaac. Something needs to change. Not just for me. People need to know the truth.'

'You don't think they know already?'

'They need it shoving in their faces then and be forced to act.'

We stepped out from beneath the street lamp, strolling past the boarded-up shops where I'd first seen him. Further up on Crocus Street, a dark car was pulled up at the side of the road.

'You can't force people to act,' you said.

Behind us a car door banged and we both turned around. Someone was walking towards us.

Why didn't we move, run away or something? Why did we just stand there and wait for him to reach us?

'Martha Honeydew, you're a filthy whore just like your mother.'

I recognised his voice straight away.

'And it's about time we rid the world of the burden of having you in it. You were a mistake that should never have happened.'

'What?' you said.

I heard a click and as he moved closer I saw the moonlight glint on the barrel of a gun.

'No, Dad.' I watched you move forward but my feet were stuck to the ground.

'I don't want to hurt you, Isaac, but I'll kill her and I'll see that some fucking low-life scumbag fries for it. Nobody'll care and in a couple of weeks nobody will even remember. Two birds, one stone. Two degenerate shits that this city will be better off without. She's no good for you – she's nothing, just some stupid worthless slag like her mother was.'

'My mother was a good woman!' I shouted and I stepped towards him now. 'But you left her with nothing! Nothing but me!'

'What are you talking about, you silly bitch?'

'You know what's she's talking about,' you replied.

We were edging around each other like it was some elegant, slow-moving dance, one pace this, one pace that, neither getting the upper hand, drifting over Crocus Street and back towards the underpass.

'I have proof as well,' I said.

'Of what?' Jackson snorted.

'Let's start with that you killed my mother – and then we'll move on to the rest.'

'You can't prove anything,' he said.

A bullet whizzed past my ear, the bang echoing so loud, the night stagnant in silence after it.

'The next won't miss,' he said.

A gun pointing at your head, the man you love at your side, your family dead, no future, no education . . . well, it kind of puts things into perspective.

* * *

'The time,' the electronic voice announces, 'is 7.30 p.m. You have: one hour and thirty minutes until your possible execution. The current stats are: 79.6% in favour, 20.4% against. We will update you in . . . thirty minutes.'

Shit.

Isaac

The white limousine pulls up at the gates of the prison. The crowd is massive; press with microphones and cameras, people with placards, tourists come for the spectacle. They're rowdy, chanting 'Death for the accused', 'An eye for an eye'.

To one side of the crowd is a smaller group, banners proclaiming 'Let there be evidence', 'Fair votes for all', but their voice is quiet and the press ignore them.

As Isaac and his mother step from the car a hush falls over the crowd, hats are removed and the jostling stops. People stand still with their heads lowered or hands on hearts.

'Jackson was our hero!' someone shouts, and from behind her dark glasses, Patty Paige smiles wide.

'Hero of the people!' another shouts and the rest applaud.

'If only you knew the truth,' Isaac mutters, but nobody hears him.

They're led along a path at the side of the building, past a tree where a sparrow sits and a barred window. At the door they're scanned for weapons.

'What's this?' the guard asks Isaac, lifting the folder.

'A speech,' he replies. 'I'm speaking on my mother's behalf.'

The guard nods and lets them through.

'This way, please,' the female security officer says, and leads them into a large room. 'I should inform you that at this point, the glass is lit to only provide a view *into* the cell. The accused at this point, *cannot* see you, or can only see *very* little.'

Isaac steps into the room.

It reminds him of a cinema or theatre. Rows of seats leading back and slowly up, lights angled towards the front, a flat space between the first row of seats and the stage.

He stops, staring at the glass screen, closer than he expected, no curtain to obscure it before the titles roll or the actors appear, no age certificate or trailers before it all begins, because there she is.

His eyes rest on her and he cannot help but step towards her until he is right in front of the glass and his fingers are reaching out to touch.

'Can she hear me?' he asks.

'No, absolutely not,' the female officer replies. 'You can call her all the names you want and she won't hear a whisper.'

He watches her sitting in the death chair, her face red and blotchy and her long hair gone. 'Martha,' he breathes.

Whatever the other officer is explaining to his mother Isaac is oblivious, and as his heart holds him to the glass, he watches Martha struggle barefoot from the chair.

Her eyes don't focus as she stumbles towards him, they're vacant or away in some deep memory, but she stops at the glass right in front of him, raises a hand and places it next to his.

'Can you see me?' he whispers. 'Can you hear me?'

Her eyes flit over him without focus.

'I love you,' he breathes.

She peers through the glass, looking at him now, then she bends down and breathes heavy on it, creating steamed-up clouds. He watches her draw a finger through it, and starting on her right, his left, the letters, blurry and awkward, begin to form:

I LOVE YOU

As he gulps, she glances over his shoulder and quickly wipes the message away with her palm.

Behind him a conversation continues, but he watches Martha.

'I'm sorry,' he mumbles.

She shakes her head, and again she breathes on the glass.

REMEMBER YOUR PROMISE

He nods and closes his eyes, and when he looks back again, she's sitting on the chair.

'There are seats reserved for you at the front,' the female officer says, suddenly next to him. 'There will also be a few dignitaries with you, notably the CEO of Life Visions, the editor-in-chief of the National News, a representative from Cyber Secure – if there are any other people you'd like sitting with you, that can be arranged, such as other family members, close friends . . .'

'Eve Stanton,' he says.

'What? The counsellor?' Patty asks. 'What do you want her for? You don't know her.'

'And Judge Cicero,' he adds.

'What?' she says again.

The woman raises a hand. 'Mrs Paige, having such people as those on the guest list will certainly increase public curiosity and therefore gather viewers. We can do a quick press release now.'

Patty nods and the two women walk away together.

The male officer turns to Isaac. 'At the agreed time, two television screens will lower from the ceiling, one at each side of the glass, both providing a live feed from *Death is Justice*. Some time before that the lighting will be altered, allowing the accused to see out as well as you seeing in.'

Isaac nods.

'She will be allowed the opportunity to make her final words in approximately . . .' he glances at his watch, '. . . fifty minutes. And don't forget, she's claimed she has a secret to tell, so it's going to attract a lot of attention. We're looking at this being the highest viewer ratings in history! It's a huge deal. It's the first of its kind – a teen girl accused of killing someone like your father –'

Isaac interrupts. 'And when do I get to speak?'

'After phone lines have been closed and votes have been verified. Five minutes before she's executed, so 8.55 p.m.'

'You're very sure she'll be found guilty.'

He laughs. 'Oh, that's a cert!'

Martha

'The time is: 8 p.m. You have: one hour until your possible execution. The current stats are: 97% in favour, 3% against. We will update you in: thirty minutes.'

Back to where they were twelve hours ago.

How time flies.

This is it: the last hour.

Make it count, Martha.

It's all minutes now. Fifty-nine minutes until my possible execution . . .

'Possible execution' my arse.

Fifty-nine minutes until I die.

Fifty-eight yet?

Oh, the glass has changed, I can see out, see properly.

Jesus, there are a lot of seats. How can they expect to fill so many? But they are! People are swarming in! I don't know any of them!

Someone's taking tickets off them and showing them to their seats. My God, this is . . . this is scary . . . oh God . . . oh shit. They're looking at me, watching me, like I'm some animal in the zoo or something. Jesus!

I want to hide but there's nowhere to go.

Death is Justice

At the desk, Kristina and Joshua are watching the screen filled with images from Cell 7 and the viewing room. His face is sombre, his movements slow and deliberate; she smiles constantly, her eyes flickering with excitement.

JOSHUA: What are you thinking to this, Kristina?

KRISTINA: Frankly, I can barely contain my excitement! I only *wish* we could be there live!

His face stretches, a grimace or a fake smile.

JOSHUA (laughing): You should've lived in gladiatorial Rome, Kristina. Seems you enjoy the spectacle of suffering!

Her smile drops, she turns from the camera to him. Ignoring this, he continues.

JOSHUA: I heard tickets were trading hands for more than four times their face value.

KRISTINA: Yes, well, quite honestly, I would've given a kidney to be there! Spectacle of suffering or not, this is a once in a lifetime viewing.

JOSHUA: Well, you kind of hope so. Certainly we hope and pray that we live in a society where this type of crime is a very *irregular* occurrence.

KRISTINA: Indeed. Oh, would you look at that!

They both focus on the screen.

JOSHUA: Oh, my . . .

KRISTINA: Well, there's a surprise. I believe in the front row we have, if I'm not much mistaken, not only our bereaved family of course, but Mr Cicero and Eve Stanton! *What*, pray tell, do you make of that?

JOSHUA: Kristina, I haven't a clue!

Martha

Eve, there's Eve, and I recognise that man too, that's Judge Cicero.

Eve, can you see me?

I try to beg with my eyes for her to look up, but she doesn't.

And Isaac. He's looking at me. He's not taking his eyes off me.

Oh I feel sick. I want to cry.

Help me, someone help me.

I didn't . . . I didn't . . .

No . . . don't do that . . . be strong . . .

Eve

'I don't want to be here,' Eve whispers to Cicero. 'I can't look at her.'

'You need to,' he replies. 'You need to be strong for her. Talk to her with your eyes.'

'This is wrong,' Eve says. 'This shouldn't be happening. But I don't know what to do.'

He leans towards her. 'The boys have something planned,' he whispers.

She frowns at him. 'The boys? What boys?'

He sucks in a breath. 'Isaac and your Max.'

'Max!' she hisses. 'What's Max doing in all this? Cicero, I can't let him get involved.'

'Shhhh,' he says. 'It's all right. He promised me it's nothing like that. He said he wouldn't even be here.'

'Then how . . . ? And when did you and him suddenly know each other?'

'This morning, with the television thing. He's good with technology, your son.'

'What?'

Martha

'The time is: 8.30 p.m. You have: thirty minutes until your possible execution. The current stats are: 97.4% in favour, 2.6% against. We will update you in: ten minutes.'

Oh God.

God in heaven help me.

I don't think I can do this.

I'm scared to die.

I want to change my mind . . .

That night, *that night*, you remember? A week ago! One whole week ago!

This time last week I had walked over the frosty park, met you at the station, walked hand in hand with you, all the time knowing, sensing something . . . *something* . . .

And then, there he was. Jackson staring at us, gun in hand, threatening . . .

Suddenly everything in perspective.

I thought I would die. Thought he'd shoot me there and then and be rid of me and have his little family back and his secret safe and all that. All he had to do was pull the trigger. He knew, I knew, you knew, that he would never be caught for it.

I'd just be one more.

Your mum, my mum, me.

Those were just who we knew about.

We'd said things had to change and as I stared down the barrel of that gun, I knew that was the time. Act now, or never.

I shouted at the top of my lungs and ran at him. He didn't shoot, too surprised maybe, and I knocked him to the ground and I heard the thud of his head against the tarmac.

But he leapt back up and grabbed me as I tried to run away.

I waited to feel the cold of the gun on my skin, but didn't.

'Isaac!' I shouted to you and I twisted and turned against Jackson, throwing a punch that glanced off the side of his face.

'Bitch!' he spat at me.

I squirmed sideways but not quickly enough. Suddenly I was on the floor again with my face stinging and my head spinning. His shoes were in front of me and I felt the thud of one into my stomach. I had no air to scream or shout.

Isaac, where are you? I thought.

I blinked the pain away and across the tarmac I saw Jackson's gun lying on the twinkling frost.

I can't do it, I thought, the air in my lungs burning hot.

Can, I argued back. *Have to.*

I tried to crawl across on my knees. Another kick came to my legs, another punch to my head. Everything spinning.

Oh my God, the worst way to die – beaten to death.

A blow against my back.

I stretched my arm out to the gun.

You have to do this, I told myself.

A thud into my arm. Recoil. Oh God, the pain. Please stop. Please help me.

Refocus. There it was. Stretch to the gun. Stretch.

Shoes came down close to my fingers, hands took the gun from in front of me. I collapsed.

I'm done. This is it.

I heard a voice. 'You wouldn't,' it said.

'Would,' said the other.

Couldn't distinguish between them. I rolled over. Saw Jackson's feet close by.

'Step away from her.'

'I can't do that, son. You know I can't. She could ruin us. We need to get rid of her.'

I looked up. He was undoing his belt. Pulling it through the loops.

'You mean she could ruin you, not us. And you're wrong – there's no *could* about it – it's *will*. She . . . no, me and her, me and Martha, we *will* ruin you and you deserve it.'

'Isaac, you're not thinking straight. The girl's got in your head.'

'No, Jackson.'

'Dad, I'm your dad.'

'No, you're not. Yeah, you adopted me, but you took me out of there so I didn't blab about you pushing my mum over the balcony and so you looked good! Give your public profile a touch of humanity! I *know* you killed her!'

'Isaac . . .'

'Don't deny it.'

'All right, if you need to hear it from me, yes – I killed her! OK? But that's not why I adopted you. It was because you . . . you *looked* at me with these big innocent eyes and all I could think of was what my life had been like living there, and what was going to happen to you.'

'What?' Your tone was mocking. 'You had some rare moment of compassion?'

'Believe it or not, yes, I did. But Patty, she turned it into something else.' He snorted and shook his head. 'Patty . . . the rest . . . it was all Patty.'

'No. Patty didn't sell drugs on the Rises, getting people addicted to get more money. Patty didn't have affairs just to prove she was still attractive, or, I don't know, for some power trip; Patty didn't push my mother off the balcony, didn't run Martha's mum over, didn't bribe people to get her own way, didn't –'

'ALL RIGHT!' His voice echoed through the underpass. From the corner of my eye I saw the belt slip through his hands and his fingers pause at the buckle.

'I don't want to be associated with you,' you said.

'You don't have to be,' he replied. 'You can walk away, live your own life.'

'You'll let the press see that? Broken family? Failed father?'

I felt him shuffle sideways towards me. 'They don't have to. We keep them sweet. We show the public what they want to see while behind the scenes we do as we like.'

'Lie to them? Manipulate the press with all your nasty contacts? Yeah, of course, because that's what you always do!'

'Just put the gun down. You're not seeing straight. We'll get rid of the girl and everything can go back to normal.'

I glanced up and saw you shake your head.

Jackson edged closer to me. I was trembling, watching as he pulled his belt through the buckle. I couldn't move.

335

'We have to,' Jackson said and he was right behind me, the smell of the belt leather in my nose, the strap nudging my shoulder as it swayed.

'Move away from her!' you said.

'No. I'm going to finish this and you're going to go home and we're going to forget the whole fiasco.'

'I said, move away from her!'

'You're a child. You don't know what you're doing.'

I was crying, desperate to run away but I couldn't move, couldn't speak.

'MOVE AWAY!' you shouted.

Behind me Jackson laughed.

'I'm warning you!'

'No, you're not. You're just a little boy in a big man's world who doesn't know how to behave.'

I felt the belt slip over my head.

I watched you with the gun in your outstretched arms, your finger on the trigger, tears in your eyes.

I felt the leather on my neck.

'You've turned me into this!' you shouted.

'The apple never falls –'

The bang of the gun finished the sentence.

I turn my back on that godawful electric chair waiting to kill me, and move to the glass. I want to tell you I'm sorry. Please, Isaac, look at me. Tell me everything will be all right. Tell me it won't hurt.

Jesus, I'm scared.

My chest's burning. I feel sick.

No ... calm down ... breath steady ... come on.

Something's going on behind me. The door's opening. There's a guard and ... what is that?

Isaac

'What *is* that?' Isaac says.

The security officer leans forward from the seat behind. 'Our new machine.' He smiles at Isaac and points to the television screens lowering from the ceiling.

'Watch. They're about to introduce it on *Death is Justice*.'

Death is Justice

Kristina and Joshua stand next to the large screen. On it an animated version of Cell 7 and an animated Martha sitting in the death chair. Straps are tied around her wrists, ankles and chest. Above her a metal crown lowers onto her head.

KRISTINA (smiling): Yes, viewers, our proudest innovation to date, I believe.

JOSHUA: Many think so . . .

KRISTINA: Let me explain.

On the screen a small door opens in the rear of the cell and a machine rolls in on pre-set tracks.

KRISTINA: This new invention is completely automated. It eliminates the need for an executioner as such.

As the machine reaches the animated Martha an arm extends and plugs into the rear of the chair. A timer appears on a display along with the stats, and a voltage meter reading zero.

KRISTINA: As the timer counts down the final votes and stats, it triggers an automatic reaction from the machine. If a 'guilty' verdict is reached, a separate timer counts down from three minutes . . .

The screen pans out to an animated man standing at a lectern in the front of the viewing area, speaking to the crowd of onlookers.

KRISTINA: . . . allowing for the final words from the victim's family.

The man returns to his seat, and as the timer reaches zero, the voltage meter reading rises and electricity courses through the body of the animated Martha. After a few minutes, the meter readings reduce and Martha's eyes close.

Joshua turns to camera.

JOSHUA: What do you think to that, viewers?

Applause goes around the studio.

KRISTINA: You see, ladies and gentlemen, what this does so well is put the justice and the death directly into your hands. You are judge, juror and even *executioner* now. The machine here takes direct information from the phone lines, converting it into action, which ultimately does away with our accused. We are all about empowering you!

Isaac

'Can it be stopped if something goes wrong?' he whispers.

The officer shrugs. 'What could go wrong?'

'Everything,' Isaac says, shaking his head. 'But I think it did a long time ago.'

Cicero turns and taps him on the arm. 'Isaac, look.'

Inside the cell, Martha is standing up.

Death is Justice

Seated at the desk, Kristina and Joshua turn on their high stools to face the live feed on the screen, the eye logo spinning in the corner.

JOSHUA: Well, the moment we've been waiting for.

KRISTINA (laughing): One of them!

JOSHUA: I can't tell you, viewers, how excited I am to hear what secret it is that Martha has to tell us. How long has she been given to speak, Kristina?

KRISTINA: She's been allowed the normal three minutes, which frankly surprised me, seeing as that is the same as the victim's family. Seems an imbalance; surely the guilty should be allowed less.

The live feed shows the guard has shackled Martha's wrists and ankles together and moved her towards the glass.

Joshua puts his fingers to his lips and looks to the audience. The sound changes, crackles, the noise of Martha's heavy breathing hanging over the studio.

Martha

Martha focuses on Isaac. Flicks a smile so small only he could notice, then she turns her attention to the audience.

'I promised you a secret,' she says, her voice small and shaky. 'I don't think it's one you want to hear and it's not one I want to tell any more.'

'Just get on and kill her!' someone shouts.

'But I need to start further back so, please, bear with me . . .' She takes a breath and looks out to the waiting faces. 'My mother . . .'

'Your mother was a prostitute!' a female voice says. 'The Rises is full of them!'

Martha pauses. 'My mother wasn't, but you're right that there are prostitutes in the Rises. Tell me what you would do – sell sex or starve?'

'I'd work!'

Martha screws her face up. 'Please, I have three minutes, I don't want to use it arguing about lack of jobs and low pay and everything, please . . .'

Her breath jutters, her eyes hover the audience, catching the gaze of each and every one.

'My mother believed in love. In truth and honesty. And trust. I like to remember her as an idealist, but really I suppose she was naive.' She glances to the clock.

'Seventeen years ago she fell in love with a man. He was good-looking, charming, he spoilt her and promised her the world. She'd grown up in poverty, her family struggling from one pay day to the next.'

'You won't get any sympathy from me!' a man shouts. 'Nothing excuses what you did!'

A few people around him turn and glare; a few fingers on lips to hush him.

'The last thing I want from you is your fucking sympathy!' she shouts back.

There's an intake of breath and Martha glances to Eve who has her hands raised as if to calm her.

'I'm sorry,' she says, her voice lower. 'I'd just like you to listen. With an open mind.' She takes a breath. 'I suppose she was vulnerable. I suppose she should've known better. She knew who this guy was, she'd seen him around and heard the gossip. Friends tried to warn her. When she was telling me about this, she said she was stupid. I don't go for that, I think she was manipulated.

'This man was clever. He knew what he wanted, took it, finished with his victim and moved on to the next. A trail of destruction followed him that became bigger and bigger over time.

'When my mum first knew him, the trail was just beginning.

'When she told him she was pregnant, he upped and left her to cope by herself. I never knew his name, she never told me. She told me it was better that way and I believed her.

'It probably would've been.'

She looks back at the clock – one minute thirty seconds left.

344

'But things have this weird habit of coming out. After she died, after she was *murdered*, sometime after, not straight away cos I couldn't face it, I went through her stuff. I didn't want to. It was private to her, but I had to. And I found some letters, and I held them in my hands; looking at her name on the envelope, a heart drawn on the back of one, I knew they must be from him. I couldn't work out why she would keep them, I knew they must be from him, my *father*, and . . . and . . . I took the papers out . . . and I read them.'

Her body trembles, she crosses her arms and rubs her hands down them, her eyes as well. She blinks and tears fall.

'With them all was another letter, typed address and all official looking. I read that too. It was from a solicitor, an agreement that she had signed, that said in return for her not contacting him, my father that is, and for keeping his identity secret, she would receive fifty pounds a month until I was eighteen. Fifty pounds a month for her silence.

'The handwritten letters were only signed with his initials and I remember staring at them, thinking it couldn't possibly be the person I was thinking of.' She sucks in a deep, ragged breath, looks at the thirty seconds on the timer and back to the audience.

'But the letter from the solicitor had his name in full. My father . . . my father . . .' She looks over the audience.

'Was Jackson Paige.'

Death is Justice

The studio is in silence. Both Kristina and Joshua are open mouthed and agog.

JOSHUA: Huh . . . well . . . viewers . . .

KRISTINA: Lies and deception. That can't possibly be true.

JOSHUA: At this point, Kristina, I do wonder why she would lie.

Martha

A ripple goes over the crowd, louder and louder.

'That's why you killed him!' someone shouts.

'Jackson Paige,' Martha shouts over the hubbub, 'was a regular visitor to the High Rises. His charity work was a cover. He had mistresses there, he sold drugs there. He didn't respect us or where he came from, he used us!'

The noise is getting louder and louder. A guard comes up from behind Martha and grabs hold of her, but she stands firm.

'He got my mother pregnant and left her with nothing. He didn't care. He just moved on to someone else. He was a liar and a cheat. He was corrupt. *He* killed my mother, not the boy who was executed, and he got off because he has money!'

'She hated him!' someone shouts. 'She was jealous!'

'She wanted him dead!'

'Execute her!'

The guard drags Martha back to the death chair, but she struggles and pulls away from him, lurching towards the glass and staring out.

'I never wanted him dead!' she shouts. 'I just wanted the truth for my mum and for Ollie. There should be proper, fair justice for all, not just people with the money to buy it!'

Eve, Cicero and Isaac stand up and they applaud.

Death is Justice

KRISTINA: And would you look at that? A strange clique there of the counsellor, the judge and the *bereaved*, don't you think? What *is* going on there?

JOSHUA: I think, Kristina, that people know a lot more than us . . .

KRISTINA: Impossible!

JOSHUA (shaking his head): There's more to this than meets the eye. This is not over yet.

The studio audience are strangely quiet, mouths wide as they watch events unfold.

Martha

'Please,' Martha says. 'I'm telling you the truth!'

'You're time's up, bitch!' a woman's voice shouts.

Martha looks out and pauses on Isaac's face watching her, tears falling down her face. For a moment she drops her head and her shoulders judder as she breathes in and out.

'I promise you that you will understand even more,' she continues, looking up again, 'when you've heard everything. You'll think back to what I've just told you and wonder. Someone once said to me that there comes a time when you choose to act or choose to be silent for ever. I'm only sixteen, but even I've seen the apathy from those who could do something, and the frustration of those who can't. This is the only thing I can do to maybe, *maybe* change things.

'From the day that trigger was pulled and Jackson fell, I've known that my role is the martyr. Someone else, someone else who's stronger than me has to carry on.'

The guard drags her to the chair and slams her into it.

'Please, stop,' she says. 'Let me carry on, please!'

The straps tighten across her wrists and around her legs.

'Stop!' she yells. 'Please!'

A cloth goes around her mouth and her eyes widen in horror. She squirms and pulls and tugs, but she cannot get free.

Death is Justice

KRISTINA: As I said, viewers: lies and desperation.

JOSHUA (quietly): Don't forget to join in the debate on your social media device, and stay tuned to follow these live events and listen to our in-studio questions. In fact, Kristina, things are going a little crazy out there in internet land, are they not?

KRISTINA: Indeed they are. Ladies and gentlemen, I'm sure you must have very strong feelings about this landmark case, but don't let the fact that she is only a teenager sway your opinions. This is the last five minutes of voting time, get your fingers busy. And don't forget, tonight you are the executioner too! Let's get those all-important numbers . . .

Martha

'The time is: 8.50 p.m. You have: ten minutes until your possible execution. The current stats are: 98.3% in favour, 1.7% against. We will update you in: five minutes with the final count.'

That's it then. I bet everyone thinks I was making stuff up. Trying to eek out time. I'm going to die and all they'll know about me and remember is lies.

She said some crap about having a secret then told us Jackson was her father – I can hear it now. *Reckon she had some vendetta against him, or she was jealous. She's a cold-hearted bitch who pulled a trigger and killed our hero.*

Only I didn't pull the trigger, did I?

It felt like hours, sprawled there on the frosty tarmac, battered and bruised. The bang of the gun in my ears. Staring at the body next to me. His eyes open and vacant. A hole in his head. One, not riddled with bullets like the papers said.

I couldn't stop staring at him.

I didn't see you collapse next to me, I just suddenly sensed you there.

'I . . . he . . .' I couldn't find words. Couldn't think or fathom or . . .

'The police will be here soon,' you whispered.

I put my hand on yours. My head started coming into focus. 'We said, didn't we, that things needed to change. This is it.'

'Martha, you should go. I don't want the police to involve you with this, I don't want them to try to blame you.'

'Let them,' I said.

And there it was.

'Let them blame me. You know, this could work, this could be it.' I knew it was over for me, everything. I had no future to go to. I'd put myself in an impossible situation with no escape.

All I'd ever wanted was justice and truth, not him dead . . . but saying I'd done it?

'Isaac, this way could work. This could really change things. Have an impact, do some good, couldn't it?'

'What?'

I watched the moonlight in your eyes and I looked up to the sky we shared. 'This is it. If I say I did it, there'll be so much media attention, and if I tell them I'm Jackson's daughter at my final words then folks will *have* to listen. You can get the evidence. Then at the victim's speech you can show them what he did. We've got it all. All that stuff at Gus's. The solicitor's letter from my mother's, the documents you photocopied. You can show them it all because then they'll be listening. It's what we've been waiting for. It's what we said. Then things will have to change. They'll *have to*!'

'No. No. I'm not letting you take the blame. *You* can show them the evidence, there'll be enough of a media storm anyway!'

I shook my head. 'No, I can't. I'm just a girl from the Rises. An orphan girl from the Rises who means nothing and is nothing.

Nobody will pay any attention to me. You know that. You are Jackson Paige's son! People will listen to you.'

'No, Martha, I won't let you do this. This is shock speaking. You're not thinking straight . . .'

'I'm thinking straighter than I have in a long time. Listen to me, Isaac! The press will just discredit me, you know they will. They'll laugh at me, and everything – that list, all those innocent people – will be for nothing. But they'll listen to you! You're educated. You have influence. People *like* you. They'll listen. I can be the martyr, Isaac, I can do that, but the fighter has to be you.'

'No.'

'It *has* to be. You have the influence and the money. People will listen to you. You can do that. I can't. But I can do this.'

Across the darkness and silence the yowl of sirens began. A hint of blue light.

See where desperation pushes you to? Where you'll forfeit your life on principle?

You took my hand. 'But . . . I don't want you to die. It's not fair. You're not guilty. It should be me.'

I was shaking, I could feel the nerves in me, but I knew this was the right thing to do.

'Isaac, this isn't about me and you any more. This is bigger than us. Think of all those people on that list. The families who never saw justice, the innocent people who were executed or imprisoned, the guilty who were never punished. *How many more?*'

The siren was louder. The blue brighter, flashing on off on off.

'We could change this and you know it,' I whispered. 'We have to at least *try*.'

You took me in your arms. 'I love you,' you said. 'Don't –'

'Let me,' I pleaded. 'For my mum and yours. For Ollie and for *everyone*. Please, let me.'

You held my face in your hands and you kissed me and as you pulled away I saw the blue flashing in your eyes.

'Promise me,' I said. 'Promise me you won't tell, promise me that you will do everything you can.'

'If it's what you want,' you replied, 'then I promise. With my whole being, I promise.'

The siren was even louder, white headlights and blue bouncing through the darkness.

'Go!' I shouted.

It's all down to you now, Isaac.

Strapped into the chair I watch as you walk up to the lectern.

I'm glad I met you.

We only had a year together, but it was the best year of my life.

In this world we could never share any more than that.

Remember the first walk we had together in the woods? Remember looking up at the dark sky pinpricked with stars? Remember sitting on the swings together? Remember making love in my flat?

'We'll share the sky,' you told me. And we always will.

I'll miss you.

I'll love you for ever.

'The time is: 8.55 p.m. and the lines are now closed. The final stats are: 98.6% in favour, 1.4% against. Your execution will commence in: five minutes.'

This is it then.

Isaac

'Ladies and gentlemen, I'm very aware we don't have much time, and I implore you to allow me to speak without interrupting, for what I have to say, I would also like the accused to be able to hear in full.

'As you know my name is Isaac Paige. I'm the adopted son of Jackson and Patty Paige. I'm certain you all know that Jackson *rescued* me from the High Rises, but I'm certain you don't all know that he was having a relationship with my mother too. He's not my father, I hasten to add.' He pauses, looks around and takes a breath.

'My mother didn't jump off the balcony of her flat – he pushed her.

'Yes, Jackson Paige is, was, a murderer. No, I can't prove that one.'

The studio audience, the audience in the viewing area, and the crowds of people outside watching the live stream, are silent.

'On the night Beth Honeydew, Martha's mother, was killed, Jackson came home drunk. I was in bed; his arguing with Patty woke me. Believe it or not, they often argued – she always won. When I looked out I could see the front of his car was damaged to the point I thought it would be a write-off. There was blood on it. I took a photo.'

From the folder he takes an A4 photograph and holds it up to the audience.

'And I took another photo of the men turning up to fix the car –' he holds that one up, 'and I have this.'

A hissy recording blurs through the speakers.

'Get it cleaned up and quick. Stupid bitch . . . no, the Honeydew woman . . . I don't know, sort it. How do you usually do it? Yeah well, I don't know, just find some car and beat it up a bit . . . find out who it belongs to and get in touch with the lawyer . . . he's good with votes.'

The voice stops.

Isaac speaks again. 'The voice is unmistakeable. And this.'

On the screen the live TV feed fades from view and is replaced by a blurry black and white video recording. The date and time are displayed along the bottom while in the middle the camera focuses on the road next to the underpass. A car, the number plate in focus, is waiting a little distance away. A woman walks from the left-hand side with a bag of shopping in one hand; as she steps onto the road, the car can be heard revving. The woman turns as she reaches the middle of the road, but it's too late. It slams into her, sending her flying into the air and over the car.

A few metres away it screeches to a halt and a man steps out and the feed focuses on him; clearly visible is Jackson Paige. As he strides towards the body, bends down to it, and then walks back to his car, the air above the audience is sucked in.

'Seems the security cameras *were* working the night Martha's mother was killed,' Isaac says. 'The neighbour's boy, Oliver

Barkova, was executed here, in this cell behind me for the hit and run killing of Beth Honeydew. He always protested his innocence.'

He glances over the audience. 'I knew Jackson was guilty, and I knew it wasn't the first time he'd killed someone. Why did he do it? I can speculate that the incident with my mother was an argument gone wrong, or the hit and run was because Martha's mum was about to go against the contract she'd signed and expose him. Or I could speculate that he was nothing more than a psychopath looking for ways to exert his power.

'I wish he was here to answer. But what good would that do? He had a system, he had people under his influence. They know who they are, and they should be ashamed. Innocent people were put to death because of them.

'The judicial system in this country doesn't work. It's wrong and it's corrupt. To convict somebody of murder and crime you need evidence. You need witnesses. It should not be done by votes that only some can afford. We need change. I knew this, but did nothing about it. The guilt I felt over Beth Honeydew sent me back and back to the High Rises; every evening I'd find myself near the spot she was killed.

'On these late night vigils, I met someone. She told me I saved her, gave her reason to breath in the mornings, but in reality, she saved me – she gave me hope in a society I thought was doomed.

'We started a relationship, but with who I was, am, and where she was from, we had to keep it quiet, at least from those on my side of the tracks. But, as they say, all good things must come to an end. When Jackson found out he put a gun to my head and told me not to associate with *slags*.'

He sighs heavily, turns and looks to Martha and the timer. Two minutes and thirty seconds to go.

'But I loved her, still do. I couldn't let her go even though he threatened to kill me. She was – *is* my everything. Yet Jackson was nothing if not a man of his word. He followed me, he tracked me down and he found me with her. With Martha.'

Death is Justice

JOSHUA: Oh my. Oh my Lord. I did *not* see that coming. Kristina, it's a love story, it's Romeo and Juliet. The wrong side of the tracks. Wrong families. It's . . . beautiful. It's . . . *tragic*.

KRISTINA: Viewers, I implore you to take no notice of this. I'm certain it can't be true.

JOSHUA: But –

KRISTINA (shaking her head): It's quite ridiculous. Apply some logic. Why would someone of his stature be with a girl like that? Think of how many beautiful girls would offer themselves to the son of Jackson Paige.

JOSHUA (frowning): It's *love*, Kristina, not logic!

He glances to the live feed then back to her.

JOSHUA: Anyway, let's hear more.

Isaac

Isaac gestures towards Martha. The audience are enrapt.

'There was an argument, lots of shouting. I never thought someone could be so self-absorbed or so narrow-minded. I'd seen him get away with murder twice, seen him destroy people's lives for his own gains. But most of all, I'd seen him pervert the course of justice. Now, there's a phrase . . .

'Justice here is a phone call. Easy, you think? Not if you can't afford it. Easy to alter and to fix. It's not a fair system.

'*I'll kill her,* he said to me when he first found out about us. And a few months later, when his ultimatum came again because we'd refused to stop seeing each other, he proved he meant it.'

On the screen is different CCTV footage. The audience watch in silence as Jackson points a gun to Martha, they gasp as he beats her, hold their breath as Isaac picks up the gun, and put their hands over their mouths as the belt goes over Martha's head.

'When Martha knocked him to the ground and I held the gun to him I wasn't doing it out of anger, I was doing it to save the person I love, and because the machine Jackson had become needed to be stopped.'

He takes a deep breath and stands tall.

White flashes on the screen as Isaac pulls the trigger and Jackson falls to the ground. The audience are silent.

'I killed Jackson Paige, not Martha Honeydew,' he says.

The screen changes again – the photograph from the newspaper, the still of Martha at the crime scene. It zooms in to the shadows and a blurry shape can be made out. It refocuses, zooms again, focuses again, clear and bright now, showing the face of Isaac as he runs away.

'It was there for you all to see, but you chose not to look. Martha doesn't want me to do this, but you know why she's taking the blame?' He raises his hands in desperation. 'Because she believes I'm in a better position to change the system than she is. She thinks no one will listen to her because she's *just a girl from the Rises*.

'I think she's wrong. And I think enough people have died for something they didn't do.'

As he steps away from the lectern, the glass screen separating the cell from the audience slides away. The audience gasp, Martha stares at it.

The display reads one minute fifty seconds.

'See?' Cicero whispers to Eve. 'I told you your Max is good with technology.'

Death is Justice

JOSHUA: How are they moving the glass? It's not supposed
to do that any more.

Kristina stares at the screen.

JOSHUA: I am quite flabbergasted. We have no precedent
for this. What *is* going to happen? She's still been
voted guilty, but now . . . Does she need to change
her plea? Viewers, I simply don't know.

The audience are silent.

JOSHUA (quietly): She's innocent . . .

Martha

Isaac jumps into the cell, rushes to Martha and pulls the cloth from her mouth.

'We have to get you out of here quickly,' he says and he rattles at the metal clasps around her wrists but they don't move.

Behind him Eve and Cicero are standing and running into the cell.

'Get her out!' Eve shouts.

The audience sit agog and shocked as security and prison guards stream into the cell and flood towards Martha.

The display reads one minute.

'I can't undo it,' Isaac says to Eve and he tugs again at the clasps.

'The power,' Eve says, 'can we cut the power? Cicero, help me try to get her legs out!'

Fifty-two seconds on the display.

Isaac tears around the cell. 'There's no cable!' he shouts. 'I can't find the cable!'

Eve and Cicero pull and yank at the metal clasps around Martha's legs. 'They won't budge. I can't get them off her!' Cicero says.

'I'm sorry, Martha,' Eve whispers. 'I'm . . .'

'It's OK,' she breathes. 'It's OK.'

Isaac looks out to the audience and up to the camera. 'How can you do this?' he shouts. 'How can you kill her now? She's innocent, for Christ's sake. Get her out!'

He turns back to Martha in the chair, tears streaming down his face as he clings to her hands.

'Tell them the truth. Let it be on record. Let people see what they've become!'

'No!' she shouts. 'No, if I do that, you know what'll happen.' She gulps and lowers her voice. 'If they can't kill me they'll take you, they'll kill you. I can't try to change anything. I've told you, I'm not strong enough. I'm not clever, not . . .'

'You are!' he whispers. 'Tell them you're innocent for Christ's sake!' he demands. 'Tell them, and tell them that I did it. They need to hear it from you! You need to change your plea.'

She stares at him.

Forty seconds on the display.

Death is Justice

KRISTINA: But . . . we need an execution . . . the viewers, the
voters can't be cheated out of what they want.
What they've *paid* for.

JOSHUA: But she's innocent. They're about to execute an
innocent sixteen-year-old girl. And what about
Isaac now he's said he's guilty?

KRISTINA: Execute them both, I say.

Joshua stares at her.

Isaac

Thirty-five seconds on the display.

'Tell them the truth!' Isaac pleads with her. 'They need to hear it from you. It has to go on record. Please, Martha, do this for me. Trust me. Tell them the truth!'

'But . . .'

'You *are* strong enough. You're the strongest person I know! Look at yourself – how hard you work to support yourself, how you cope without your parents, the happiness you bring to Mrs B and to me, the friendship you offer to people like Ollie and Gus. You are strong. You are a good person. Tell them the truth! If they're going to kill you, you'll go to your grave with everyone knowing you're innocent – because you are!'

Martha looks out at the sea of expectant faces, then to the guards blocking the cell from people trying to clamber in, down to Eve crying as she pulls in vain at the clasps, and to Cicero trying to break the machine, to the timer counting down . . . thirty . . . twenty-nine . . . twenty-eight . . . and finally to Isaac.

So little time, and so few options.

'I . . . I didn't do it,' she breathes. 'I didn't shoot Jackson Paige.'

Her eyes hold on to Isaac's.

'Go on!' he pleads. 'Tell them who did it!'

Tears fall down her face and she shakes her head slowly side to side. 'Isaac,' she whispers. 'Isaac killed him. But he did it for me.'

Twenty-five seconds.

'I told you, didn't I?' he shouts. 'Now let her out!'

He pulls and tugs at the clasps but nothing moves.

'LET HER OUT!'

Tears pour down his cheeks and he takes Martha's face in his hands and stares into her eyes.

'I'm so sorry,' he says. 'So sorry. I should never have agreed to this. I can't . . .'

Twenty seconds.

He spins around again. 'STOP THIS!' he shouts at the top of his voice.

'Isaac, you have to move.' Eve pulls at him.

'Come on,' Cicero says.

Fifteen seconds.

'Someone has to pay!' a man in the audience shouts.

'I spent good money to watch an execution!' another adds.

A guard grabs Eve and drags her away. 'Isaac, you can't do anything; you need to move! The electricity . . . if you're touching her . . .' she yells across the cell.

Another guard pulls at Cicero.

Thirteen.

'You're monsters!' Isaac shouts, the air vibrating with the force of his voice.

The crown starts to lower onto Martha's head. Isaac pulls at it and tries to yank it from the stand, but it's solid.

A guard grabs him, but he spins and lands a punch across his face.

'Why are you doing this?' he shouts. 'She's innocent! I did it, I told you that. She told you too! I'm guilty, not Martha!'

'Isaac, listen,' Martha says.

Nine.

He turns to her, tears streaming down both their faces. 'Let me go,' she whispers.

'No . . .'

Seven.

'I've done what I wanted – it'll go in the papers. People will know. Now you have to let me go.'

Six.

He shakes his head again.

Five.

'You *have* to. There's no beating this now for me, but you can fight it in the future, just like we planned.'

Four.

'But . . .'

Three.

'Let me go, and make a better future. Promise me,' she says.

Two.

Tears fall down his face.

'Let me go,' she says. 'And promise me you'll fight.'

One.

'I promise,' he breathes, and he lets go of her hand.

AFTERMATH

Martha

There's a clunk. The lights go out.

There's no pain.

Did I die that quickly?

I didn't feel anything. I can't see anything. Everything's dark.

I just sit, not sure what's going on. It sounds like people are moving around me. Voices are mumbling. Feet shuffling. I blink, look around, nothing changes.

Is that it? Am I dead?

Is this the afterlife I questioned?

I try to move my hands, expecting them still to be stuck but they pass through the clasps with no effort. My ankles too.

Maybe I'm a ghost.

I lift a hand and touch my face.

I think there's breath coming out of my mouth. I think . . . *think* . . . my chest's moving up and down.

I open my mouth. 'Isaac?' I croak. My mouth's dry – but I can feel it. If I can *feel* then that must mean . . .

Or my imagination?

I reach my arms and hands out, carefully take my weight on my feet and shuffle forward. My feet are still shackled. 'Isaac?' I say again, and I can hear my own voice.

'Martha?' Hands reach out I feel his arms around me. 'Martha, Martha, oh my God, Martha, you're alive.' He squeezes me tight and I hold on to him. His face is on mine and the wet of his tears too. Our bodies shake and my hands move over him to make sure it is actually him.

'I love you,' I say to him. 'I love you, I love you and I'm sorry.'

'You're alive!' he says again.

I smile because, yes, I am. I really am.

We collapse to the floor together, clinging to each other in the darkness.

'How did that happen? How did it stop?' I say.

'It must've been Max,' he replies, his fingers brushing away my tears.

'Max?'

'Eve's son . . . It doesn't matter . . . you're out . . . you're safe . . .'

'What's going to happen now? Shall we run? We *should* run, get out of here. Find safety. Come on, let's go. Quick.'

Torchlight flashes. Faces leap around me like ghosts.

'I don't think we can,' he says.

'Get the emergency lights up!' a voice booms.

Somewhere a door creaks open. More boots and shuffling bodies.

'We can try,' I whisper. 'Come on!'

I go to stand but suddenly his fingers let go and his hands pull away from me.

Mumbled voices shout and the sound of boots is louder and closer.

'Isaac?' I say, and I reach out to him. 'Isaac?' I say again, but I can't find him now.

I tumble onto all fours, groping around for him.

'Isaac!' I shout. Feet stand on my fingers, bodies bump into me. I can't find him.

'Isaac, please, where are you?' I shout again.

Green lighting flickers. I look up and scan through the strange half-lit shadows it's making. It's like I'm in a dream – no, more like a nightmare. Or maybe I *am* dead and this is some trick of hell.

It flashes now, the green lighting. On off on off on off so quickly like some special effect from a film or some psychological thing to disorientate or make you throw up.

But through it all, I see him.

His legs kicking out as he's dragged backwards, his body bucking against the arms holding him, his mouth contorted in pain or frustration.

They're pulling him to the cell door!

I stand and run at them. 'Isaac!' I yell.

For just one of the flashes of green lighting we make eye contact, but I stumble and slip and it's gone. I pull myself to my feet and run towards him, watching through the flickering as he kicks out against the guards. But another guard comes, three of them now, all trying to overpower him. A hand goes over his mouth, the crook of an arm around his throat, his legs lifted from the floor as another and another and another guard join in.

'No!' I yell.

But behind him the cell door opens. White light tumbles in and I raise a hand in front of my eyes as it near blinds me.

For a second I peer out from behind my fingers and see the dark shape of him as he disappears into the light of the cells beyond. More shadows of guards than I can make sense of; he's powerless.

I run at the door.

Maybe I can get a foot in, maybe I can make them stop, change their minds, let him go. But it slams shut before I get there. Solid. Dark. Immovable. The hope of white light is gone.

Barely half a metre away from him, but I may as well be in a different world.

With no shame or self-consciousness or worry that I *shouldn't*, I sob and I sob and I don't give a flying fuck who sees me or who comments. I want to batter down this door and beat the living crap out of the guards for taking him. I want to scream at the fuckers who decided on this system. Make them feel the pain of loss, the hopelessness of watching someone die who you know is innocent. I want them to feel everything I've felt and gone through – the grief and the hatred and the anguish and the loneliness and the confusion and fear and this interminable bloody, fucking, bastard *despair*.

I shout at the door.

I bang my hands on it.

I shout and scream.

I kick it.

Punch it, yank at the handle and try to shake it from its frame.

'Bring him back to me!' I yell. 'Bring him back!'

I do everything to get through that door until I collapse exhausted onto the floor.

You useless cow, I tell myself. *You selfish, useless cow.*

'It's all a mistake!' I try to shout but my throat and my mouth are dry.

But he's guilty, isn't he? He said so and so did I. They'll be getting him ready for Cell 1 like they do with all the prisoners and in a week's time it'll be him in here, sitting in that chair, waiting for the timer and the electricity. Who's going to vote him innocent when there are no 'mitigating circumstances' allowed, no grey areas?

How's he going to fight on now?

You *have to fight it*, a voice in my head says. *With everything you've got and every way you can. He's in there now instead of you. You have to fight it!*

A hand touches my shoulder. I turn and Eve is crouched next to me. I nod to her. With her is Judge Cicero – he's telling the guards to leave me alone.

The flashing of the green slows and stops, replaced by white again, just how it was before.

Behind us the screen flickers back to life and the over-sized eye blinks down at us before fading away.

Death is Justice

The studio audience sit in silence. Kristina and Joshua watch the screen with their mouths open. Kristina's face is a rock, her eyes are cold and her body is stiff. Joshua sniffs quietly, takes a tissue from his pocket and dabs his eyes.

AUDIENCE MEMBER 1: We want our money back! She should've fried!

Applause sounds.

AUDIENCE MEMBER 2: She was found guilty!

AUDIENCE MEMBER 3: Who cares if she said she was innocent? Too late, I say.

AUDIENCE MEMBER 4: I say we should execute them both for lying!

Joshua raises one hand, his other to his ear. He nods cautiously.

JOSHUA (quietly): Ladies and gentlemen, I think there is no doubt that we've all been witness to something quite remarkable this evening that I don't think even I can sum up in words. Emotions are running high. There are many issues to be debated and discussed that we must not lose track of. Accusations of corruption at the highest levels, insinuations of an inadequate legal system, demands for changes within, allegations of murder. The near-execution of a teenager who was clearly innocent. A veritable soap opera. Could you ask for any more drama? Well . . .

He touches his ear again.

KRISTINA (interrupting): It has indeed been a –

JOSHUA: If I may continue, Kristina? Yes, quite what happened to the power in the cell and with the death chair remains unknown but a full investigation will doubtless be launched. However, to turn our attention to what is happening at the moment, may I direct viewers this way.

He stands and strides across the floor to the screen on the right-hand side. It blurs, flickers and a room comes into view – a bed, a sink and a toilet. A window high up on the wall. Everything white and bland. The young man in it wears white overalls with chains at his wrists and ankles. Seated as his head is shaved; he pauses and looks to camera. Isaac.

JOSHUA: Yes, ladies and gentlemen, further to the revelations that he shot Jackson Paige, Isaac Paige is now being prepared for in Cell 1 of death row. Of course you can follow his journey here with daily updates. But in the meantime . . .

The screen changes. Martha in Cell 7, Eve and Cicero with her, the chair, a reminder of how close she came, looming behind them.

JOSHUA: I feel we are at the beginning of something. This young lady who has battled against poverty, against being an orphan, against loneliness, loss and injustice, who has been thrust into the public eye in her own private fight for right may well be the hero we didn't realise we were missing. A hero to guide us through difficulty and to a better society. I'm sure all media will be following her closely, and I look forward to it. I can honestly say I am proud of this show for bringing her to your attention.

The audience applaud. Kristina is silent.

Martha

Everyone's leaving.

Isaac has gone.

I'm alive.

Am I glad? I don't know. In front of me everything looks difficult and I don't see how I can be the person for this fight.

I don't have any money. Nowhere to live now. I'm underage with no parents or legal guardians – they'll put me in one of those care institutions. What future is that?

I shake my head. This is impossible. I should've died in there. Isaac should be here, not me. I don't know what to do.

Listen to yourself, my head says to me. *You're not weak. You don't give up. You never have before, so why would you now?*

You know what to do – you fight and you fight and you fight, I tell myself. *You've shown people what Jackson did. They know he killed your mum, and Isaac's. You've done that – you and Isaac. You owe it to yourself to carry on. You owe him too. You can* do *it.*

Outside

Martha takes Eve's hand and together they walk across the floor and out of the building, Cicero at their side.

It's dark but streetlights form pools and light streams from windows; flashes come from media cameras and peoples' phones a short way off, and it all mixes together like a fairground at night time. Confusing and disorientating.

They walk along the path and stop.

'That's what the tree looks like from this side,' Martha whispers. 'I never thought I'd see it.' She stares at it for a moment. 'It's much bigger than I thought.'

A sparrow rests in it. They walk on.

A crowd of people are waiting at the gates, a few journalists with cameras and microphones, some demonstrators who look like they've given up with their placards but others, those demanding a fairer and better system, lift theirs high. Gus has gone, and he is nowhere to be seen.

Cicero stops at the front of the crowd.

'What's he doing?' Martha asks Eve.

'I don't know.'

'If I could have your attention, please,' he says.

The crowd turn to him.

'Are your cameras on? Microphones?'

They nod.

'I'm sure you're all aware of what has just happened in there, and I'm sure you will all understand when I ask for some privacy for Martha in the coming days. However, right at this moment, there is something I must do.'

He pauses and looks down to an envelope in his hands.

'Shortly before . . . this evening's events, Isaac Paige handed me this. He said that if he was unable to share it after the *proceedings*, then I was to in his place. I don't know what it says, but . . .'

He tears open the envelope and pulls out a piece of paper. For a second his eyes scan over the words, then he takes a deep breath and looks up to the crowd.

'I'll read it to you. This is written by Isaac. They are his words.

'*While I was aware of what was going on in society and our judicial system, it took meeting Martha for me to really understand its impact. I saw her quiet frustration at the loss she, and others, encountered through my adoptive father's callousness and the power he held over others, and I came to realise something must be done. I never planned to kill him, nor for Martha to take the blame. Together we had an idea – that we could seek justice for her mum, for mine, and for Oliver Barkova. We hoped that could lead to change. But this idea for fairer justice relied on perverting the course of justice to do it – for Martha to take the blame for my actions. Hypocrisy, I came to think. But I'd made a promise – in haste because there was no time to argue – but still a promise, and I would not break it.*'

Cicero turns to Martha and continues reading.

'*Martha, if I don't have chance to tell you, I need you to know a few things. Firstly, you were wrong. I know you won't like that, but you were. You doubt yourself and your abilities but so many don't. Take strength from those around you, accept help when needed, and always stand by what you believe. The only things stopping you are yourself, opportunity and, unfortunately, money. You can barely afford to eat, let alone study, let alone lead a fight for change. For this reason I've signed everything I own over to you. Not a lot for a sixteen-year-old boy, not usually, but as my father, to my surprise, left everything, bar a small living allowance for Patty, to me, I think you'll find it will be sufficient.'*

Cicero pauses to clear his throat.

'Secondly, in this envelope is something for you that was my birth mother's – a puzzle ring. I used to play with it as a child. It's difficult at first, she used to tell me, but persevere and you'll get there.

'I hope you choose to wear it and to remember me, wherever I am right now, and I hope it inspires you to keep trying.

'You lit my life, Martha Honeydew; now it's time for you to light other people's too.

'I love you and always will, Isaac.'

Cicero reaches into the envelope and pulls out the ring, five pieces linked together but that have fallen apart.

He drops it into Martha's hands.

'I will,' she whispers. 'Always.'

Death is Justice

Joshua looks away from the screen. He takes a tissue from his pocket and again dabs his face, but can't hide the tears. The eye logo in the corner blinks slowly and closes.

JOSHUA: Oh my, ladies and gentlemen, what a show, *what a show*, we've had for you this evening. This whole week, in fact. It's been emotional. It's been a rollercoaster. And I don't mind telling you, I'm exhausted. Kristina?

Kristina's hair and make up are still perfect and she still sits bolt upright in her usual seat at the high desk, but the audience's eyes are now on Joshua.

KRISTINA: Indeed, but don't forget to keep those voting fingers –

JOSHUA: And Jackson not leaving his money to Patty? What *is* going on there?

He looks over the audience, takes a deep breath in and stands up. A spotlight follows him as he walks across the studio floor, leaving Kristina in shadow. He stops at the screen, staring at an oversized image of Martha in the cell, tears on her face as her eyes look upwards.

JOSHUA: Martha Honeydew . . . what a girl.

He looks back over the audience, a slow grin creeping across his face.

JOSHUA: Ladies and gentlemen, I can't wait to see what our good lady Martha is going to get up to next, nor what will become of Isaac at the end of another seven days, but until then, it's time to sign off from this *monumental* episode of *Death is Justice*. Let's hope we'll be able to bring you an exclusive interview with our Martha, and maybe pose the question to her – is death justice? This is An Eye For An Eye Productions saying goodnight, Viewers, and thank you for tuning in.

Acknowledgements

This book would not be in your hands without the help and support of a lot of people, and I feel incredibly fortunate to have had them by my side.

Big thanks to a group of people who always welcome me back from out of my own head, make me laugh, remind me that there is life outside of my laptop and have offered me the most wonderful friendships over the last few years, all while getting wet, muddy, sweaty, out of breath or trying not to drown: John Sharp, Stephen Johnson, Martin Ball, Simon Sharp, Tracey Wilkinson, Kate and Richard Conway, Jo and Steve Hunt and, of course, Jackie Hall.

Thanks to Peter Bretan for his sensible name suggestion and for drinks and cake while standing in the middle of a lake on New Year's morning.

When I was first thinking about *Cell 7*, I read an essay by historian Liz Homans entitled *Swinging Sixties: The Abolition of Capital Punishment*, and I'd like to thank her for such an informative and interesting read that really sparked me to think 'what if . . . ?'

Thanks to Ian Durant for taking the time to chat and offer insight into the current legal system in the UK, and to Miriam Barber for the introduction.

The YA community is such an incredibly supportive place and I feel honoured to be part of it, so thanks go to all of the Manatees (you know who you are!) and the Author Allsorts. You guys are the best.

Special thanks go to authors Rebecca Mascull and Emma Pass, who both read early drafts of this and have been my rocks, my sounding boards and my worrying partners. Your support, your friendship and your kindness mean more than you could ever know.

Huge thanks to my wonderful agent, Jane Willis (at United Agents) who, in my house, is referred to as Agent Jane, complete with super-agent cape and super-agent powers, for her enthusiasm from the very beginning and her continuing support. Also at UA, thanks to Julian Dickson and Emily Talbot, and for all things film and TV, thanks to Yasmin McDonald.

I feel very privileged to have been welcomed so warmly into the Hot Key family and would like to thank Emma Matthewson for all her advice and hard work at helping this become a better book. Thanks to Jenny Jacoby for her keen eye (and I promise no more 'mutters'!), to Ruth, Monique, Rosi, and to James Fraser for a stunning cover.

And finally, thanks, love and promises of cheesecake go to my brilliant family. My husband, Russ, my children, Jess, Dan and Bowen, my dad Richard, my step-mum Ann, and my brother Colin. I love you all.

Kerry Drewery

Kerry Drewery is the author of two other highly acclaimed YA novels tackling brave topics: *A Brighter Fear*, 2012 (Love Reading 4 Kids Book of the Month and shortlisted for the Leeds Book Award) and *A Dream of Lights*, 2013 (nominated for the CILIP Carnegie Medal, awarded Highly Commended at the North East Teen Book Awards, shortlisted for the Hampshire Independent Schools Book Awards). Kerry and fellow YA author Emma Pass organised a hugely successful UKYA Extravaganza at both Birmingham and Nottingham Waterstones. Before writing full-time she was a BookStart Co-ordinator for BookTrust. She was a finalist in a BBC Scriptwriting for Children competition and has a first class honours degree in Professional Writing. Kerry lives in Lincolnshire between the countryside and the sea, in a house filled with books, films and dogs. Follow Kerry on Facebook at facebook.com/KerryDrewery, Tumblr kerrydrewery.tumblr.com and Twitter @KerryDrewery

Look out for the next gripping book
in the series . . .

7 DAYS

Martha Honeydew is free,
but the public are hungry for blood and now
Isaac's days are numbered.
Literally.

COMING SUMMER 2017

HOT KEY BOOKS

Thank you for choosing a Hot Key book.

If you want to know more about our authors
and what we publish, you can find us online.

You can start at our website

www.hotkeybooks.com

And you can also find us on:

We hope to see you soon!